Shadow of Guilt

A COMPENDIUM

OF STORIES

by

Barbara Anne Machin

Grosvenor House
Publishing Limited

The right of Barbara Anne Machin to be identified as the author of this
work has been asserted in accordance with Section 78
of the Copyright, Designs and Patents Act 1988

The book cover is copyright to
https://www.istockphoto.com/gb/portfolio/chainatp

This book is published by
Grosvenor House Publishing Ltd
Link House
140 The Broadway, Tolworth, Surrey, KT6 7HT.
www.grosvenorhousepublishing.co.uk

This book is a work of fiction. Any resemblance to
people or events, past or present, is purely coincidental.

A CIP record for this book
is available from the British Library

ISBN 978-1-78623-674-6

DEDICATION

I dedicate this book to my husband Clive for his encouragement
and for believing in me.

Shadow of Guilt
By Barbara A. Machin

CHAPTER 1

Clare ran to the waiting car, her normally cheerful face etched with worry. Behind the wheel was Mr Moorland, the director of the company she works for, Moorland & Dickenson. She had been working in Holland for the last 12 months, setting up some new offices. Moorland & Dickenson was an advertising agency and had offices all over the world. Clare was one of their best sales people. She had received a phone call from Mr Moorland to tell her she must come home, for Julie was in hospital. Julie was Clare's younger sister. As a child Julie had suffered from rheumatic fever and it had left her with a weak heart.

'It really is very kind of you to fetch me yourself, Mr Moorland. How is Julie?'

'I'm not sure, Clare, we will soon be there,' he replied with a sympathetic smile. 'Are you sure you don't want to nip home to change?'

Julie shook her head. 'No, I'd sooner go to the hospital first and make sure she's on the mend.'

Clare and Julie's parents had been killed three years ago in a head-on collision. Both her parents were only children so there had been no aunts or uncles to help them through that tragic time. Julie had been Clare's responsibility ever since. Why did I take this secondment? Clare thought, biting her lip.

Sometime later she was sitting in the consultant's room, staring at the clinical white walls. She could not believe what he had said.

'I'm so sorry, Miss James, we were unable to save her.'

'It can't be true,' Clare had replied through a mist of tears.

Clare felt as if someone had hit her between the eyes, her heart was thumping and she had to grip the arms of the chair to stop herself sliding to the floor. The doctor's words were whirling around her brain. Julie, dead. How could this be possible?

The doctor's voice broke through her thoughts.

'We did everything we could to save her; we really are so sorry, Miss James. We were hoping you can shed some light on why Julie went against our advice, given her heart condition. Julie was aware of the risk she was taking. Her heart was very weak. She already knew that if she was to marry, children would be out of the question.'

'Children?' Clare asked, stupidly.

'Yes, the child survived. A healthy little boy. Once you have composed yourself, Miss James, we can take you to see him.'

'But how... it just can't be possible... Julie wasn't married.'

'My dear Miss James, I can assure you that it was possible. You don't have to be married to have children. We live in a modern world,' the doctor replied, smiling faintly.

Clare tried hard to concentrate and take in all that was being said. How could Julie have been pregnant, let alone have kept it from her. Besides, she had still been a child herself – just 18 years old two months ago. At 21, Clare had become mother and father to Julie, protecting her and always making sure she rested and took her medication.

'Do you have any idea who the father is, Miss James?' Dr Linham's voice cut in.

Her voice was a mere whisper as she replied, 'No, I didn't even know Julie had a boyfriend.' Clare was in a daze and try as she might she just could not take in the reality of the doctor's words.

'Will your parents be able to take the baby?'

asked the doctor with a worried frown on his face. Clare stared at the nurse who stood slightly to the side of the desk, willing her to say it was not true. But instead Clare heard her own voice explaining that their parents were dead and had been for the last three years.

'I am slightly older than Julie and have always tried to look after her since Mum and Dad died.' She bit her lip. 'We have been on our own for quite some time. Julie was far too delicate to go out to work. But she did a little typing at home, so when my boss asked me to go to Holland we discussed it and decided it was a brilliant opportunity and that the extra money would be handy. Julie assured me that she could take care of herself. I just don't understand. Why did she not tell me? At least we could have sought medical attention. I rang home twice a week and at no time did she mention anyone. I have been in Holland for 12 months. I came home for two weeks in the summer and there appeared to be no problems.'

The tears welled in Clare's eyes again.

'If only I hadn't gone away.'

Dr Linham cleared his throat and said in a kindly manner, 'Don't blame yourself, Miss James, this could have happened if you had been at home and leaving for work each day.'

The sympathy was just too much for Clare, and with her hands covering her face she sobbed loudly.

'Nurse, get Miss James a cup of tea, would you,' said Dr Linham. Looking at Clare he thought how young and vulnerable she seemed.

Clare was dainty, around 5ft, and had curly, chestnut hair and blue eyes. Her flawless skin was creamy and she was very slim, almost like a young boy. This was often accentuated because most of the time she dressed in jeans and a sweater.

Eventually Clare stopped sobbing, and gratefully accepted the tea handed to her by the nurse.

Dr Linham cleared his throat.

'We need to decide what is to be done with the child; he is a healthy little boy and needs a stable home.'

Clare turned and stared at him with determination in her eyes.

'What do you mean? He is all that is left of Julie and she would expect me to look after him for her. There's no question at all about his future. I will take him. He will be loved as if I am his mother and he will have a stable and a loving home.'

Clare looked at the doctor, fear now replacing her tears. She was aware that Dr Linham was shaking his head. However, the child would be her only relative.

'But, Miss James, are you certain? It's a heavy responsibility for one so young; it will mean a lot of sleepless nights. You won't be as free as you were. Are you expecting to return to Holland? And there will be not as much time for boyfriends, you know.'

'I don't have any boyfriends and no, I won't be returning to Holland. I most certainly can look after Julie's baby. I'm not that young. Lots of girls bring babies up at 21. I know I can manage. I will just need to leave him at the hospital while I deal with Julie's funeral and then I'll pick him up.'

'Of course, of course, Miss James, that will give us time to set up some support from the social workers and for you to arrange home visits with the nurse.'

Clare stood, shook hands and said, 'Thank you for your kindness, Dr Linham.'

Clare's heart was heavy with grief as she left the hospital. She allowed the kindly Mr Moorland to drive her home.

'Ring me in the morning, Clare, you must be tired now. Mr Dickinson and I will help to arrange the funeral.'

Clare forced a smile. 'Thank you, Mr Moorland, that would be a great help, and thank you again for everything.'

'I'll see you in the morning, then.' Mr Moorland smiled and gave her a kindly pat on her hand. Gazing down at her white face, he said, 'You know, Clare, things have a way of working out. I know you might not think so now, but they will.'

Chapter 2

Clare stood looking down at the little bundle of humanity. Her heart was bursting with feeling as she realised that the baby was the image of her sister. His blue eyes appeared to recognise her however she probably imagined it.

'How do you propose to go to work and look after him as well?' the social worker asked. 'You must also consider your financial position and your ability to provide for the child.'

Clare dragged her gaze from the tiny bundle and was amazed at the strong grip he kept on her finger, as if to say, Don't leave me.

'No, I won't leave you,' she crooned, smiling down at him.

Clare's blue eyes held the social worker's gaze. 'I still have the money from the sale of our parents' home, and I own the flat. Also, I have some savings, so I'll manage quite well.'

'I will put Julie's share into trust for Julian, and I can type well, so I'm sure to find plenty of work I can do at home.'

The social worker smiled. She could see that the baby would be well looked after.

'I must warn you, Miss James, that if the father comes forward he will have first claim on the child.'

'He's not come forward so far though, has he?' Clare said flatly. 'Julian is a month old and no one has claimed him. No, I will take care of him. If his father was bothered why has he not been in contact with us? He must have known Julie had a sister. No, I'm sure if he had been bothered he would have tried to contact us by now.'

'Yes, I'm sure you are right but we do have to cover these eventualities.'

The social worker paused.

'Julian. Is that what you intend to call him?'

'Yes, after his mother. She would have loved him.'

The social worker smiled. 'I'm sure she would, and I'm satisfied Julian will be well looked after. However, I will need to set up regular visits and will ensure you have as much support as we can give. How about a weekly visit, say for the first two months?' 'That will be fine, and thanks for your help. Everybody has been so kind.' The social worker was there for a medical appointment and Clare was happy to have discussed most of the issues she was unsure of on realising the social worker would be the one supporting her.

Clare made her way out of the hospital with her very precious bundle held close to her heart. She was pleased to have met the social worker already and managed to talk through her appointments, as the social worker was at the hospital to support someone else and had been introduced to Clare. She had already bought a pram and enjoyed the short walk to the flat.

CHAPTER 3

Clare surveyed her small flat. It had always been compact and neat but it looked far from that now, with what seemed like endless piles of nappies, toys and babies' bottles scattered around.

With a little smile Clare realised she was loving every minute of looking after her small nephew. She now had a regular income from three typing contracts and her company had provided her with several accounts to work on. She could manage these accounts, which involved selling and designing advertising space, from home. The firm had assured her that it would also recommend her, where possible, to other companies. Julian slept most of the day, enabling Clare to work. It was waking to feed him in the night that she found most difficult because it left her tired in the mornings. He was worth it, though, and she would soon get used to it, she thought.

'Just a couple more contracts and then we are home and dry, young man,' she cooed.

Clare bent over her tiny nephew and tickled his tummy.

'You keep me awake tonight, young man, and we won't be able to buy your milk tomorrow. I'll be far too tired to go out to the shops.'

Julian gurgled happily, his toothless smile and sunny face acknowledging Clare.

He was a happy, contented baby and was gaining weight healthily, and the first few visits from the social worker had gone well.

If only I knew who your daddy was, Clare thought, I would give him a piece of my mind.

Her eyes clouded for a moment.

On second thoughts, I don't want to know. He might try to take you away and I could not bear that.

'I need you, angel,' she said, stroking his soft cheeks. Once again Clare marvelled at the likeness to Julie – the clear blue eyes, the way his face lit up when he smiled.

'Oh, but your granny and granddad would have loved you.' Mum, Dad and Julie had missed so much, she thought.

The shrill sound of the doorbell interrupted Clare's thoughts. She groaned, expecting it to be Keith, who supplied the paperwork for one of her typing contracts.

Although Clare appreciated a little company of her own age after a long day looking after Julian, Keith was dropping in a little too often. She needed time to catch up on the work left over from the night before, and to do the chores; babies meant endless washing. She went to open the door, pinning a smile to her face. After all, Keith was an old family friend.

A stranger stood at the door and Clare's heart lurched as she looked into his clear grey eyes. He was tall and lean, with dark untidy waves of hair falling over his forehead. He smiled down at her as if he recognised her.

Clare began to blush as she realised his eyes were appraising her body, lingering on her small, pert breasts then moving down to her shapely hips and small, slippered feet. Clare was tongue-tied and couldn't take her eyes from his face.

He brushed the dark untidy waves from his broad forehead, as if by habit. He was six feet of sexy manhood and when he spoke his voice was deep and cultured. Clare gave herself a mental shake; there was no room in her life for men anymore.

'You must be Clare. Julie told me you were pretty but she was wrong; you are beautiful.'

He raised his gaze and his brows drew together as he heard the cry Julian let out. Julian was telling Clare that he was hungry.

'I'm here, darling,' Clare called, and turned swiftly without another thought, with only Julian's welfare in her mind. She lifted Julian from his pram to soothe his cries and, as if by a miracle, the wails stopped and he gave Clare one of his toothless smiles. At least Clare liked to call them smiles; they were more than likely wind, she thought wryly.

'Just like women, they never plan in advance,' came the caustic comment. Clare turned in astonishment. Whoever he was, he had followed her into the flat.

'Who invited you in?' burst out Clare, angrily bobbing her head up and down and glaring into the smiling grey eyes.

'My name is Adrian Loring, and I invited myself in. It looked as if you needed some help. Is it feed time?'

Clare nodded as Julian once again began to grizzle.

'Right,' said Adrian, 'I'll warm some milk. You hold the fort.' Clare's mouth opened in amazement.

'Go on woman, practice your witchery, whatever it is you women do. I know my way around.'

Clare stared at Adrian's disappearing back. Was he Julian's father? If he was she could understand why Julie had fallen for him and been swept off her feet. Instantly she thought that he would have been too old – what would he be, 35, or maybe 36? Twice Julie's age. Still, you could quite easily be taken in; he seemed to ooze charm.

She felt the same now as when she had first set eyes on Julian – a quivering in the pit of her stomach, a melting of her senses, an immediate bond.

Clare shook her head in disbelief. Take hold of yourself; it's just fear you are feeling, she reasoned, fear that if he was Julian's father he would want to take him away. Whatever she did she must let him think that Julian was hers. She was not going to let anyone take him away from her; Julian was hers now and that's how it would stay.

Taking control of herself she followed Adrian into the kitchen and watched angrily as he opened drawers and cupboards to locate the utensils he needed.

Clare could not keep the sarcasm out of her voice as she said, 'You certainly know your way around, Mr Loring, and it looks as if you almost live here.'

Adrian stared back into the accusing blue eyes.

'Not really,' he replied, giving Clare a puzzled look. 'Julie reads, corrects and types my work. However, I've been known to make the occasional coffee when Julie has not been well. It's some time since I've seen Julie. I've been away for a couple of months researching my next book.'

He looked around. 'When will Julie be in? I left my last book with her and she promised she would have it ready for the publisher when I returned.'

Clare stared into his eyes, lost for words. What could she tell him without raising any questions about Julian. He obviously wasn't aware of Julie's death, which would make sense if he had been away for two months. Clare realised she needed to be careful.

Adrian stared and held Clare's gaze, his eyebrows slightly raised. He was awaiting some kind of response.

The kettle gave a shrill whistle and, turning towards it, he said, 'Let's feed the child first, then we can discuss my book.' His voice was gentle. Clare returned to the lounge and sat down, and from the kitchen could hear the coffee cups rattling. Adrian returned just as Clare was gently placing Julian back in his pram. He then placed a steaming mug of coffee besides the chair she had vacated and settled himself into the large chintz armchair opposite.

'Julie never told me you were married,' he said enquiringly.

'I'm not, and I don't believe you need to know my business,' Clare answered sharply. Something like relief seemed to flicker across Adrian Loring's face. He raised his eyebrows in reply, making Clare blush crimson with embarrassment as she read his thoughts. He thinks Julian is mine. It's best if I leave it that way, she thought. Better to be branded the scarlet woman than this man knowing the truth.

Adrian cleared his throat. 'Now, about my book.'

Clare met his steady gaze.

'Julie has gone away,' she lied, 'and I'm sure when I check Julie's desk I will find it finished. If not, I will ensure it is finished and returned to you. If you leave your phone number I will ring you as soon as it's ready.'

'It was very sudden of Julie to go away. She didn't tell me.'

'Did Julie always give you a rundown of her whereabouts?'

'Well, no,' Adrian answered, frowning.

'Well, she has,' Clare stammered, 'and she won't be back for a couple of months.'

Adrian studied Clare and said, 'I find it hard to believe she would leave no message for me, particularly as she gave me her word my book would be ready for today.'

'I assure you, Mr Loring, I am a very good typist myself and will make sure you have it as soon as possible. We won't let you down, and of course the sooner you leave the quicker I will be able to check any outstanding work Julie has left.'

'Will you have time among all these domestic chores?'

Clare raised her head and looked into his eyes. 'I have said it will be ready and it will.'

'In that case, I will leave you these notes as well.' He reached for a tattered brown briefcase she had not noticed before. Clare took the bundle of notes. Here was another contract. However, she was not sure she wanted this one, just in case he was Julian's father. The less he came to the flat the better.

At that moment the doorbell rang shrilly and Clare groaned, thinking that this must be Keith – just what she could do without. She needed to gather her thoughts and to still her churning stomach.

Clare hurried to the door, hoping that Adrian would take this as a dismissal. As she expected it was Keith, who was standing there impatiently.

'Hello, poppet,' he said as he bent to kiss her cheek. Clare stared at him in amazement. Why did he do that. He knew she didn't like it. He had hinted on many occasions that he was more than fond of her and Clare had made it clear they could only be friends.

At that precise moment a voice broke in. 'You are not very fussy over anything, are you Clare – who's typing you poach or who's boyfriend you take, are you, poppet?' Adrian said snidely, emphasising the 'poppet'. He must have followed her into the hallway but before Clare had time to think of a suitable retort he shot her a look of pure contempt and said, 'I'll call you in a week's time. I will expect my work to be ready.' With that he pushed passed them and left without a backward glance.

Colour suffused Clare's face. 'Well, of all the bad mannered men I've met he takes the biscuit.'

'Yes, you are quite right,' said Keith. 'That Loring chap is a very unpleasant character and if you have any sense, Clare, you will keep him at a distance. While you were away he was always hanging about Julie, in fact I wouldn't be surprised...' He looked knowingly at Julian and tapped the side of his nose, leaving Clare in no doubt as to what he was implying. Clare looked at him, taking in his sly expression and weak chin. There was nothing in Keith's personality that Clare liked, however, he had supplied her with work so she had to put up with the constant dropping in at any time with the excuse that he needed to check the contents of a report.

Clare and Julie had known Keith for most of their lives. He was the son of a friend of her late father and as a child he had often visited Clare's home with his parents.

Mentally Clare began to compare Adrian with Keith; Adrian was so strong and dependable-looking, while Keith looked a little vain and self-centred.

Still, her mother had always counselled her not to judge a book by its cover and, thinking of Adrian Loring, her mother was most likely right.

All the same, she would have to be careful where Adrian was concerned; if he did prove to be Julie's lover he would find out about Julian sooner or later, and get to know how and why Julie had died.

Hopefully the six months would be over quickly and the adoption papers would be signed. Then it would be too late.

Keith's voice cut across Clare's thoughts.

'You're not getting bored of playing the doting mother, are you?'

She looked at Keith in amazement.

'How could you ask that? Of course I'm not.'

Keith took no notice and blustered on.

'I don't mean to interfere, Clare, but it might have been better had you put him up for adoption, better all round. You could have got on with your own life, then. Honestly, Clare, you need to have some time to yourself, and what about me?'

'What about you, Keith?' Clare stared at him, her face full of curiosity.

'You know how I feel about you; I've told you countless times.'

'Keith, you are a good friend and that's all,' Clare replied, embarrassed.

Keith continued as if he had neither heard nor noticed the look on Clare's face.

'I've told you before, I love you and always will.' Clumsily he gripped Clare's shoulders and began smothering her face with wet kisses.

'Please don't,' she gasped, panic rising in her breast. Never before had Keith tried to force himself on her. Clare pushed with all her strength against his chest.

'Please!' Keith let her go and stepped back. Clare caught her breath and stifled a sob. This was all getting too much.

'You can't blame a chap for trying,' blustered Keith. 'I've always been fond of you.'

'I'm sorry, Keith. I think of you as a dear friend but I will never love, let alone marry anyone. Julian will be my life from now on.'

'You don't mean that, Clare.'

Clare looked at Keith. He was good-looking in a feminine sort of way but his face lacked character. There was no trace of Adrian Loring's strength and lean fitness; you could tell Keith would lean to flabbiness in a few years' time. His hair was a mousy brown, his eyes a muddy colour and he was just slightly taller than Clare herself.

Clare had kissed several men over the years but had not experienced anything quite as unpleasant as Keith's clumsy approach. By nature she was kind and caring, and found it difficult to hurt anyone.

'Let's forget it, please,' Clare begged. 'Let's pretend it never happened.'

Keith nodded his reply with a sulky look on his face. His ego had been crushed; he was like a small boy who had not managed to get his own way.

'Please, Keith, let's try to keep our relationship on a friendly business footing; let's not spoil it. Now, would you like a cup of coffee? I'm just about to make one.'

Keith nodded, not daring to look at Clare. Damn Adrian Loring. He had given Keith quite a shock. Adrian had seen him in a nightclub with his secretary and a week later had found Keith at Julie's flat wearing a dressing gown. Adrian's sarcastic comments had aroused Julie's suspicions and Julie had kept asking what he had meant. Keith had always had a cruel streak, had lost his temper and pointed out that Jane, his secretary, was much better in bed. Keith had thought he could talk Julie around, but not this time. She had told Keith she was expecting his child, but she would rather bring it up herself rather than have Keith around as its father. She had threatened to ring Clare and ask her to come home if he didn't stop bothering her.

Keith mopped the sweat from his brow. He was in so much debt. He had realised that the banks would not extend his loan and the £300,000 Julie and Clare had received from their parents' estate would go a long way towards putting him back on his feet. The solution was to marry either Julie or Clare. He had been on the point of making a play for Clare but always she laughed and rebuffed him, and then to cap it all she went to Holland. Things were getting desperate, so he had decided to pay attention to Julie. Things were going really well until that Loring chap stepped in. Keith had been sleeping with Julie since Clare went abroad, and he had persuaded her to marry him by special licence. They would tell Clare once they had married. Just another two weeks and he would have been home and dry. Keith was now desperate. He needed to catch Clare while she was vulnerable. Thank goodness that Loring chap had gone. He needed to persuade Clare not to have anything to do with him. And he certainly didn't want her to keep that brat. Children were not his cup of tea. Keith started to think of Clare's slim figure and small breasts. It would be quite good to bed her, he thought. Clare was relieved when Keith decided to leave. She dreaded any repetition of his earlier behaviour.

CHAPTER 4

Clare pushed Julian's pram. He was gurgling happily and his contented blue eyes were wide open and watching Clare as she spoke baby words. His head was now covered in a light brown fluff. It wasn't as dark as her and Julie's hair but never-the-less it was hair.

Julie parked the pram in the supermarket and put Julian into the baby park, which was close to the checkout. Only when she was satisfied that there were ample nursery attendants did she enter the store to collect the badly needed shopping.

She looked like any other young mother: her grey trouser suit matched perfectly with a red sweater; her brown curly hair shone with the vigorous brushing she had given it, although in a slight hurry to complete picking up the goods she needed. She'd added just a touch of pale pink lipstick; it was all the make-up she needed. Clare had no idea of the picture of health and vitality she created as she wandered along the aisles.

At that precise time Adrian Loring was making his way into the store and spotted Clare ahead of him.

Something about Clare intrigued him. How could someone so worldly-wise look so fresh and innocent.

Yet there was a deep sorrow showing in her young face. Adrian wanted an excuse to speak to Clare and walking towards her. He thought there would be no harm in asking how his typing was going. Then he saw Julian in the baby park and stopped to tickle his chin.

The nursery assistant on duty eyed him suspiciously and he was forced to explain himself. His voice was deep and rich.

'I'm just about to catch up with his mother.'

'Oh,' the girl said, mistakenly adding, 'you are his daddy.' At that moment Clare reached the checkout and heard the end of the exchange. She noticed the admiring look the young girl was throwing him from under her eyelids. If only she knew, Clare thought, disapproval written across her young face.

Hearing the girl's words and seeing Adrian standing there, with one large hand extended because Julian's small fist was clutching his finger, brought fear and anger blazing into Clare's eyes.

She acknowledged Adrian with a nod and paid for her purchases, hardly daring to look or speak.

'I saw you come into the shop and I thought it would be a good opportunity to ask how my book was coming along,' said Adrian.

'I've finished your typing. You can call for it whenever you want.' She had misunderstood the conversation between Adrian and the attendant, was tired and angry and realised she could no longer play this cat and mouse game. Better for it to be out in the open.

'Mr Loring, I think you had better come to my flat. We both know that your typing was not the only reason you visited Julie. We have a lot to discuss. It would be far better putting our cards on the table.'

'Really, Miss James, you intrigue me. Well, there is no time like the present. Shall we say in 30 minutes' time at your flat, or would you like me to fold the pram and put it in my car?' He pointed to the black Jaguar parked outside.

'No, I can walk back, thanks,' Clare replied and without a backward glance made her way to the door. For some minutes Adrian stood watching her walk away.

At the flat Clare lifted Julian from his pram and carried him into the bedroom. She took off his outdoor clothes, changed his nappy and gently laid him down.

'Now, you be a good boy and have a little sleep.'

She had just an hour before he must be fed, just long enough to thrash out his future.

Could she appeal to Adrian's better nature, she asked herself. That was supposing he had a better nature. Perhaps he would be reasonable. Somehow she doubted it. Had she not heard him declaring to the nursery assistant that he was Julian's father? Clare realised she needed to be careful and think about the future.

'Best get him out of my hair,' she mumbled. There was no way she would relinquish Julian.

CHAPTER 5

The doorbell rang. Clare looked at herself in the mirror. She looked presentable but pale. The stress of the last hour had taken its toll.

'Do come in, Mr Loring. We both know why you are here so let's get straight to the point,' she said following him into the lounge.

As Adrian turned to face her she saw the huge teddy he held awkwardly in his arms. He placed the teddy on the settee and sat down beside it.

'For the boy, unless you feel you would like it.' Then, as if he had only just heard her, he asked, 'What have I come for?'

'Oh don't act the innocent with me, you know why.'

By now Clare was becoming angry. Gone were her good intentions. 'If you think you are going to use Julian as an excuse to make use of me like you did Julie I won't let you.' Clare faced him, looking like a young tigress defending her cub.

'How could I make use of you, Clare?' he asked in a carefully controlled voice that held a touch of anger.

'You need not act the innocent with me, Mr Loring. I know you are Julian's father; did I not hear you telling the nursery attendant?'

Once started Clare was unable to control her tongue. All the pent-up anger and hurt poured out.

'It didn't bother you leaving Julie here pregnant to fend for herself? How could you take advantage of her? Her heart was weak, she wasn't strong enough to have children, and now she's dead and you don't care. I won't let you take him away from me. I won't. I will fight you all the way. I can give him love. He's all I've got.'

Clare began to sob uncontrollably. All the grief and pent-up emotions of the last two months poured out of her in an uncontrollable flood.

Adrian moved to the arm of her chair and placed his arm protectively around her.

'Don't cry,' he soothed. 'I'll make some tea and then we will talk sensibly. Promise me you will stop crying.'

Clare's sobs became quieter and more controlled. Adrian went into the kitchen, put the kettle on and made some hot sweet tea. It was good for shocks and she looked all in.

Placing the tea in her hand, he said, 'Now, not a word until you have drunk this and calmed down.' Then he watched as she sipped the tea. All the fight left her. She began shivering like a frightened child, pale and tired.

'Are you telling me that Julie is dead and that the child is Julie's? When did she die?'

'Two months ago.' Clare's voice was dead and flat.

'I was called back from Holland on emergency leave, but it was too late.'

'And you hold me responsible?'

'No, no, I don't want you to be responsible. I will look after him,' she cried, tears threatening to erupt once more. 'I only want you to go away and leave us alone.'

'Wouldn't that be just a little too easy for a villain like me?' he asked in that same quietly controlled voice. 'No, my dear little Clare, you are not going to get away with it that easily. I know you are upset but if I am the child's father, as you say, I have rights. I must shoulder some of the responsibility.'

'No, please let me keep him,' she implored. 'When would you find time to look after him? You could only be a part-time father. How would you concentrate on your books?'

'Yes, that would be a problem,' Adrian said. He had a strange look on his face. 'Yes, you are right. Yes, Julian needs a mother as well as a father. But first, just to see you are not lying, I would like to see Julie's death certificate and Julian's birth certificate.'

'You think I would lie about something like Julie's death?' Clare's anger was returning.

She went to the sideboard and took the two documents from the drawer. Thrusting them into his hands, she said, 'Look, see what you have done. Do you think I would lie about someone I loved?'

Adrian studied the documents and said at last, 'No, 'you're not lying, and as you have pronounced me the father you have two alternatives: either I take Julian and look after him or,' he smiled, 'you continue to look after him as my wife. The choice is yours.'

'But that's stupid. I hardly know you,' Clare said in amazement.

'You seem to know all you want to know about me,' he said, raising his eyebrows and holding her gaze with his clear grey eyes.

'I really don't understand you, Mr Loring. Would ruining my life as well as Julie's give you some sort of satisfaction?'

'I'll give you exactly 30 minutes to give me your answer. In the meantime, I need a strong coffee. It's not every day you become a father,' he said wryly. 'And I warn you, I'm not a patient man, Clare.'

With that he went back to the kitchen, leaving Clare staring after him.

Clare thought to herself, What a mess. What have I done?

Clare's heart was thumping so loudly she was sure he would hear it banging against her ribs as she tried to understand the situation.

Marry him or he would take away Julian; what choice did she have. Clare tried hard to think of a way out. However, each new thought led her back to his proposition. He was Julian's father but she would be the one to raise Julian and give him that love that he needed. Perhaps a marriage of convenience was the answer.

Wearily she went into the bedroom and stood at the side of the crib looking down at Julian. His features had changed in the past few weeks. Clare could easily see Julie in him, but try as she might she could not see any similarity to Adrian. He did remind her of someone but she couldn't think who. Perhaps it was Adrian. How could she leave him? He was defenceless; he needed her.

'Come and have some coffee,' Adrian said in a gentle tone from the doorway. Silently Clare followed him into the lounge. All the fight had left her body. Taking the cup she refused the sandwiches he had made. They drank in silence.

'Well,' Adrian said as he put his cup on the tray. 'What is it to be?'

Clare looked at him, feeling far from brave. She wished the floor would open and swallow him up along with her problems, but this wasn't going to happen.

'You have left me no option,' she said in a small voice. 'I can't and won't give Julian up; I love him like my own, as I loved Julie. In these last few weeks he has been so dependent. I've given him all the love and all the attention he has needed. So I could no more give him up than if he were my own.

'So, Mr Loring, I have to say yes for my sake, as well as Julian's, but are you sure you want him? I promise he will be well looked after.'

'Yes, I'm sure,' Adrian replied with a faint smile. 'You might not believe it, Clare, but I'm sorry Julie is dead. I found her a very pleasant person; she was too young to die.'

Clare looked up in contempt. 'Is that all you can say? If she hadn't been having your baby, and you hadn't taken advantage of her, we would not be having this conversation. This would never have happened. And Julie would still be alive.

'Tell me, Mr Loring, those nights when you…' Clare's voice trailed away and she could no longer look him in the eye. 'Tell me, did you love Julie?'

Clare raised her eyes when no answer came. She looked hopefully at him, hoping that at least she would see a good reason for her sacrifice.

'No, Clare, I didn't. I will only ever love one woman and she is not aware of it yet. You see it was love at first sight. Do you believe in love at first sight, little one?'

'I don't believe in love, Mr Loring, it only brings heartache,' she replied cynically. Clare felt a deep pain in her chest. Julie had died in vain and all hope of ever liking this man had vanished with his callous words.

'Well, now we have agreed on a course of action I will call tomorrow and bring someone to babysit while we shop for a ring and some necessary items.' Looking down at her slacks, he added, 'I can't have my bride looking like a boy on our wedding day.'

Clare cut short her retort as he wagged his finger and walked slowly towards her. She felt like a rabbit caught in a trap and could neither move nor drag her gaze from his face as he reached and pulled her onto her feet. She didn't struggle as he pulled her to him.

Looking into her eyes, he murmured, 'If we are going to be married, we might as well act as if we are happy about it.' He gripped her under her chin and kissed her with such passion it sent her senses reeling. For one short moment she tried to fight her feelings then found herself responding to his caresses. Clare felt him tremble, then abruptly he let her go.

'Would you like me to stay for a while so you could have a rest?' he said, lifting an eyebrow. 'I can listen out for Julian.'

'I have managed for the last two months,' Clare said sarcastically. 'I'm sure I can manage a little longer.'

Adrian took her by surprise and brushed his lips once more across hers.

'As you wish. Until tomorrow, 10 o'clock sharp.'

He smiled mockingly as Clare dragged her hand across her mouth as if to wipe away any trace of his kiss.

CHAPTER 6

Looking around the flat that had been her home for the last three years, Clare took in the plain magnolia walls and wall-to-wall cream whipcord carpet. The small items of antique furniture she had rescued when her parents' home had been sold. The treasured Worcester china was displayed in the corner cabinet; she noted the gold curtains with matching Chinese hearthrug. It was only a tiny flat but the furnishings were tasteful. Adrian had told her that they would be packed and stored away until she had decided what to do with them.

The last few weeks had passed so quickly and, after making her way to the bedroom, Clare watched Mrs Pringle deftly dress Julian. Mrs Pringle was a small, plump woman with a lovely homely smile. In other circumstances Clare would have really liked her, but childishly she resented the part Mrs Pringle would play in looking after Julian; Mrs Pringle had been living in the flat with her for the past few weeks, after being hired by Adrian to care for Julian while Clare cleared any outstanding work. All the doors were open and a chauffeur waited patiently for them outside. He was to take Julian, Clare and Mrs Pringle to the church and then drive Julian and Mrs Pringle to The Laurels. He would then return to the church.

Clare glanced down at the solitaire diamond on her finger, and carefully touched the soft folds of lace that made up her cream, calf-length dress.

Adrian had certainly spared no expense; he had insisted that if a thing was worth doing it was worth doing well and had arranged a church wedding with all the trimmings. Clare felt guilty about the amount of money he had spent; she hoped to goodness he could afford it.

It was going to be the fairy-tale wedding that every girl wished for, and the bridegroom was handsome. Clare could have loved him if circumstances had been different. She recalled the way he looked at her with those grey eyes, the polite, cultured tones of his voice and the quizzical smile he gave her when he caught her looking at him.

The chauffeur's voice cut across her thoughts. 'Miss James, Mrs Pringle, it's time we left.'

Later, standing beside Adrian at the altar wondering who all the guests were, Clare felt herself trembling, even though it was a warm day.

She tried to speak in a clear voice without showing her inner turmoil. As a young girl she had always imagined her wedding day would be the happiest day of her life, but Clare felt no joy as Adrian slipped the wedding band on her finger and the vicar pronounced them man and wife.

Panic began to rise in her throat as Adrian bent to kiss her lips, but the warning look he gave her stilled any protest. There was no going back now. She was Mrs Adrian Loring. Walking back down the aisle Clare watched the smiling faces of the 50 or so guests. Neither she nor Adrian had close relatives present. Adrian explained that his mother lived in Paris and that she was not in good health, so Clare would meet her as soon as he could spare the time for them to visit. Most of the guests were colleagues of Adrian's, from work. Putting his arm around her waist he led her back to the car. At the reception Clare felt as if her face was aching as, with a forced smile, she greeted the guests, cut the cake and posed for photographs. One of Adrian's friends, John Bloomsbury, slapped Adrian on the back and said, 'We all thought your only interest was old relics and work. You are a dark horse. What a catch!'

After the reception they travelled back to Adrian's home in silence, both staring out of the window, deep in thought. Only once did he make any contact on the long drive through the countryside, reaching for her hand and squeezing it as they shared a companionable silence. It was as if he wanted to comfort her, but Clare childishly snatched her hand from his grasp.

CHAPTER 7

The tall building amid the trees that gave the house its name took Clare's breath away. The lawns rolled away from the long drive and looked like green velvet. The windows glistened like many-jewelled eyes, twinkling and inviting. Clare gasped.

'You mean this is The Laurels?'

'And why not!? Had you decided that I was a penniless author who lived in one room? If so, *Mrs* Loring, you are wrong, once again.' He stared at her searchingly, as if he was waiting for a particular reply. But Clare was too busy gazing at her new home.

Adrian opened the door and held out his hand but Clare ignored it and climbed out without his assistance.

Almost at once she realised she had made a mistake, because he quickly gripped her elbow, his fingers digging into her flesh and hurting her. Adrian ignored her gasp of pain.

'You can go now, John, take the night off,' he told the chauffeur with a smile. 'Mrs Loring and I won't be requiring you until tomorrow.'

Clare could not escape his grip so was forced to wait until the chauffeur stepped into his car and drove to the back of the house.

'Let me go,' she cried, 'you are hurting me.'

'Not until I have given you a lesson in how a good wife acts. Never, never treat me like that in front of my staff or by God you will know you have married me.'

Clare tried to pull her arm free. 'You mean you are a bully as well as a coward.'

Adrian thrust her away from him, almost causing her to fall as he let go, and strode towards the door without a backward glance, leaving Clare to follow in his wake.

She hesitated inside the door to admire the polished wood floor, the antique mahogany table bearing a huge silver bowl full of rust-coloured chrysanthemums, and the sweep of the huge stairway.

'Begging your pardon, your ladyship, I'm Mrs Downs, the housekeeper. Sir Adrian asked me to show you to your room. Your luggage has already arrived and has been unpacked.'

Clare stared at the old lady standing at her side; she had not noticed her when she followed Adrian in.

'What did you say?' Clare asked quite rudely. 'Did I hear you right? Did you say *Sir* Adrian?'

'Of course, your ladyship,' Mrs Downs replied, eyeing Claire with a puzzled frown. 'Perhaps when you have settled in you would like me to take you along to see your nephew. He puts me in mind of the master when he was a wee boy himself. It's good to have a babe in the house again and if I might say so, madam, I'm right glad his lordship has married you; you are a right bonny lass. Just what the old house wants again, a family.'

'So Julian looks like Sir Adrian, then?' quizzed Clare. 'In a manner of speaking, but all babies are alike.'

'Oh, I see.'

'If you could follow me.'

'Of course.'

Clare, still distracted by Mrs Downs's remark, following her up the wide staircase until she stopped outside a door.

'Here we are. This is your room. Sir Adrian said everything must be perfect for your homecoming. He ordered the roses especially for you.' Mrs Downs smiled.

Clare gazed around the room. The walls were white and the floor was covered by a thick, springy, silver grey carpet. Pale pink satin curtains hung at the windows and a huge bed with a pale pink cover that matched the curtains dominated the room. Dark rosewood wardrobes lined the walls and vases of red roses were dotted around, filling the room with a heady perfume. Looking once more at the bed, Clare felt her cheeks go hot with embarrassment. Surely he did not expect her to sleep with him.

'And this is the bathroom.' Clare glimpsed a pale pink and grey bathroom with gold fittings.

'I will leave you to have a wash and change. Dinner is at eight and I need to supervise Cook. Sir Adrian will be in the study when you come down.

'Now, I did say I would take you to the nursery. I'll come back in half an hour. Would that be okay?'

'That's fine, thanks.'

Cook, housekeeper, chauffeur... why had he not told her? She had no idea. He was so rich and he had let Julie die an unmarried mother. Anger filled her small heart like poison.

Clare opened the nearest wardrobe to look for her clothes and gasped as she saw the rows of neat suits. There must be some mistake, she thought, and hurriedly dragged the other wardrobe doors open, eventually seeing her own clothes. He could not possibly expect her to share a room with him. She would have to speak to him.

Clare rummaged among the newly acquired suits and dresses that Adrian had insisted on buying, until she found a pair of jeans and a sweater, and, after locking herself in the bathroom, took a bath. If he thinks I am going to sleep with him, she fumed inwardly, he's in for a shock. Please, he couldn't, she prayed.

Unlocking the bathroom and coming out she found Adrian lounging on the bed and in a flash realised she had made him angry again. He quickly stood up, glaring at her.

'What's the meaning of them?' He inclined his head angrily towards her jeans. 'I'll give you two seconds to choose a suitable dress and if you don't comply I will choose one and dress you myself.' His tone brooked no compromise.

'In fact,' he said, a slow smile appearing on his face, 'I would take great pleasure in it.' His glance slid down from her face to her slim hips. 'A great pleasure, little one.'

Clare's heart skipped a beat at the thought of his strong hands taking off her clothes and quickly she pushed the thoughts from her mind. Her voice trembled into life.

'How dare you. I'm not Julie and it won't be as easy to take advantage of me. I married you to stay near Julian. You can't tell me what to do and how to dress. I will wear jeans whenever I like, and I don't expect to share your room.' She rushed to the wardrobe and pulled out some of his suits.

'Oh, but you will, Clare, because... .' He stepped across the room in two strides, 'Because you are my wife.' He spoke with such anger that any protest was stifled on Clare's lips. Looking into his face Clare realised the futility of any more arguments. He took from one of the wardrobes a deep blue cocktail dress with a matching jacket.

'This will do, I think. Do you need any help?' He gave it to her.

'No!'

After a moment's silence Clare still stood in the same spot clutching the dress to her.

'Well,' Adrian demanded with an underlying threat in his voice, 'what are you waiting for, Clare?'

Clare glanced at the door.

'So you want me to leave the room, my little puritanical maiden? Just this once,' he said, placing one finger under her chin and gently stroking her cheek.

Clare looked into his eyes and was puzzled by his gentle look. All the anger had left his face and his closeness and the way he looked at her disturbed her greatly.

Her heart beat hard beneath her ribs. Why did he make her feel this way?

'Please,' was all she could whisper.

Understanding that Clare was near to breaking point Adrian nodded. 'I will be waiting in the lounge. Do you think you can find it?'

Clare nodded her head dumbly.

'Don't keep me waiting,' he replied, turning on his heels and closing the door gently.

Feeling utterly spent Clare sank onto the bed to gather any remnants of self-control. Mechanically she began to undress again and, after taking some sheer nylons from the drawer, began to work on the image that Adrian seemed to think so important. Standing before the mirror she gasped at her reflection. The dress fitted perfectly, moulding itself like a second skin to her small breasts and slim hips. Its deep blue colour matched her eyes.

Quickly she applied a touch of lipstick to give her a little colour. With her smooth creamy skin she needed no other make-up. With a last look in the mirror she slipped on a pair of silver sandals, picked up the matching jacket and bag and, steeling herself, left the safety of her room. She made her way carefully down the curving staircase to the hall, taking in the luxury that surrounded her. She stopped in the hall and looked about her. Most doors were closed but one stood slightly ajar.

Straightening her shoulders Clare carefully pushed open the door. The room was dominated by a huge fireplace and furnished with the dark polished wood of a large Chesterfield suite. The beige carpet was thick and springy. Gold velvet drapes adorned the windows and, once again, bowls of sweet-smelling flowers were on several tables placed by the walls and chairs.

Adrian had not heard her enter. He was sitting on the Chesterfield sofa with his long legs spread out comfortably before him. He was staring moodily into the fire and appeared to be deep in thought. Clare waited, unsure of herself. Then he turned, sensing her presence. That strange lopsided smile appeared and what could only be admiration glowed in his eyes. Pulling himself to his feet he paused and gave her a long slow look.

'Your photographs did not do you justice,' he said. 'I certainly have a very beautiful wife. Would you like a drink, to light the fires, perhaps?'

Clare's cheeks blazed red. Damn, she thought, why do I turn to jelly every time he speaks. I will have to have more control. She scolded herself silently.

Taking in the look on her face, he said, 'Perhaps not. Come and sit down. I won't bite.' He held out his hand. Slowly she walked towards him, her blush subsiding with his easy manner.

'When can I see Julian?'

'I've told cook we are going out, so we'll go up before we go out, poppet.' It was as if a mask had fallen from his face.

'Why did you not tell me you were Sir Adrian Loring?' asked Clare, in an attempt to make conversation.

'Would it have made any difference? Would I have been more acceptable, little Clare?'

When Clare did not answer he changed the conversation.

'I thought it would be nice to dine out tonight, and besides, I want to show off my beautiful wife. Or would you like a more intimate dinner, just you and me?' He raised an eyebrow in a mocking manner. 'There's still time for me to ring Mario's and cancel.' 'What about Julian?' Clare asked, ignoring his suggestive remarks.

'He has Miss Pringle and a house full of people to watch over him. Stop clucking like a mother hen. You are no longer alone, Clare,' Adrian added in a gentler tone. 'You can spend as much time or as little time as you want with Julian, but not at my expense. I expect a little of your time myself and tonight is our wedding night and I intend to make it memorable. Clare,' he whispered, reaching for her and fondling her bare neck, 'you look lovely. The dress really becomes you – much better than jeans. But something is missing.' He reached into his pocket, took out a slim case and held it out to her. Clare stared at the box stupidly.

'Well, don't you want to see what's inside?' he asked, and, not waiting for an answer, said, 'It's my heart; please take care of it.'

Opening the box he drew out a slim chain holding a heart made up of tiny diamonds.

'But I can't,' Clare gasped. 'It's far too expensive.' 'Nonsense,' he replied, walking behind her to fasten it around her neck. 'I don't want people to think I don't look after my wife.'

Clare felt his hot breath as he bent to kiss the nape of her neck, and a delicious shiver ran through her body.

Driving the feeling away she asked sarcastically, 'And how am I to pay for it?'

Adrian gave a throaty laugh and said, 'I'm sure we will think of a suitable way.'

CHAPTER 8

The Rolls Royce was comfortable. Clare was glad of its dim interior and, sitting beside Adrian, could not control her chaotic thoughts. She wished she could stay there all night to stave off bedtime. The thought of that large double bed gave her butterflies.

All too soon the car scrunched to a halt and they were outside the very popular and exclusive nightclub, Mario's. Clare had often heard people talk of it and its exclusive patrons but never thought she would dine there.

She was careful to stay in her seat and wait for Adrian to open the door. She did not wish to anger him again. Adrian led her into the foyer, whispering, 'That wasn't so hard, was it, little one.' Once inside the restaurant he was instantly recognised by the owner, who fussed around them like royalty. Obviously Adrian was a frequent visitor. Clare felt a stab of jealousy when she thought of all the women he must have escorted here. Instantly she banished the thought from her mind, controlling her emotions to ensure she did not betray Julie.

Clare was not used to wine, and the two glasses she drank with her meal made her feel warm and pleasant. Relaxing in the luxurious atmosphere, she glanced around at the other tables, which she could barely see in the dim light, and wondered what it would have been like had they been in love and married. Suddenly she remembered Adrian and felt his eyes on her. Glancing from under her lashes she thought how handsome he was with the wave of hair over his forehead beginning to fall forward. She wanted to push it back, to feel that dark hair entangled in her fingers. Without a word Adrian filled her wine glass.

'Has it been so bad?' he asked gently.

Clare returned his look and dumbly shook her head. She was reluctant to answer in case he read her thoughts. What was this madness, she silently asked herself. Adrian stood and held out his hand.

'Shall we dance?'

Clare nodded her assent, unable to drag her eyes from his. Gently he led her to the dance floor and they swayed in perfect rhythm. Clare leant against him, feeling his hard lean body close to her, and her mind strayed once again to wonder what would have happened if they had met under other circumstances. For some reason Adrian affected her sanity. The music stopped and Clare felt his lips brush her hair. Still holding her close to him he led her back to the table and without speaking a word beckoned to the waiter.

'Add it to my account.'

Bending close to Clare's ear, he whispered, 'Go and get your jacket. I will wait for you by the door.'

Clare hurried to the cloakroom, unaware of the admiring stares they were attracting from other diners. She pulled on her jacket and paused for a moment by the mirror in the cloakroom. The face staring back from the mirror was flushed and her blue eyes were deep with passion. Please, God, give me the strength to resist him. Please don't let him play with my feelings.

'Well, well!' Clare turned to look at the blonde woman leaning against the wall. 'So you are the little chit that stole Adrian from me,' the woman said in a hard voice. 'How did you manage that?' she sneered. 'You can't be as innocent as you look. I've never seen you at The Laurels. You must have come onto the scene while I went away. Absence makes the heart grow fonder, I was told. What a fool I was to go away. I left the field clear for you.'

Clare shrank back as the woman walked nearer. She was much taller than Clare.

'And now he's married you. But he'll soon tire of you. Adrian likes someone with a little fire. You won't satisfy him; I know how to please him.'

Suddenly she made for Clare, and grabbing her by the shoulders, hissed, 'He's mine in more ways than one. He'll come back to me.'

'Let me go,' Clare gasped, pulling herself free and escaping through the door. Just as she made for the foyer door she saw Adrian, who was obviously looking for her.

Adrian looked at her white face and silently cursed himself. The poor child is terrified of me. He swore under his breath. The comfortable truce that had existed between them had vanished. They drove back to The Laurels in silence, each turning over their own particular problem. If only they could read each other's thoughts. Clare followed Adrian into the hall, frightened and unsure of what to do next. Adrian broke the silence.

'Go up and see the little one,' he said in a tired voice, 'and then go to bed.'

Clare did not move; she could only stare at him and suddenly his face blazed with anger.

'Go on, get out of my sight before I change my mind,' he hissed, then turned on his heels and strode away.

Clare quickly climbed the staircase, unable to check the sudden tears that were coursing down her face; the whole day had been too much for her. She closed the door and stood with her back to it. Julie, oh Julie, why did I go away and leave you? What have we done? With a heartrending cry she threw herself on the bed, crumpling the pretty blue dress and eventually crying herself to sleep without visiting Julian.

CHAPTER 9

Clare was gently shaken awake.

'Your tea, madam.'

The events of yesterday rushed back into her mind and somehow the blonde woman from yesterday took centre stage in her confused thoughts.

'Thank you,' Clare said, accepting the tea tray. She assured the girl that she could pour it herself. To Clare's great astonishment, the maid then walked to the other side of the bed and picked up an empty coffee cup from the bedside cabinet. She also retrieved a pair of blue silk pyjamas.

'I'll take these down for the laundry.'

Reaching the door the maid turned and smiled at Clare.

'I hope you don't mind me saying so, madam, but I think it's all been so romantic and you make a lovely couple. His lordship is so handsome.'

Clare stared at the closed door trying to remember the previous night. All she could remember was that she'd been too tired to look in on Julian and instead had lain on her bed. She could not remember undressing herself yet there was no sign of the blue dress she had worn yesterday. She suddenly realised she had slept in her underwear. The colour rushed to her face when she thought of the possibilities. Jumping from the bed she rushed to the bathroom, intending to cool her hot skin under the shower. Try as might she could not blot out the image of the empty coffee cup and the blue pyjamas. Half an hour later she emerged from the bedroom much more composed.

Clad in her favourite garb of jeans, sweater and comfortable blue sneakers she went in search of Julian. He was her main worry. Had he settled down? Did he like Mrs Pringle? And most important of all, had he missed her? Since bringing him home from the hospital she had not left his side, until then.

Clare quickly found the room that was now the nursery; the walls were painted in sunshine yellow and decorated with prints of nursery rhyme characters. The wooden rocking horse had obviously been well used and was not newly acquired. Everything needed to look after a child was in that room. Sitting on a chair was a pleasant-faced nurse holding a freshly washed Julian. Clare could see that her Julian was happy and well looked after, and her heart gave a little pang of regret as she realised he didn't seem to have missed her at all.

The nurse looked up and instantly recognised Clare.

'Good morning, madam.' Then, looking at Julian, she said, 'There you are, my lovely, you have a visitor.' The nurse put Julian gently into Clare's arms. 'I will be in the dressing room, madam, if you require me.'

'Please don't call me madam. I'm Clare, please call me Clare.'

The nurse smiled her thanks.

Like a mother who had been deprived of her child for too long, Clare held Julian tight in her arms. Her brown curly hair rested against his small downy head and she crooned, 'I'm here darling, Auntie Clare is here.' She was unaware of the picture she painted from the open door and that Adrian had been watching with a tender look on his face. Turning silently he left.

Clare stayed in the nursery until lunchtime, helping to feed Julian and laying him down for his nap. She had a pleasant morning. Although she was not feeling hungry she felt in better able to face Adrian, and felt she may as well get it over with. Slowly she made her way downstairs in search of someone or something to occupy her time. Her mind told her she did not want to see Adrian, but underneath she wondered where he was. She glanced down at the rings sparkling on her left hand and, as if to blot out the truth, she thrust her hands deep into her pockets out of sight. Timidly she opened the door of the room she had been in last night and there, sitting on the Chesterfield with his head in his hands, was Adrian.

'Have you a headache?' she asked.

Without raising his head to look at her he asked, 'Why would you care if I have?'

Clare didn't answer but Adrian answered for her. 'No, I didn't think you would.'

He rose to his feet and his voice hardened as his glance slid over her. 'I imagine you would like to lunch alone, as you saw fit not to join me for breakfast. Very well, I can see you won't miss me so I will be dining with a friend. Please tell cook I won't be in for lunch or dinner.'

With that he strode out of the room, throwing over his shoulder a last comment.

'Oh, by the way, I meant every word I said about your dress sense. I expect you to dress like a woman. Is that clear.' Without another word he was gone.

For the rest of the day Clare wandered around the house and grounds, taking in the lovely gardens and trying to help where she could, mostly in the nursery and kitchen. She was not happy with the inactivity. She had worked hard, even when her parents had been alive, and theirs had been a comfortable happy home. Now, all three people she loved had gone. She sighed. She could not imagine spending the rest of her life with her hands idle. She made a mental note to speak to Adrian about helping around the house. There must be something she could do.

At 10 o'clock Adrian had still not returned home and, bored with her own company, Clare decided to go to bed after taking a last peep at Julian, who was contentedly sleeping. There was a slight flush on his cheeks. Clare bent to kiss him and smelt the familiar baby soap and talc. She mouthed goodnight to the nurse and left.

Once in bed Clare lay awake, her nerves on edge. She was half-fearful and half-curios as to when Adrian would come home.

At around 2 o'clock in the morning Clare heard a noise, and keeping her eyes tightly shut she pretended to be asleep. She was sure he must hear her heart thumping; the blood was also pounding in her head. Clare felt Adrian's breath on her face and smelt the whisky on his breath, but she remained rigid and still. With a chuckle he gently kissed her cheek and then heard his soft padding across the floor and the rustle of clothes and shoes being dropped. Clare almost panicked and fled from the bed as it gave under his weight. However, fear kept her there, lying still and breathing evenly. She need not have worried, because he lay down facing the other way and was soon sleeping heavily. It was the sleep of a man who had indulged in a little too much drink. Eventually Clare's eyelids began to droop. She tried to fight the urge to sleep and became aware of Adrian's arm tightening around her. She was uneasy but eventually drifted off.

CHAPTER 10

Clare awoke to a knock on the door and was about to answer when she heard a curt 'Come in' from Adrian. Everything came flooding back: Adrian coming home; her pretence of being asleep. Quickly she shut her eyes.

'Oh no you don't, sleepy head,' Adrian said, giving her a playful dig in the ribs. Clare slowly opened her eyes and met his amused gaze. She shot him a furious look. He held her gaze for a few seconds then swung his legs out of bed, dismissing the maid with, 'We can manage now.' He sat on the side of the bed not looking at her, his dark hair falling in untidy waves across his forehead. He was bare to the waist and his muscular body was tanned and fit.

'Sugar or lemon?' he asked as he poured the tea. 'Lemon,' she whispered.

'Did you sleep well?'

'Yes.' She nodded, not daring to look him in the face.

They sipped their tea in companionable silence. To any onlooker it would have appeared to be a normal picture of domesticity, the most natural thing in the world, and it didn't make sense that she was partly afraid and for some reason strangely attracted to this man who was now her husband.

Adrian drained his cup and placed it on the tray, all the time watching her from under his eyelids. Suddenly he leant over and caressed her bare arm, and Clare shivered as a delicious feeling rushed to the pit of her stomach.

Not taking his hand away or his eyes off her he gave a deep pleasant laugh and said, 'Do you know, little wife, how lovely and desirable you are?'

'Is that what you told Julie,' Clare spat out.

Adrian's hand stilled then continued tracing a path along her arm. Clare tried to control her treacherous heart; it would be so easy to betray the memory of her sister with this man. She searched for a new weapon.

'And what about your other friend, the blonde, do you sleep with her?' she asked bluntly.

His eyes searched her face. 'Blonde? You must mean Rhonda. She is the only blonde I know well. How do you know about Rhonda? Has one of my staff been gossiping?'

'No.'

'Good. I wouldn't like to think you made a habit of gossiping with staff. How did you know then?' The softness had left his voice.

'I met her in the powder room at Mario's.'

Taking her by surprise he bent to kiss her on the lips.

'She means nothing, my sweet, believe me.'

With that he sprang from the bed and made for the bathroom. Getting out of bed herself Clare pulled on a robe and began hanging up his clothes and making the bed. By the time he returned she had found clean underwear, jeans and a sweater, purposely ignoring the new clothes he had insisted on buying and laying her own clothes on the bed in readiness. She looked up as Adrian emerged from the bathroom, showered and freshly shaved, with a towel secured around his middle.

'Very domesticated,' he drawled, 'but I can think of a better way to show your wifely talents.'

His hand hovered over the towel as if he was about to remove it and scooping up her clothes, Clare bolted past him, slamming the bathroom door shut. Standing with her back to the door she heard him call, 'I can wait, but not too long, sweetheart.'

Clare emerged dressed in the jeans and sweater to find Adrian lounging on the bed quietly awaiting her return. In an instant he was on his feet.

'You obviously intend to ignore my request to dress correctly,' he said icily. 'I abhor those awful trousers.'

'I'm sorry. I don't intend to offend you, Mr Loring, however, I haven't been raised to wear model gowns to clean in. Good clothes should be looked after. Besides, I feel more comfortable in clothes I've paid for myself.'

'And I, my dear Clare, do not intend you to be a cleaner in our home. If I needed another cleaner, I would employ one. You have a different role altogether, Mrs. Loring.'

With that he walked slowly towards her, pulled her into his arms and crushed her to him. Whispering her name he claimed her lips and slowly explored her mouth with insistent kisses. Clare suddenly stopped struggling and responded, pressing herself to him, allowing him to arouse a passion she was unaware she was capable of. Gently he held her away from him.

'Lesson one. Lesson two will come later,' he said suggestively. 'You had better come down for some breakfast. You are far too thin, Clare. I'm not the ogre you think I am. Later we will talk. That way we might stand a chance.'

Clare nodded her head and her small pink tongue moistened her lips. Sooner or later she would have to face the obvious. She had married him, and the bargain had been that she could stay with Julian. Clare now knew that marriage meant more than living together, and somehow deep down she knew she could not hold out against him.

Sitting opposite him at the breakfast table everything seemed normal. Clare poured his coffee and served both of them breakfast from under the covered dishes, as he held the plates. She ate just toast, and drank some orange juice and two cups of coffee. Breakfast had never been her strong point. Adrian, however, appeared to enjoy his cooked breakfast.

'Is there anything in particular you would like to do today? I'm afraid I'll be busy until around lunchtime, but after that I'm all yours,' he said, lifting an eyebrow.

Clare gave a ghost of a smile. 'Nothing special.'

'I don't suppose you would like to help me, then?'

'How?'

'Read and check my new book, and perhaps do a little typing. My secretary left a few months ago. That's why Julie was typing for me.'

A look of pain crossed Clare's face at the mention of her sister, and carefully she fought to control her feelings.

'Yes of course I'll help you. It will be good to be busy again. Can I just go to see Julian first?'

Adrian sensed the change of mood.

'I'll come with you,' he said gently.

Silently they made their way upstairs and Clare was soon engrossed in cuddling her small nephew, kissing his rosy cheeks and murmuring sweet words.

'Lucky fellow,' Adrian said, causing Clare to look up and blush.

Much later Clare began typing Adrian's manuscript. There was so much she didn't know about this man she had married. His book was about an archaeology dig he had just returned from, and he had made some exciting discoveries. Clare had not realised that he was *the* Sir Adrian Loring, the famous archaeologist. Adrian sat opposite at a huge oak desk. The French windows were thrown open; it was warm and sunny outside and for the first time in weeks Clare felt at peace. They both worked in silence. Clare was absorbed in the contents of Adrian's book and his work appeared to be both interesting and exciting.

Suddenly their peace was shattered by the scrunch of footsteps on the gravel path outside. Both Adrian and Clare looked towards the French windows to see who their visitor was. Clare's heart felt a quick stab of hurt as Rhonda appeared.

Before she had time to wonder what relationship existed between them Rhonda stepped through the French windows, cooing, 'Adrian, darling, surprised to see me? I have missed you so much. I just had to come around as soon as I arrived back. I'm ready and willing to come back to work.'

Rhonda stopped there.

'Oh! You have employed a temp. Well, I'm back now. You know no one else understands your needs better than me,' she said, hinting at something more. 'I'm sure she has been satisfactory, but we both know you would prefer me.' She pouted, staring at Clare as if she had never met her.

Adrian got to his feet. 'On the contrary, Rhonda,' he said, walking around the desk, 'this is my wife, Lady Clare Loring.' He pulled Clare to her feet and kissed her tenderly. 'She understands my needs better than anyone, don't you darling?' The long silence embarrassed Clare and she visibly squirmed in Adrian's tight embrace. Addressing Clare he said, 'Run along, sweetheart, and ask Mrs Downs to send coffee for two and then dress yourself in something pretty. We are dining out. About half an hour. Is that enough time, sweetheart?'

His voice seemed to linger seductively as he uttered these words.

Clare nodded mutely. She almost felt sorry for Rhonda. He was obviously tired of her and was trying to make her jealous. God, what a perfect performance. At least Rhonda was still breathing. She should be grateful. Julie had forfeited her life. Yes, he had said how sorry he was but he was not grieving. What a heel he must be. Julie had had such a short life. Please God, let her have been ignorant of Adrian's selfish ways; let her have felt loved.

Adrian could not have spent long with Rhonda, for while Clare was sitting at the dressing table he came into the bedroom, slipped off his polo shirt and, much to Clare's embarrassment, took off his trousers. Clare pretended to fiddle with her watchstrap, as if she was having trouble fastening it.

He chuckled. 'Later, Clare, there's a time for everything.'

Five minutes later he was dressed in navy slacks and a white silk shirt. The neck of the shirt was slightly open, showing the dark hair on his chest.

Bending over her he reached for her wrist to see why she had been struggling with the strap.

'It's already fastened,' he said, tilting her chin with his free hand. His lips brushed hers. Pulling her to her feet he looked at the green linen dress, matching shoes, and bag.

'You look lovely, Clare.'

Not letting go of her hand he led her downstairs to the car.

She watched him from beneath her eyelids. He did not mention his talk with Rhonda, short as it was. Had he arranged to see her again? Clare wondered. A cold hand clutched at her heart.

Why had he married her? He had only to prove paternity to the courts and he would have been given Julian. Clare was aware that she really had no rights. With his money, he would not have needed to look after Julian himself. She was still trying to work it out when they pulled up outside a small but exclusive Italian restaurant. Once more the owner, Giovanni, addressed Adrian as an old friend and fussed around Clare, kissing her on both cheeks and declaring her a most beautiful bride. He wished them many bambinos and a long and happy life, then insisted on fetching his wife, Maria, to meet Clare. They then bustled off to supervise the preparation of a special light luncheon, which would be served with one of the restaurant's best wines. Clare met Adrian's gaze and at once dropped her eyes, deliberately ignoring what she read in his look.

Adrian was happy to sit in companionable silence, while Giovanni served the meal. Clare ate very little; her appetite had suffered since Julia's death. Placing his knife and fork down, Adrian covered her small hand.

'Please, Clare, don't hate me. I can't bear to see you so unhappy. All I want is your happiness, our happiness. Would you believe me if I said I had never made love to Julie, ever? And that, although I will always care for both you and Julian, I'm not his father?'

Clare stared back in anger and disbelief.

'How could you? How could you deny your own child?' Clare's thoughts began to run riot. Adrian was lying. Why else would he have married her? Poor Julie. Why was he such cad?

The words 'I love you, Clare' died on Adrian's lips and staring at her white face he realised he had failed to gain her trust. The skin tightened across his cheekbones as he struggled with some unknown emotion. He then sank into a thoughtful silence and turned his attention to his meal.

When he was ready to leave, he held her chair then in silence followed Clare towards the door, only pausing to assure the disappointed Giovanni that the meal was excellent and that they just could not eat anymore. Stooping, he kissed Maria on the cheek and assured the couple that they would call again.

After the short drive home Adrian escorted Clare into the house, telling the housekeeper there would only be Clare to provide dinner for. He then turned to Clare and said sarcastically, 'Don't wait up for me.'

Clare watched his disappearing back, and bit her lip. With a sinking heart she realised she was disappointed that he was not staying with her. What was she thinking of, she scolded d herself. Why did she long to be with the man who had treated her sister so badly. Once again she felt as if she was betraying her sister's trust. Slowly she made her way to the nursery to spend the rest of the day with Julian. Being with Julian was the only thing that soothed her aching heart.

CHAPTER 11

Clare checked the time once more. It was 10.35 in the evening and for the last hour she had been lingering in the kitchen, her coffee cup empty. The room was familiar now and was by far her favourite. The huge Aga cooker produced just enough warmth to take the chill off the room, the rows of copper pans hanging on the walls gleamed, the red tiled floor was scrubbed clean and in the middle was a large wooden table. Two old armchairs were at either side of the Aga. Clare occupied the one opposite the door. Her gaze always returned to that door and after a month of living at The Laurels she was no nearer to making a pact with Adrian. Each day began the same, with Clare waking to find the sleeping Adrian in her bed. Then followed the pretence of contented early morning tea and breakfast taken together. For the benefit of the staff a picture of happy domesticity was enacted. However, he no longer attempted to kiss or caress her. Adrian would then leave for work and never returned home until 2 or 3 o'clock in the morning. Clare wanted to clear the air and over the last few weeks she had become a favourite of all the staff. She helped with tasks, although Mrs Downs had on many occasions shaken her head and chided Clare with 'Whatever would the master say.'

Sighing, she realised that tonight would be a repetition of every night for the last month. She took her coffee cup to the sink, washed and stacked it. She was so wrapped up in her thoughts that she did not hear the kitchen door open. Looking up, she saw Adrian watching her from the doorway. He looked slightly the worse for drink. He was wearing an old pair of cords, an open-neck shirt and a rust-coloured sweater; his cords were covered in mud and grass stains. Walking to the sink he washed and dried his hands.

'You're back,' stated Clare, stupidly.

'Yes,' he answered, 'and I would love a cup of coffee and something to eat.'

'I'll get you something.'

Clare set to work filling a plate with cold meat and salad. She put the kettle on.

'I won't do you any bread. It will be too heavy to sleep on.'

Setting the plate and coffee before him, she said lamely, 'Don't drink too much coffee it will keep you awake.'

Adrian suddenly smiled that lopsided grin. 'Perhaps I would like to stay awake,' he said, smiling suggestively.

Clare suddenly lost her nerve. His smile was having the same effect on her as before and turning, she almost broke into a run towards the door. Adrian was too quick for her. His hand shot out and gripped her wrist.

'No, please wait for me,' he said in an urgent tone.

Clare looked at his face. It seemed drawn and tired. Without further protest she sat down on the other chair. Through half-closed eyes she sat and watched him drain his cup, then stood up to wash his cup and plate. She could feel his eyes on her.

'I'm going to bed,' she said lamely.

'Good. I'll come with you. That will save you the bother of pretending to be asleep. It could prove more interesting, don't you agree?'

Clare started to quiver and felt that same strange sensation fill her stomach. Finding nothing to say her eyes locked with his. Somehow, she knew it would not be hard to give herself to him and in an instant the truth dawned on her. In just a few short weeks she had fallen in love with this man.

'Julie, Julie, I have no right to love him,' she said silently.

But she knew she could not deny him.

'Clare, look at me,' Adrian said softly.

She dropped her face. He put his fingers under her chin and gently raised it to face him. Slowly he caressed her cheek.

'Tell me you don't hate me.'

Clare was mesmerised and tongue-tied. Pulling her to him he began to slowly explore her lips. Clare did not struggle, and returned his kisses. All she was aware of was the desire to remain locked in his arms. Urgently he slipped his hand beneath her jumper to grip and caress her quickly hardening nipples. She was no longer embarrassed when he lifted her and carried her up the curving staircase, lying in his arms with her head resting on his broad chest. He pushed open the bedroom door and kicked it shut behind them and, after lowering her to her feet, continued to kiss and explore her mouth, his hands roaming unchecked over her hips and thighs. Clare answered with a passion that shocked even her. His hands shook as they fumbled with the zip of her jeans.

'Now why could you not wear a dress instead of jeans, my darling, like any other woman?' he whispered.

Those whispered words were like a dose of cold water on Clare's emotions and she suddenly began to struggle.

'I won't let you use me! I'm not like Julie and Rhonda.' She scratched his face in the struggle.

'Why you little she cat.'

He swore softly and tightened his hold on her, making it impossible to break free. His lips pursed in anger. 'You're a tease, Clare, giving a glimpse of paradise with one hand then snatching it back with the other. The time for playing games is over. You are my wife and I have every intention of having what is mine by rights.'

Swiftly he lifted Clare onto the bed, pinning her down with his body. He removed her jeans and flimsy undergarments with ease. Savagely he lowered himself upon her and her body was consumed with blinding hot passion. Clare no longer pulled away from him but met him, her small hips moving with pleasure.

Afterwards, Clare lay by his side without moving. Tears silently trickled down her face. The act of love had been rough but had only served to feed her desire. She was ashamed of her feelings for this man; she had been putty in his hands.

Adrian was now breathing evenly. He still had one arm across Clare as if to prevent her from leaving the bed. His head was close to hers.

'Clare, I'm sorry I hurt you. If I had known you were a virgin... .' His voice trailed off.

Gently he covered her half-naked body and pulling her close he soothed her tears. He lay watching her long after she had fallen into an exhausted sleep. Her long dark lashes rested on her cheeks and tears still glistening like tiny diamonds on her ivory skin.

God, he thought, she looks so vulnerable and defenceless. Tomorrow he would step up his search to find out who Julian's father was. He needed to wipe the slate clean. If she would not accept the truth, what could he do – offer to release her from the marriage? He closed his eyes. He knew he could not bear that – the thought of someone else making love to her pained him.

He lay awake, recalling taking his manuscript to Julie.

'Who's this,' he had asked, picking up a photo on the side table. Julie had smiled.

'That's Clare, my sister.'

'Is she married?'

'No, but she's working away.'

From then on he had been unable to get that picture out of his mind. He had vowed that sooner or later he would meet Clare; he had fallen in love with a photograph.

He pulled Clare close, willing her to feel his love, then slipped out of bed and, with a grim look on his face, quietly went to the bathroom to change. Before leaving the room he gently kissed her and whispered, 'I love you.'

CHAPTER 12

Clare awoke at peace with herself; her dreams had been filled with Adrian whispering his love for her. For the first time in weeks she could think clearly. Perhaps she had misjudged him; perhaps he had not known that Julie was pregnant. Julie must have been willing. The feeling that she had betrayed Julie had faded away. How could she have been so stupid and not recognised that Adrian had really tried. Perhaps he could learn to love her, for she was now aware that she would never love anyone but him. All she could think of was his endearing mannerisms, the way he pushed back those dark waves of hair from his eyes, his lopsided grin and the passion when he looked at her. She had judged him without a hearing; everyone was innocent until proven guilty.

Looking at herself in the mirror she thought that everyone would tell the difference. There was a sparkle in her eyes and a glow to her skin that had not been there the day before. Humming the popular ballad *True Love* she went to shower, then, choosing a day dress of shadowed red silk that accentuated her slim figure and suited her dark looks, she again surveyed herself in the mirror. She was aware that she had dressed to please Adrian. Whatever had happened in the past she was willing to forget. She had married him, for better or for worse, and it was up to her to make it for the better.

Opening the dining room door Clare expected to find Adrian having his breakfast. However, the room was deserted. Disappointment was etched on her young face. She poured herself a cup of coffee and sat down.

After what seemed an eternity Clare decided to tidy up and go in search of him, but first she would help with the breakfast dishes. Putting the used dishes onto a tray she carried them to the kitchen and insisted on helping to wash up. After spending the morning trying to make herself useful and visiting Julian, Clare decided to finish some of Adrian's typing. At 4 o'clock there still was no sign of Adrian and Clare decided there was just enough time to take a walk before dinner. This would give her time to think. Not bothering to put on a coat Clare made her way outside.

Why had Adrian left without a word? Last night he had truly made her his wife and since then she had been far more positive; all problems were surmountable. She had woven dreams around herself, Adrian and Julian. After all, Julian deserved to be raised in a happy home. She pictured her chubby nephew gurgling and sucking his small fist. It brought a smile to her face for the first time that day.

Clare made her way across the lawns and down the drive, then wandered through the gate, enjoying the late afternoon sunshine. Losing all trace of time she just walked, not bothering to take note of the distance or route she had followed.

Suddenly it started to rain. Clare stopped and realised she was lost, and she was shocked to realise that she had been walking for two and a half hours; it was now 6.30 in the evening.

She wandering around, trying to get her bearings, then started to walk back the way she thought she had come. It would take ages for her to get back. The rain was a fine drizzle, the type that seemed to wet you more than a good downpour. Shivering slightly, she followed the badly lit road and, after quickening her pace, she imagined what a sight she must look. Her dress clung to her slim figure, her hair was soaking and springing into tight curls around her head. She pictured the roaring fire at The Laurels and sighed. Why do I always make a mess of things?

Suddenly, the headlights of a car appeared and dazzled her. She stepped onto the pavement and tried to shield her eyes from the glare. She thought about how warm and dry it must be in that car.

Her heart gave a lurch as the car skidded to a halt beside her and Adrian jumped out of the driver's seat. 'What on earth do you think you're playing at?' Anger stirred within her and she answered in quiet, controlled manner.

'I decided to go for a walk.'

'Without having the decency to inform anyone of where you had gone?'

Clare lifted her head and gazed at him in amazement. 'Like you inform me every day of where you go – or would Rhonda mind?' She spat out the words, anger and the misery of being cold getting the better of her. Adrian took a step towards her. His skin was stretched and white over his cheekbones.

'Get in,' he ordered, 'before I do something I will regret.'

Opening the passenger door he bundled her inside and pulled a travelling rug over her.

'Get out of that dress. It's soaking.' He held the rug around her.

He then found an old coat in the boot which was covered in dried mud. It was dry and warm, however, and smelt of Adrian's cologne. After tucking the rug around her legs he slammed the door shut and climbed into the driver's seat. Stealing a look at him, Clare realised she had angered him once more. Little droplets of water shone on his dark hair and his mouth was fixed in a tight, hard line. The car's engine sprang to life with a roar and soon it was sliding to a halt outside The Laurels. Adrian jumped out of the car, opened the door for her and picked up the rug. Clare looked up at him, unaware of what he was thinking as he took in her bare legs showing below his jacket. Holding the blanket around her shoulders he hurried her into the house. Luckily for Clare no one was there to witness Adrian pushing her up the stairs before him. Once inside their room he instructed her to strip off her remaining clothes. Clare just stood, holding the coat around her.

'Take them off or I will,' he commanded, adding as an afterthought, 'I've already seen every inch of you.'

Turning, he strode to the bathroom and ran her a hot bath and after settling Clare in the bath went in search of a hot drink.

Soon after, Clare had settled herself under the covers and he returned with a sandwiches, hot milk and a pot of coffee for himself.

Clare ate a sandwich and drank her milk, and looking up whispered, 'I'm sorry if I worried anyone.'

'So you should be,' he replied more gently. 'Have you finished?'

Clare nodded.

'Right, I'll be back in a minute.'

Taking the tray he left the room. A warm drowsiness overcame Clare and she struggled to pull herself back from sleep as she became aware of Adrian caressing her breast. She turned to him and felt the hardness of his body. Passion rose within her as his hand slipped between her thighs. This time Adrian's lovemaking was gentle and slow, and over and over again he caressed her until she shyly begged him to love her. With a low cry he took her to him. Afterwards she was content to lie in the circle of his arms, resting her head on his chest. Both Adrian and Clare fell into an exhausted sleep.

CHAPTER 13

Adrian slipped out of bed making sure he did not wake the sleeping Clare; he had risen early. He needed to be in Paris by 8 o'clock that evening. He had fully intended to take Clare with him but had a little business to attend to before catching the flight. Adrian didn't want Clare to be aware of his impending visit to Keith Charnwood and for this reason decided to leave Clare behind this time. By the time he returned home he would have the whole mess sorted out. After checking that he had the solicitor's papers in his briefcase, he quietly bent over the sleeping Clare and softly brushed her lips with his.

'I love you,' he whispered, and left the room, closing the door quietly.

Adrian left Keith's office with a huge smile on his face; he now had documents signed by Keith giving up all claims to Julian. Keith was a very unsavoury character, but it had been worth the money he had paid to ensure Clare's happiness.

He smiled and rubbed his hands. Before leaving Keith he had paused, turned, and said, 'Oh, by the way Keith, this is for Julie.' Keith had gone down with a bump as Adrian's fist slammed into his face.

Clare awoke to the rattle of teacups on the tray. The maid smiled at her and set the tray down.

'Good morning, madam. It's a lovely day.'

'Yes, a beautiful day,' Clare agreed, smiling.

Reaching for a cup, Clare noticed an envelope propped against a single red rose. She held it in her hand until the maid left. A small smile lingered on her lips as she thought back to the previous night.

Ripping it open she read,

'Dear Clare. By the time you get this note I will already be in Paris. I have an important meeting to attend. I will also be calling on Mother, who, by the way, is thinking of visiting. When I return I will have some information for you. It might make you decide you want your freedom, so I think this short time apart will give both of us time to think, and make the right decision to ensure Julian's happiness as well as ours. By the way, little one, last night was wonderful. Must dash, your Adrian.'

Clare held the note in her hands, grossly misinterpreting its contents. Her eyes misted with tears. He had never meant any of the words he had whispered in the height of passion. Was she just another conquest? Why had he come in to her and Julie's life? Things had been so uncomplicated before. How she wished she could turn the clock back. His note was plain enough. He regretted the bargain they had made. But what of Julian? He must surely care for his own son. Clare lay back, tears clouding her vision. All at once she realised what she must do. Swinging her legs off the side of the bed, Clare made her way to the bathroom, and once under the shower scrubbed herself clean, as if she were trying to wash the last few weeks away. Quickly dressing in trousers and sweater, she threw open the wardrobe, searching the shelves for her battered suitcase. She could only find the leather cases with the initials 'C.L.'. Adrian thought of everything. Selecting the smallest, she began to pack a small selection of clothes, taking care not to pack any that Adrian had purchased. Clare realised that it was easy to pack but it would not be as easy to visit Julian for the last time. Thinking of him brought her back to reality. She could not go back to the flat. That was already sold and her solicitor was forwarding the cash to her bank account. Besides, Adrian did appear to be quite fond of Julian and in her heart of hearts Clare knew that he would be cosseted and well looked after at The Laurels. Had she the right to deprive him of all this? Covering her face with her hands Clare began to sob uncontrollably. It was more than half an hour before she could control the hurt.

As if in a dream she went once again to the bathroom, and after washing her face and applying a little more make-up she sat down and wrote a short note to Adrian, telling him that she was sorry to have blamed just him – it was wrong of her. Julie had been 18 and old enough to have made her own decisions.

Becoming his lover was just one of those decisions. 'Please take care of Julian,' she wrote. 'Although I love him very much he needs your love and guidance.' Taking the note and placing it on Adrian's desk in his study, Clare squared her shoulders and went up the stairs to Julian's room. As she opened the door she fixed a bright smile on her face.

She picked up his small wriggling form, and hugging him to her breast she whispered, 'Forgive me, Julian, I'll always love you.'

After giving his plump cheek a last kiss Clare placed him back in his cot. She took a last look around the pleasant room as if to imprint it on her memory – the sunshine-yellow walls, his cot with the mobiles bouncing above. Clare hurried out taking care to keep her eyes averted from the nurse in case she saw the stark misery in her eyes.

Walking along the corridor to her room Clare could sense the faint smell of lavender polish. Over the last few weeks she had come to love this house and the people in it. She picked up her case and walked to the bedroom door. Then, turning on impulse, Clare put the red rose in an envelope and pressed it on the dressing table. She then placed it in her handbag. A lump came into her throat and she fought for control as she gazed around the room, the room in which Adrian had made love to her. She then gathered herself , firmly grasped the suitcase and turned away.

Clare slipped out of the house without bumping into anyone, and, keeping close to the trees, reached the end of the drive and walked quickly through the gate. Once out on the road she waved down a taxi, asking for the nearest railway station. Clare slumped in the back, trying to calm her chaotic thoughts. After paying the fare, she made her way to the booking office. Scanning the departure board on the way her eyes picked out the 10 o'clock train to Windermere in the Lake District. She asked for a single to Windermere. Hopefully she would be far enough away to enable her to forget her short married life.

CHAPTER 14

Clare was tired and hungry by the time her train approached Windermere. She picked up her bag and case as it pulled in, alighted onto the platform and made her way out of the station. She needed a place to stay and looking up she noticed a small hotel, The Lakeside Arms. Clare went in and rang the bell on the reception desk.

'Can I help you, miss?' asked a smiling young man.

'Yes, I'd like a room, please.'

'You're in luck. How long will you be staying?'

'I'm not sure. Can I book for two weeks? If I need to stay longer I'll let you know.'

'I think we can manage that, miss. I'm sorry, I meant Mrs.'

Clare realised he was looking at her wedding ring. In her rush to leave she had forgotten to take off the ring.

'Mrs Loring, Clare,' she said but almost as soon as she had said it she thought, Damn, I've given him my married name. Mind you, Adrian was hardly going to follow her and drag her back.

'Molly,' shouted the young man, 'we need clean towels for room 18. We have a new guest.'

Clare was later told by the chatty Molly that he was her younger brother.

'Follow me,' she said, and smiled at Clare.

A bright red carpet and gold curtains decorated the reception area. The hotel had a homely feel and Clare felt that she had made the right decision. She was not too worried about money after the sale of her flat her parents' home, and felt she could pick and choose. With Julia's half of the funds she would open a bank account for Julian. It was his by rights. Now she could look for a small flat to rent or buy, and she would get the job she needed to keep occupied.

'Here you are, Mrs Loring,' Molly said. 'My dad or John will be up in a minute with your case.'

'Please call me Clare. It would be nice to be able to talk to someone my own age.'

'Thanks! I will. Come down to the kitchen when you are ready. I'm sure you we can find you a cup of tea. You look as if you need one.'

'Thank you, Molly, I'd love that.'

Molly smiled and left her, quietly closing the door.

Clare looked around the room. It was quite pleasant and clean, and it had matching curtains and bedspread, patterned with blue and lemon roses, and a blue carpet. On the dressing table was a bowl of forget-me-nots. Clare could not help thinking of the room she had recently shared with Adrian. It was strange that even now she longed to be with him; deep down she knew that she would never want anyone else. Giving herself a mental shake, Clare went into the bathroom. The day was nearly over and she felt a little sick; she needed to eat something. She looked at her reflection she slipped downstairs to find the kitchen. In the corridor she saw a door marked 'Private'. She knocked gently.

'Come in,' shouted Molly. She was sitting at a table with a lady who looked like an older edition of herself.

'Mother, this is Clare. She will be staying for a couple of weeks.'

Molly's mother looked up from the book she was writing in.

'Hello, love. Sit down and make yourself comfortable. My name's Annie.'

'Hello, Annie.'

'Molly, pour that tea, love.'

'Would it be possible to buy a sandwich? I didn't get time to eat on the train.'

'Of course, love.' Clare drank the tea and ate in silence.

'Will your husband be joining you?' Annie suddenly asked. The shrewd woman had taken in the pale face, sad eyes and violet shadows beneath them.

'No, we have decided it's best if we part.'

Clare's eyes met the kindly eyes of Annie.

'I'm sorry, love. I'm too inquisitive for my own good. I wasn't meaning to pry, but you look so lost.'

Clare had to fight back the tears. Sympathy was the last thing she needed.

'Don't be. All I want is to find myself a job and somewhere to live. That way I will have a fresh start.'

'What sort of job?' asked Molly.

'Anything. I'm a secretary but I'll consider anything.'

'Mum!'

'Hang on, Molly, you are going too fast for me. Well now, let me see. I think what Molly is getting at is that our receptionist-cum-general help has left and we could do with a replacement. The wage won't be much but it would help us and perhaps give you thinking time. There would be free board and lodging, that's if you're interested.'

Clare was amazed.

'You have a trustworthy face,' added Annie.

Tears rained down Clare's cheeks and she searched in her pocket for a handkerchief. Annie came around the table and put her arms around Clare's shoulders.

'There, there, love, it can't be as bad as all that.'

Clare found herself enveloped in Annie's protective arms. 'It will all come out in the wash,' she soothed. 'Finish your tea and then go and lie down.'

Clare wiped her eyes.

'I'm sorry. So much has happened in the last few months.'

Molly and Annie nodded.

'We understand, love. You will feel much better in the morning.'

CHAPTER 15

Clare soon got into the hotel's routine. She kept the books, helped out generally and acted as receptionist. The work was varied and different from that she was used to. Annie and her family quickly became firm friends and took Clare to their hearts. Gradually Clare found peace of mind. She thought of Julian and Adrian every day but was now able to cope. Adrian, she knew, wouldn't miss her, but what of Julian? Had he grown? Did he miss her?

When Clare had a day off she would go sightseeing, and visited Kendall and Coniston. The lakes were lovely and Clare liked to watch the speedboats roar around Windermere like free spirits.

One morning, two months after her arrival, she was looking in the mirror readying herself for breakfast when she suddenly felt queasy. I must have eaten something last night that didn't agree with me, she thought.

'You look dreadful,' she said to her reflection. 'For someone who thinks they have conquered Everest you look very green.'

Her eyes looked too large in her small face.

'You look as if you need a tonic, my girl,' she said to herself.

Only yesterday she had said, Molly, 'I need to buy some new jeans; the air must suit me and I appear to be gaining weight.'

Suddenly Clare dropped her hand to her stomach; it no longer felt flat. As she slowly rubbed her hand over the smallest of swellings an awful suspicion screamed at her. How stupid she had been. The pain that filled her breast was so real she had to clutch at the nearest chair for support. She was pregnant. She slowly lowered herself down before her legs gave away and sat with her head in her hands.

Why? Why me? Clare now knew how Julie must have felt. Please, God, don't let her have suffered this awful pain.

Searching her mind Clare made excuses. Adrian had been away. I'm sure Julie would not have known that he didn't want her. He would have married Julie to look after Julian, as he had married her. Quickly Clare pulled herself back to the present just as vomit rose to her throat.

She sat on the bathroom floor next to the toilet, waiting for the sickness to abate. Then, after washing her face and composing herself, she told herself that she must go down to reception. There was a lot to do. But still she lingered, going to the window that looked out on the lake. Hungrily she pictured Adrian, his slate grey eyes, the way his dark hair fell over his forehead; she could almost feel his touch on her skin. This won't do, my girl, she told herself, and wearily turned towards the door to make her way downstairs to the kitchen.

Annie and her family had been so good to her and she did not want to let them down. Besides, it was the middle of the holiday season and they were already short-staffed. There would be time for thinking and planning soon enough. How was she going to tell Annie, though, who had accepted her as a daughter? She could not ask Annie to help her look after a new-born child.

For a second Clare allowed her thoughts to travel back to that nursery, the one that her lovely Julian occupied. Would Adrian, if he knew, love and take care of this baby, too? Clare's heart hardened. This was one child she would not allow him to take away. It would only be a small part of Adrian. With a pang she wondered if the child would look like her or Adrian. Would she have to watch her child grow up and be reminded daily of the person she loved? She knew she must carry on as usual until she had figured out what to do.

'Morning, love,' said Annie, looking up and smiling. 'What's it going to be – a full English breakfast?'

Clare shook her head.

'No, just some toast and coffee will be fine, thanks.'

Annie eyed Clare sharply. 'Are you all right, lass? You look a little pale.'

'I'm fine. I must have slept heavily and I have a little bit of a headache; it will soon pass.' Clare did not like lying to Annie, who had been so good to her, but she needed time to think.

'Right,' said Clare, forcing a smile. 'I'll start on changing today's menu and check that we have enough clean linen.'

'Well, don't do it all yourself,' Annie replied, giving her a thoughtful look. 'Give Molly a shout. The job will be done much quicker by two of you.'

Clare forced a smile, nodded and left the room.

Molly and Clare spent a full morning changing menus, checking linen and confirming bookings.

'Right,' Molly said, looking at Clare. 'I'll just take the water jugs in. You give our John a shout. He can take over the reception and you and I can have our lunch. We've earnt it.'

Clare smiled. 'I'll just go and clean myself up and then send him in.'

Just as Clare and Molly were about to leave, the door opened and Clare turned to go back to the desk.

'Why, Lady Loring!' The voice stopped Clare in her tracks.

'Mrs Pringle, how are you? Clare asked in a stilted fashion. Not for the first time that day she felt sick. This time, however, it was for a completely different reason. She was unaware that Annie had walked in and was standing next to Molly.

'How is Julian,' she said in a small voice. 'Has he cut any teeth.'

'No, but they are troubling him, your ladyship.'

Mrs Pringle eyed Clare.

'Sir Adrian said you had gone to visit relations down south.'

'Yes, I had,' Clare said lamely. She tried to change the conversation.

'And what are you doing visiting here, Mrs Pringle?'

'I came to see my sister who lives in Ambleside. She has been poorly and Sir Adrian kindly gave me the time off.'

Clare nodded. There were lots of questions running around in her mind. Not all of them were about Julian. Had Adrian missed her? Had he tried to look for her? Then common sense took over. He had lied and told them she was away on a visit. Why?

'I called in here because I needed something to eat and drink. It looks a lovely little place.'

Clare said nothing.

A voice broke in. 'Thank you, miss.' It was Annie.

'I'm sorry you were disturbed. How can I help. I'm the proprietor.'

Clare mouthed 'Thank you' to Molly, turned quickly and fled the room. Hot tears blinded her eyes but she refused to let them fall and she swiftly made her way to her room. Would this nightmare never end? Memories crowded back into her head and every time she thought of Julian another face appeared. She saw Adrian smiling down at her with his lopsided grin, Adrian holding her close at Mario's. and, particularly, Adrian holding her close in bed. The pain these visions caused in her chest was intense, and placing her hands over her heart she dropped to the bed and gave way to a storm of bitter tears. Two shocks in one day were just too much for her.

'Adrian, oh Adrian,' she whispered.

'Clare, are you all right, dear?' Annie called.

Clare tried to answer but could only manage a small moan. Annie opened the door and joined Clare on the bed.

Folding her to her breast, she said, 'There, there child. Nothing is this bad. Old Annie will take care of you but if you keep upsetting yourself it will be bad for the baby.'

Clare pulled away sniffled.

'How did you know?'

'By your face, lass. I can always tell. You still love him, don't you?'

Clare's voice was barely a whisper. 'Yes.'

'Does he not love you?' Annie asked gently.

'No.' Clare lifted her chin, something she always did when she was facing up to unpleasant problems.

'How do you know? Has he told you?'

'No he hasn't. I just know.'

'How?'

Before Clare could answer, Annie said reproachfully, 'And you have a little boy. How could you leave him?'

'Please, Annie, I can explain. Julian is not mine

He's my sister's child and she died giving birth to him. Adrian is his father. I was going to look after him myself but Adrian found out and wanted him. The only way I could keep him was to marry him; he gave me the choice: marry him or he would take Julian. What could I do, Annie? It was a marriage of convenience. I thought he needed me to look after Julian but he didn't want me to do that. He engaged a nurse. No, Adrian never loved me,' she repeated, as if to convince herself.

'Convenient for whom – you or him?'

'Both of us I suppose. I was able to stay with Julian and he had his son. But why he insisted I marry him I don't know. He had only to do a DNA test and he could have proved he was the father.'

'Clare, why did Mrs Pringle address you as your ladyship?'

'Because Adrian is Sir Adrian Loring and I didn't know that until after I married him. I was out of the country when he met Julie. She died before I got to the hospital. Oh, Annie, it's such a mess. What am I going to do?'

'Child, you will stay here with us if that's what you really want. If you don't want to see him you don't have to. Everything will come out in the wash.'

Clare gave a ghost of a smile.

'That's just what Mum would have said.'

'You are like a daughter to me, Clare, and your baby will be part of the family.'

Clare threw her arms around Annie and kissed her on the cheek.

'I don't know what I would do without you. I've only known you a short while but I love you as if you were my mum.'

Annie smiled. 'You are a good lass. Now wash your face and come down for lunch. You are eating for two now.'

CHAPTER 16

A week later Clare was making her way to reception when she heard Annie's raised voice.

'No, you will not see her, not unless she wants to see you.'

Swinging through the oak doors to reception, Clare stopped dead in her tracks. What little colour she had drained from her face and as she swayed as if to faint her blue eyes locked onto his grey eyes.

'Adrian,' she whispered, and slumped to the floor.

In two strides he was kneeling down next to her and had gathered her in his arms. He laid her on a settee and knelt down beside her.

'Clare, my little one, I'm here. I'm going to take you home.'

By this time Annie was by his side.

'Go away, woman, and let me speak to my wife.'

Annie stood her ground, her normally smiling face ready to do battle.

'I'm staying. It's my hotel.' Folding her arms she watched, giving a sigh of relief as Clare's eyelids fluttered open. But then Clare's body began to tremble violently.

'Get a brandy,' Adrian ordered.

'Please, Clare, don't be frightened I would never knowingly hurt you.'

Annie returned with a glass of water.

'I said brandy,' barked Adrian.

'Do you want me to send him away, Clare?'

'For the last time, woman, no she does not.'

Annie sniffed.

Adrian held out several forms to Clare and said, 'These prove I was out of the country when Julia conceived her baby. Clare,

58

darling, please listen. Believe me, I never slept with Julia. I hired a private investigator who spoke to the janitor of the flats. Julia hardly ever went out. Her only other male visitor was Keith Charnwood and he quite often stayed overnight. I went to see him and he signed a document giving up all claims to Julian. It's here, too. Will you read it? Will you do that for me, please? And if you still want me to go, I will, although I could not bear it if you sent me a way.'

Clare could not believe what she saw in his eyes. Slowly she unfolded the papers. One was from his solicitor and stated that Julia would have been four months pregnant when Adrian first took his manuscript to her. Then she looked at the others.

'You paid Keith Charnwood?' Clare gasped.

Adrian put his finger to her lips.

'And it was worth every penny. You won't hear from him again, I promise you.' With a lopsided grin he added, 'I left him with quite a black eye and a bruised face.'

The other paper was a letter from the janitor of the flats, stating the dates and times of Keith's visits. The writing danced up and down before Clare's eyes. She stared at Adrian in disbelief and her anger flared.

'You made a fool of me. You tricked me into agreeing to marry you.'

'Clare, would you have had me, believing what you did?' Gently he took her hands into his. 'Clare, how old are you – nearly 22. I'm 35. I was scared. I fell in love with a photograph, your photograph in the flat. I can still see Julia's face when I asked her who you were. She was so proud of you, and was singing your praises all the time. I couldn't wait for you to come home. I just wanted you, to make you mine. You, my darling, presented me with an opportunity. I took it. Oh, Clare, look at me, darling.' Out of his top pocket he took a tiny diamond heart on a chain. 'I once gave you my heart.' Slipping it around her neck, he said, 'It will never belong to anyone else, my darling. Please take care of it.'

Clare looked at him and melted in his arms.

'Clare, darling, I love you,' Adrian whispered. 'Never leave me again.'

Tears of joy misted her eyes. Both she and Adrian were oblivious to Annie who was still standing next to Adrian holding the water.

Adrian brushed the tears from Clare's eyes.

'Now, Clare, don't cry again,' Annie said. 'Think of the baby.'

Adrian looked astounded.

'Baby? You don't mean our baby? You clever girl.' He hugged her to him.

Annie's voice cut across their happiness.

'Now, will you two stop cluttering up my reception? Take him to your rooms, Clare, and by the way you have been eating one another you must be hungry.'

Adrian jumped up, whirled Annie off her feet and planted a big kiss on her cheek.

'I'm the luckiest man in the world.'

'Go on, you big oaf,' Annie chided.

'But what about Rhonda?' Clare said.

'There never was a Rhonda. She was only my secretary. She left when I made it clear I wasn't interested.'

'And the mud and grass on your cords?'

'Clare, darling, I had to get away. I was mad. So I went to the site and continued to dig. You will have to get used to that. I'm an archaeologist. Although if I need to go out of the country you will come with me. I've no intention of you getting away a second time. Rhonda won't be bothering us again.

'Please, Clare, don't look at me like that. I can't live without you. I'll even put up with those godawful trousers if I have to.'

His voice became seductive and his grey eyes held hers.

'Tell me you love me.'

'I love you, Adrian,' Clare whispered. 'And I love you Mrs Loring,' he whispered.'

The door opened and shut again.

'Molly, the food can wait, get the best room ready,; Annie said. 'These two won't be going home tonight.'

The following day Clare stood hugging first Molly and then Annie, and kissed John on the cheek. She made them promise to visit her soon. Adrian returned from putting their bags in the car and reiterated Clare's invitation.

'By the way, Clare, my mother had hired a nurse for herself and has flown over, so you already have a visitor. She wouldn't go until you came back. I wonder how she will take being a grandmother.'

After more hugs and kisses, Clare and Adrian stepped into the car where, holding her in his arms, he said, 'I love you, Mrs Loring, don't ever leave me.'

Clare smiled back, her eyes shining.

'I love you, Mr Loring. I won't.'

Glorious Sunset
By Barbara Machin

CHAPTER 1

'You are very fortunate, Miss Broderick. You are now the proud owner of Briar Cottage and all its contents. Here is an itemised list of the contents, and also a banker's draft for £10,000.'

Vanessa looked at Mr Knight. 'I'm amazed. Mother and I thought Uncle Harry had died years ago. I remember visiting with Mother and Father when I was a small child. My dad and Uncle Harry fell out. This has come totally out of the blue.'

'Well, Miss Broderick, you must have remained in Henry Broderick's heart, which is fortunate for you. Now, could you sign the receipt for £10,000 and instruct me on how you wish to commence. Do you plan to dispose of Briar Cottage?' the solicitor said, adjusting his spectacles on his hooked nose, 'or do you intend to keep the property?'

'I'm not sure, Mr Knight. If you could have the necessary paperwork drawn up placing the property in my name, I can then discuss it with my mother and we can proceed as and when I have made up my mind.' They shook hands. 'I will contact you as soon as I have decided on what action I will take. Thank you once again for your help.'

'It's a pleasure,' said Mr Knight, smiling.

'It's no good, Mother, the doctor said you need a change, and if the air in Scotland will be better for your health then we must move up there and give it a try. We can always change our minds if it's not beneficial.'

'But what about your job, Vanessa? Baldwin & Kent have been good to work for, surely. It has always seemed to suit you. I dare say you won't find another job so easily, especially in a strange place. The cottage is a little isolated, as I remember.'

It's true, thought Vanessa, trying not to show her troubled feelings in her brown eyes. She had enjoyed working at Baldwin & Kent where she was PA to the owner Carl Hudson. Childishly she had given him her heart. True, Carl had never suggested anything other than he be an employer, and in her heart, Vanessa had begun to expect nothing else. She was not beautiful but she had her good points. She had long blonde hair curled under in a pageboy style, large brown eyes that were her biggest asset, a short straight nose, fair complexion and a neat slim figure.

'Vanessa Broderick, you are not listening to me,' her mother said, reprovingly. Vanessa looked up with a start.

'I'm sorry, Mother, what did you say?'

'How do you propose to find another job quickly?'

'I should have no trouble at all. This house has been far too big for us for a long time, and the cottage Uncle Harry has left me will make a marvellous home. It's as if he knew. We need a fresh start, Mother, and besides, with the money Uncle Harry has left and the money we would get for the sale of this place we should have quite a nice little nest egg. And when I do get a job it will be a bonus. Mother, it will be great, all that fresh air and countryside. And best of all, I know it will do you good.' Vanessa put her arms around her mother's thin shoulders.

It had been the nights that Vanessa had hated the most. Her mother had recently suffered several severe asthma attacks, making it difficult to control the increasingly regular coughing bouts which left her fighting for breath. Vanessa's mother had steadily lost weight and seemed to have suffered more since her father had died two years ago. Only last week Dr Hanley had suggested a move to the country. Fresh air and good wholesome living might do the trick, he had said. He felt that living in the town with its factories and traffic fumes would only make the attacks more frequent. Then out of the blue came this golden opportunity. Uncle Harry, who Vanessa could only vaguely remember, had died and left them a small cottage. Vanessa had not thought twice. Comparing the benefits to her mother against her futile infatuation with Carl was a no contest; her mother won hands down.

'The estate agent has already got a buyer lined up for us, Mother, and we will be able to move up to Briar Cottage on 1 September. That will give us plenty of time to sort out any items we intend to take with us. The rest can go to auction.

'According to the catalogue of items still in the cottage we won't need all this furniture; it's fully furnished. It's bound to be a like a bachelor's home, but that can't be helped. According to the solicitor Uncle Harry never married. Once we arrive we can quickly make it to our liking; some pretty curtains and covers will do the trick. I'm sure we will have a wonderful time, just you wait and see if we don't, Mother. We can even grow our own vegetables; there is quite a sizeable garden at the back. You must be just a little excited?'

'You know once we get there, I'm sure I will settle down, Vanessa. It's just that your father brought me here as a bride many years ago and we never had any other home. Don't be too disappointed if I miss it a little from time to time.

'We did talk of moving but the time was never quite right. Still, I think he would be pleased for us. Perhaps he and Harry, wherever they are, have patched up their quarrel.'

'I won't, Mother, and I promise you, if you're unhappy there I will bring you back. Besides, Father would have wanted you to go if it will help improve your health.'

'Perhaps you are right, Vanessa. You're so like your father, so thoughtful and helpful. I don't know what I would have done without you since your father died.'

'Don't be silly, Mother. I'm your daughter, aren't I. I love you.' She gave her a quick kiss on the cheek. 'I will have to tell Carl I'm resigning. He will have plenty of time to replace me.'

The next six weeks were spent packing their possessions and making arrangements for their departure. Vanessa noticed that her mother was becoming a lot more positive about the move, making suggestions and being slightly more brutal when it came to disposing of items with memories. Vanessa contacted the solicitor and gave him their moving date. She also asked him to employ a cleaner from the village to clean and air the cottage. Vanessa thought that, as Uncle Harry had spent six months in hospital before he died, the cottage might be a little neglected. It was better to be on the safe side.

Over the next few weeks Vanessa pushed Carl to the back of her mind, trying not to think of the selfish way he had asked her to reconsider her resignation, saying that it wasn't convenient for her to leave at that time.

'Can't your mother move to Scotland on her own?' he had said, adding, 'If not, I thought you had relations in Essex. Wouldn't it have been a better idea to send her to them?'

Vanessa had hotly replied, 'No, she can't, and I think that is an outrageous suggestion. I'm moving to Scotland in September with my mother. Secretaries are not indispensable, you know, so I suggest you get used to it.'

Carl had stared at her, open-mouthed. What on earth had got into her. She was usually so amenable.

Vanessa had marched out of his office slamming the door behind her and muttering, 'Selfish beast.' She had then begun viciously slamming files around, sorting out outstanding queries and loudly slapping documents into relevant files.

For the rest of the day no one had dared speak out of turn. Mr Hudson's placid secretary had suddenly shown some spirit beneath that cool exterior. Vanessa stood firm on her decision. Carl only wanted her as a secretary because she could do her jobs so efficiently. It was time she stopped mooning over him and cut loose. No more day dreaming; it had to be reality or nothing in the future. In any case, the matter was out of her hands. Her mother needed her far more than him, or anyone else come to think of it. She would be satisfied with looking after her in the future.

September arrived quickly. It was sad leaving her childhood home but Vanessa looked at her mother and realised she must be making a great effort not to show her own sadness at leaving the house and all the memories it held, happy and sad.

Soon they were travelling towards a small village in Scotland called Cleish, but Vanessa was oblivious to the countryside flashing by. Despite the conviction that she would put Carl out of her mind, there was a raw feeling where her heart should be. She had childishly given her heart to him, and try as she might it was hard to forget him. At least he would never know her true feelings; she was glad of that, at least.

She remembered the day she had started at Baldwin & Kent, at the tender age of 20. Carl had instantly captured her affections and she had worshipped him from afar. He wasn't much older than her and had taken over his father's business. Vanessa had been employed as a copy typist, but had later become his personal secretary. From then on Vanessa had hero-worshipped. Now she must put him, and the pretty brunette she had helped train, out of her mind. Carl was not for her.

She pushed the stabbing doubts over how they would manage in their new life to the back of her mind.

'Vanessa, dear, shall we find the dining car? I'm getting a little peckish. Wouldn't you like a bite to eat, too? I noticed you didn't eat any breakfast.'

'I wasn't hungry then, Mother,' Vanessa lied, 'but I must admit I could manage a bite now.'

Together they went in search of the dining carriage and once inside found that all the tables were full except one, which was occupied by a haughty-looking man with dark hair who was wearing a kilt and sporran. Vanessa crossed the floor to the table.

'Would you mind if we joined you?'

'As I have finished you are welcome to the table. Otherwise I would have said that I prefer to dine alone.'

Curtly nodding a silent goodbye the man left and Vanessa stared open-mouthed at his disappearing figure.

'Well, I've never met anyone quite as rude as him, Mother.'

'Don't take it to heart, Vanessa, he was not really rude, just straightforward. I'm sure that with someone like him you would always know where you stood.'

'Well you couldn't say he was a friendly person, could you.'

'No,' laughed her mother, 'you couldn't say that. He obviously likes his own space.'

They looked at the menus.

'Right, Mother, what would you prefer?'

'Just a sandwich and coffee, please.'

Vanessa ordered sandwiches and coffee for two, aware that she was now quite hungry.

Returning to their seats both Vanessa and her mother felt satisfied and sleepy and Vanessa realised that her mother needed to rest.

'You have a little sleep, Mother. It will be a while before we reach Cleish. I can read awhile and wake you up when we are nearer.'

Vanessa read her magazines, forcing herself to stay awake while her mother slept. Watching the lonely fields and moors of Scotland rushing past, her thoughts wandered to the rude man in the dining carriage. He had been quite handsome. She recalled his dark looks, his tanned and healthy skin and eyes that were blue with a hint of steel. His eyelashes had been almost as black as soot. Vanessa could even picture his flaring kilt as he turned and left them.

'Cleish, Cleish,' called the guard as he walked along the train corridor.

'Mother, wake up,' Vanessa said, giving her mother a gentle shake. 'We're nearly there. We'll soon be at the cottage.'

Her mother's eyelids flickered open.

'Oh, I'm sorry, dear. Have I been asleep long? I'm sorry I left you to your own devices.'

'That's all right, Mother, I've been reading.'

Vanessa reached for their two small bags and led the way off the now-stationary train. Looking around the deserted station she realised it was the smallest station she had ever seen. It had just a waiting room and a ticket office, and was manned by two guards. The one thing she had forgotten to do was to ask the solicitor to have a taxi waiting for them on their arrival.

'Sit down, Mother, while I find a porter to help us.' She motioned to a bench on the platform.

Inside the ticket office she found an old man with a wrinkled face and gnarled hands. In her estimation he was far too old to be working. Smiling at him she asked politely, 'Could you please ring for a taxi. We are not sure how far we have to go.'

'Och! You'll no get a taxi at this time of night, missy, noo!' He shook his grey head.

'Please, are you sure? It's only 8 o'clock,' Vanessa replied, aghast. 'My mother's all in and we've had a long journey.'

'I canna help that, there's no taxi to be had tonight.'

As she turned Vanessa caught sight of the rude man from the train just beyond the ticket barrier. She bit her lower lip and hurried across to him.

'I wonder if we could hire your car to drive us to Briar Cottage,' she said, eyeing the battered Morris he was throwing his luggage into.

'We will pay,' she said, noticing his frayed cuffs on his well-worn tweed jacket. 'I really wouldn't ask, but Mother suffers from asthma and I have no idea how far Briar Cottage is.' Her brown eyes looked worriedly into his. 'The ticket collector has told me there is no taxi after 8 o'clock.' Vanessa stood looking at the unknown man, helplessly. 'Please.'

'I've stressed that I prefer my own company,' the man replied. 'However, if you haven't had the good sense to make proper arrangements before arriving, I dare say I have no alternative.'

'Well,' gasped Vanessa, 'if that's your attitude you needn't bother. I'd rather die than impose on you. In fact, I would rather walk a hundred miles than trespass on your precious privacy.'

She made to turn, only to see her mother approaching.

'There you are, Vanessa dear. I was beginning to think you had forgotten all about me.'

'Allow me,' the stranger said, opening the car door and helping Mrs Broderick in. He placed the two small cases on the seat beside her.

'I have just been hired to drive you to your destination,' he said mockingly, daring Vanessa to deny it.

Vanessa was fuming. She held her tongue. If I create a scene and we get out, it will mean a long, lonely walk in the cool night air. She realised she could manage to walk but her mother couldn't, so had to accept the stranger's begrudging help.

Holding the door open he indicated that she should sit in the front, next to him. Glancing at the back seat of the car she realised that it would be impossible for her to sit next to her mother because the space was filled with luggage. It would have been churlish to refuse, so a very red-faced Vanessa climbed into the front seat. Whoever he was, he certainly did value his privacy. Vanessa hoped their paths would never cross again.

The man tuned the car radio to the classical music channel and they listened to five tenors singing. Vanessa lost herself in the music. Ten minutes later he manoeuvred the car up a lonely track and they stopped outside a cottage gate.

'Would you like me to come in with you to check if everything is okay inside?'

'No, thank you,' Vanessa replied, politely declining his offer. 'We can manage quite well from here and don't want to take up any more of your time.'

Vanessa struggled with her handbag clasp, pulling out of her purse a note.

'This should cover the cost of you coming out of your way. I'm sorry again that we inconvenienced you. It was very kind of you.'

Without a word he gave Vanessa a withering look and got back into the car, leaving Vanessa with her hand outstretched still holding the money.

'Well, good night to you,' she said, watching the disappearing car. 'I hope we never have the pleasure of meeting him again, Mother.'

'Really, Vanessa, don't take on so. He wasn't all that bad. It must have been out of his way. Perhaps he's tired, too. I think I'm inclined to agree with him, It is a lonely spot. We really should have allowed him to see us in and check the gardens.'

Vanessa gulped and peered down the path into the gloom. All she could see was a low thatched roof and what appeared to be roses climbing around the doorway.

'Well, we can't stand out here for the rest of the night, Mother. Let's go in, shall we?' She was trying to sound more cheerful than she felt.

They made their way to the door where Vanessa dumped the cases at her feet. She fumbled for the latch key the solicitor had forwarded to her and pushed open the door.

'Well, it certainly smells nice, Mother,' she said wrinkling her nose at the pleasant smell of beeswax and lavender.'

They were pleasantly pleased at the scene that met their eyes. They walked into a sizeable hall with a polished wooden floor. It had plain cream walls, a hall table bearing a phone, and a small occasional table on which was a vase of freshly picked roses. The first door opened into a large sitting room, again with a polished woodblock floor. The floor was covered with a Persian carpet, huge chintz-covered chairs, a welsh dresser filled with willow pattern dishes, and a gleaming oak table. There were more freshly picked roses. Someone had kindly set a fire ready for lighting in the large open grate.

'Why, Vanessa, it's beautiful,' Mrs Broderick gasped.

Vanessa's previous doubts and worries disappeared as she looked around.

'I told you we would like it,' she said, her face wreathed in smiles as she hugged her mother.

After taking off her coat she stooped and lit the fire.

'I'll go and find the kitchen and make a nice cup of tea. You sit down and relax. It won't take long.'

Once inside the kitchen Vanessa could not help but be impressed. It was as homely and as well looked after as the other rooms. A large oak table with chairs dominated the room, and there was an old-fashioned kitchen range that had been polished until it shone. There were rows and rows of gleaming pans and spice jars, and two old armchairs either side of the range, which Vanessa could see would be useful for both cooking and heating. Obviously Uncle Harry had loved his home comforts, even if he was a bachelor.

But how am I going to boil the kettle without lighting the range? she thought. She certainly didn't feel like making a fire in here. All she wanted was a drink and her bed. They were both tired from the journey. She then spotted a modern electric cooker in the corner, sighed with relief and filled the kettle.

'It won't be a minute, Mother. I'll soon have it made.'

Sipping tea in front of the now roaring fire, Vanessa and her mother sighed with contentment.

'I'm glad we have that long journey behind us, Vanessa. I've a good feeling now we are here. I'm sure we can make it our home.'

Vanessa looked at her mother.

'Yes, I knew it would be a good move for us.'

After a few more minutes she damped down the fire and put a fire guard around it.

'Come on, Mother, if the bedrooms are as good as the rest of the house, we won't have any work to do. It's absolutely perfect. Let's unpack in the morning when the rest of our luggage arrives.' Vanessa picked up their hand luggage and followed her mother up the stairs.

She chose a bedroom under the eaves. It had plain walls painted in primrose. The carpet was a pale lilac and covering the bed was a plain lilac bedspread. Vanessa marvelled at the cosiness of the cottage once more. Uncle Harry couldn't possibly have chosen the décor; he must have had the help of a woman. Perhaps he had interior decorators to help. It was quite strange that he had never married.

Sliding between into the snowy sheets she could smell lavender again. In fact, you would never have guessed that the cottage had been empty. Vanessa fell asleep, her dreams a comfortable jumble of cleaning ladies and Carl, along with the periodic appearance of her rude man.

CHAPTER 2

Vanessa awoke to the strange sounds of the countryside – the pleasant chirping of the birds while cows were mooing in the field. She lay in the lavender-scented sheets, listening to the gentle rustle of the leaves as the wind played between the branches. The warm sunshine lit up the room and tickled her face, and with a contented sigh she stretched, breathing in the smell of freshly cooked bacon.

She sat up and quickly jumped out of bed, and, not bothering to put on a robe, opened the door. With a guilty start she wondered just where and how her mother had managed to get bacon and eggs at this time in the morning, and with a grimace she realised that she had forgotten about food as well as transport from the station.

Guiltily she ran down the stairs, unaware of how young she looked in her faded, flowery pyjamas and with her face devoid of make-up. It was a warm morning and, only expecting to find her mother downstairs, she had not bothered to put on her woollen dressing gown. Bursting into the kitchen, Vanessa found her mother sipping coffee at the kitchen table with a gentle-eyed woman with grey hair.

'There you are, Vanessa, you are just in time for breakfast. You were sleeping so soundly it seemed a pity to wake you, dear.'

'You should have woken me. I'm nothing but a lazy tyke. I meant to get up and have your breakfast ready. It's because that bed was so warm and comfortable that I didn't want to get out of it.'

'Vanessa, let me introduce you to Flora. She knew we were moving in and kindly came along with some groceries. Without her we'd have had nothing in.'

Vanessa turned to Flora. 'It must have been you who put the fresh milk in the fridge.'

Flora smiled her answer.

'But how?' Vanessa said. 'Oh, I know, you must be the lady the solicitor hired to clean the cottage up. I must say, you have made a marvellous job. It's as if it has never been empty. It's spotless and it smells lovely.'

'Well, I must be running along,' Flora said, rising from her seat. 'Goodbye, Mrs Broderick, Miss Broderick.' A look of pain had appeared in Flora's eyes.

'No, wait, we must pay you for the groceries,' said Mrs Broderick. 'You were very kind to bring them for us.'

'There's no need. You can get your solicitor to forward the money onto me. He knows where to find me.'

'Flora, please come to visit us again. My mother and I would be really pleased to see you. Thank you again for everything.'

Flora smiled sadly, nodded her head and left. Mrs Broderick saw her to the door.

'Oh dear, she seemed upset, Mother. What did I say?'

'I don't know, dear. Nothing that I could see. It's such a pity – she seems so nice.'

'I do hope she does call again. She would be good company for you, Mother. Something very sad must have happened to her. She had such sad eyes. We must find out where she lives and invite her to tea one night to make friends with her and to make amends for whatever I said.'

'Yes, I'd like that, Vanessa. Now have some breakfast before you catch your death.'

'All right but I'm not a bit cold. It looks lovely outside. I'll just have some coffee and toast, then I'll get dressed. I want to explore the village and get a few things we need. We're a couple of miles from the village. If we could buy a small car it would be great, especially for work and shopping, and we could explore the area together.'

'I don't see why not. We have quite a little nest egg with the sale of the house and the money Uncle Harry left you, and you can take your time getting a job, there's no rush.'

'All the same, Mother, I don't want to miss any opportunities. I'll have a quick look while I'm in the village. It won't hurt to get the lay of the land. You know I don't mind work, Mother, you know I like to keep busy. And in fact, I'll feel better if I'm working. I can walk into Cleish, do the shopping, find the garage and see if they have any cars for sale that are suitable.'

Jumping up and planting a kiss on her mother's cheek she added, 'I'll bring something nice home for dinner. Are you sure you'll be okay? Once we have a car you can come with me.'

'I'm fine, dear, stop fussing. Go on and get yourself dressed.'

'Bye, Mother,' Vanessa shouted from the door, and gazing around her as she walked, Vanessa noticed the garden was not as well kept as the inside of the cottage and made a mental note to make that her next job. The roses were growing wild around the door and the borders were overgrown with weeds.

She made her way along the hedgerows that were still heavily laden with dew. It looked like tiny diamonds hanging from the tips of the leaves. Vanessa dragged her fingers along the wet green hedges, watching the rivulets of water travel down the back of her hand. Revelling in her freedom and the freshness of the morning, she almost danced along the lane, humming a popular tune and oblivious to the fact that this lane was used by vehicles. A loud hooting broke the stillness and Vanessa realised that she had strayed into the centre of the road. She was on the point of apologising to the driver when she realised it was him again, her rude man.

'Do you always wander around the countryside like a lost animal,' he said angrily through the window.

'Not normally. Mother forgot to tie me up this morning. There's no need to be so rude. Would you shout at your dog like that?'

He looked surprised and before he could answer Vanessa had turned on her heel and was making her way along the narrow lane towards the main road. Inwardly fuming she wondered why she let this rude man bother her so much. She ignored the old Morris as it chugged past. Whoever he was he must have seen the funny side because he was smiling.

Vanessa continued towards Cleish and her temper had improved by the time she got there, although she was still a little red in the face. Anyone would think he owned the road the way he carried on, she thought. Lazily she gazed into shop windows. The village wasn't as large as she had imagined and had just one main road and a few shops. She would only explore the main shops today. She didn't want to leave her mother on her own for too long. There would be plenty of time to explore the side streets later.

Spying the local post office, Vanessa decided to ask where the local employment exchange was and if they could advise her where she could get a good second-hand car. She entered the shop and smiled at the owner.

'Hello, could you tell me where the local employment exchange is, and whether there is local garage?'

'You'll noo find any exchange here, and if its labour you want, you'll find it in yon case there. As for the garage, there's only one; you'll find it right at the bottom of the main street. Ask for Jock McKenzie, he will soon fix you up. You're new here, aren't you?'

'Yes, I've just moved into Briar Cottage with my mother. It's a lovely cottage.'

Suddenly the owner's attitude changed, as if Vanessa had some contagious disease.

'It's nearly lunchtime. If you would care to shut the door behind you when you leave.'

'Thank you, I will. I'll just look in the showcase if you don't mind. I won't delay you long.'

Quickly Vanessa scribbled down the details of the only two job possibilities.

Her mother had been right: she would find it hard to get a good position here.

Once outside the shop she examined the details. One was for a shop assistant at the only clothes shop in Cleish, and the other was for a clerical person to help catalogue a shipment of valuable books owned by the Laird of Cleish. Applicants were to apply to his private secretary at Cleish House. The latter certainly sounded the more interesting. She would make her way to Cleish House directly after lunch. Suddenly, out of the corner of her eye, Vanessa caught sight of the postmistress and two other female customers watching her from behind the window display. They were eyeing her with mistrust. What on earth have I said to offend them? she wondered. First, the rude man and now the locals. Never before have I met such disagreeable people. If this continues I'm not sure I will have made the right decision to come to Cleish. Never mind nothing ventured nothing gained.

Turning on her heel she beat a hasty retreat in search of the garage and away from prying eyes.

It was no more than a small repair shop with one petrol pump, half-hidden behind a rusty station wagon. Vanessa surveyed the garage thinking, wryly, You can hardly call this a garage; I might never have found it.

Making her way to the cluttered doorway, she shouted, 'Hello! Hello!' into a dim interior that smelt heavily of paint, petrol and thinners.

'Is there anyone there?' she called. She took her hand from the doorpost only to find it covered in oil.

'Ugh,' she said, turning to leave, and bumped into a small man with a dirt-streaked face. He was wiping his hands on an oily rag.

'Canna help you, miss?' he said with a broad grin, his gaze appraising her from head to foot.

Ignoring the admiring look, she said, 'I'm looking for Mr McKenzie, Jock McKenzie, please.'

'Aye, I'm Jock McKenzie, lass, how canna help you?'

'I'm looking to buy a small car, Mr McKenzie. I was told that you might be of help.'

'My name's Jock. I would prefer to be called that.' He smiled. 'No need for formalities here, lass. Now, how much do want to pay?'

'Well, I like something reliable but not too expensive, Jock.' She smiled back at him. This was the first pleasant person she had met in Cleish.

'You won't want anything too big then, will you.' Vanessa nodded her agreement.

Jock beckoned her to follow him to the back of the garage where there was a pillar-box red Austin Mini with a black roof.

'I could let you have this for £1,000. It's a good little runner and has only had one owner. Is that too much?'

'No, the price is fine. I'd like to have a test drive, though, if I may.'

Jock told Vanessa about the car's good points. Its mileage was low and it had belonged to a lady who lived close to the village. Her situation had changed and she wanted to sell.

'Won't she still need it if she lives outside the village?' asked Vanessa.

'No, she moved into the village quite recently.'

'It's quite gorgeous. I dare say she could hardly bear to part with it,'

'Aye, you could say that, and her home as well. It's a crying shame.'

Gallantly he opened the door for her saying that he wished she had called when he was a little cleaner. She was a town girl, he surmised. You could tell by the orange woollen dress and the fashionable shoes.

'Are you staying here, miss?'

'Yes, I've come to live in Briar Cottage with my mother.'

'So you are Harry Broderick's mysterious relation.'

'I'm not mysterious, far from it. You knew Uncle Harry, then?'

'Aye, we all knew Harry and Flora. It's a small community. Everybody knows everybody here. You'll see – everyone will soon know how many showers you take,' he said, laughing.

'I'm not sure I like the sound of that!'

'We are harmless, you'll see,' he replied.

Vanessa suddenly had a thought: Flora.

'Who was Flora?' she asked.

You don't know about Flora?'

'No, I'm afraid I don't. Should I?'

Jock suddenly clamped up. It seemed he didn't want to talk about Flora anymore.

'Look, the Boar's Head's over there. They serve a lovely cup of coffee. Would you think it an awful cheek if I asked you to have a cup with me?' he said on impulse.

Vanessa looked at him and decided she liked him. He was so different to Carl. He had an open and honest face and a down-to-earth look about him. He had not been rude to her and she had to start making friends somewhere. She might as well start now.

'Call me Vanessa,' she said, smiling. 'I'd love a cup of coffee with you.'

Jock smiled and cheekily said, 'I'm going to bless the day God sent a blonde angel into my garage.'

Vanessa laughed at his compliment.

'Now, now,' she replied and wagged her finger at him.

Jock drove them to the pub and they walked towards its old doorway.

'They don't seem to mind my oily hands.'

Inside was a long, low-ceilinged room with dark beams and walls covered in old brasses. Several young people, who were either drinking beer or enjoying a coffee, greeted Jock, and a man wolf-whistled.

'Where did you find this pretty lass, Jock?'

'The angels sent her, she was captivated by my obvious charm and agreed to come with me,' he quipped.

Vanessa cheeks blushed pink with embarrassment. She was not used to being complimented by so many young men. Sipping her coffee, she listened to the jocular remarks bandied about between the young people. What a difference to the people she had met earlier that morning; these pub-goers were a really nice set of people.

Among the group was a girl with red hair and freckles sprinkled across her nose. She had deep blue eyes and leaned slightly to the plump side. Anyone with half an eye could see that she worshipped the ground Jock walked on. A silly little pain fluttered in Vanessa's heart. She had been exactly the same with Carl. Please let Jock notice her, thought Vanessa. Don't let her love be wasted as mine was.

Despite Vanessa arriving with Jock the young girl was still friendly and made Vanessa feel welcome.

'My name's Kathryn McPherson. I work in the stables at Cleish House.'

'You do? I'm so glad,' Vanessa said. 'They have an advert in the local post office for someone to catalogue books. I'm going to apply. In fact, I'll do it after I've had my coffee. It would be fun to know someone who works there if I get the position.'

'I'll just finish my coffee, then,' said Jock, who had been listening, 'and then I'll run you home.'

'Perhaps I'll see you at Cleish House, Kathryn, Vanessa said, rising to leave. 'And if it doesn't work out perhaps you would like to drop in at Briar Cottage some time. You will always be welcome.'

'Briar Cottage?' repeated Kathryn, her blue eyes clouding over for a few seconds. Just as quickly her expression cleared and she smiled.

'I'd love to.'

'Well, what do you think of her?' asked Jock as he drove the now quiet Vanessa back home.

'Of Kathryn?' she asked, deliberately misunderstanding.

'No, silly, the car.'

'Oh! I'd quite forgotten all about that. How awful of me. I will take it, of course but can I have a quick test drive tomorrow before I pay you because you have driven me here, she said laughing, and it is just what I want.'

'Great. I'll check it over for you and bring it over tomorrow afternoon, then you can run me back and perhaps we can go for a drink at the Boar.'

'That would be great, Jock, and you can meet Mother. I'm in a hurry now but we look forward to seeing you tomorrow.'

Jock pulled up at the gate and jumped out to open the door for her.

'I'll see you tomorrow, then,' he said, smiling. He jumped back in and roared down the lane.

'Bye then, Jock,' she called after the already disappearing car.

Vanessa ran down the path. She felt much more positive after her productive morning and it looked as if she would fit in, after all. Lunch was spent telling her mother about her new friends and recounting little antidotes and conversations. She didn't tell her mother about the attitude of the postmistress and the other women who had watched her from the window. There was no need to upset her mother, she thought, frowning down at her plate of salad. Vanessa told her mother all about the car.

'You really will like it, Mother. It's not too big, and it was only £1,000, a lot less than I thought we would have to pay.'

'I do hope its reliable, dear. You made your mind up a little quickly.'

'I'm sure it is, Mother. Jock seems a very nice person. I'm sure he wouldn't rob anyone, and I think I'm a good judge of character. Gosh, Mother, is that the time? I've seen a job I would like to apply for. I want to get it done today before the position is filled. I'll just go and change.'

CHAPTER 3

Vanessa felt good as she walked to Cleish House. On reaching its long driveway she stopped and patted her navy and white suit into place, making sure there were no creases. She had brushed her hair until it shone and clipped it into a neat French pleat. As she made her way along the tree-lined driveway she marvelled at the extensive velvet-green lawns and gardens. There were long banks of rhododendrons and azaleas. As she neared the top end of the grounds she saw someone pruning roses. Something about the way the man held himself stirred Vanessa's memory. He was obviously the gardener but why did she think she knew him? What was so familiar about him? She approached the tall figure.

'Hello,' she said in a friendly fashion, meaning to pass by. The figure turned to face her. Vanessa gasped.

'You!'

She caught the full, cold stare that her rude man gave her. The rude man she had dubbed him and the rude man he would stay.

'Have you lost your way again?'

'No,' she answered carefully.

'Then I believe you are on private property... Miss... what was your name?

'Broderick, and I'm here on business, if it's anything to do with you. I certainly don't intend to have a gardener ordering me away.'

With that Vanessa turned on her heel and left him staring after her. She quickly walked to the house in case she angered him anymore. The nerve of him, she thought. Why does he keep turning up like a thorn in the side?

Reaching the door, Vanessa rang the bell and glanced over her shoulder. Her rude man had vanished. Uneasily she followed a

83

maid into a large study full of crates of half-opened books. The walls were already lined with shelves of neatly stacked books; someone must be fond of reading, she thought.

'Would you wait here please?' the maid said with a smile.

'Thank you,' replied Vanessa.

Idly she picked up a small book of poetry by Robbie Burns; Vanessa had inherited her father's love of reading, and his love of books. She hoped she would get this job; her qualifications were good. However, how many applicants had there already been? She would love to work among these beautiful volumes. Vanessa thought of her sparse collection still packed in boxes back at the cottage. When would she find time to unpack them?

'Good afternoon,' came a cool voice. A tall dark-haired woman entered the room. She had black hair piled high on her head and she wore a severe black dress. Her only other colour was the scarlet lipstick on her thin lips and on her nails. For some reason her hands made Vanessa think of claws. The woman held out her fingertips.

'I am Aysha Collins, and you are?'

'Vanessa Broderick.'

They sat down.

'What qualifications do you have that makes you think you will be suitable for this position, Miss Broderick?'

Vanessa proceeded to list her previous positions, and the merits gained at college.

'Yes, I can see you might be what we are looking for. However, I have one or two minor details I need to speak to the laird about. If you don't mind waiting for a moment or two longer, I may be able to give you a decision.'

Aysha Collins soon returned and gave Vanessa a sharp look.

'It looks as if we can offer you the position. Here are the details of the salary and holiday entitlement,' she said, handing Vanessa some papers. 'Is that satisfactory?'

'Yes, very satisfactory.'

Aysha Collins held out her scarlet-tipped hand once more.

'We will expect you a week on Monday then, 9 o'clock sharp. The laird insists on punctuality.'

Promising to be on time, Vanessa left Cleish House.

The rest of the week was spent in exploring the district with her mother in the little red Mini.

They drove all over Scotland, their visits including Dunoon and the Trossachs, which looked spectacular in September with the trees turning a russet gold. They climbed to the Rest and Be Thankful summit where they turned south to Lochgoilhead. The road was steep and winding and Vanessa thanked her lucky stars that her father had insisted on driving lessons being part of her education. They had lunch out almost every day and returned home to cook their evening meal in the comfortable kitchen. This was the room they loved and used the most, Vanessa reading while her mother crocheted. As the week went on Vanessa found that she had been accepted by the younger locals but that the older residents still seemed to eye her suspiciously, and seemed to become tight-lipped when they found out she was Harry Broderick's niece. Jock McKenzie went out of his way to be friendly, calling at the cottage on some pretext or other. He would sit in the comfortable sitting room recounting colourful tales of the local shinty matches.

'The season starts in September but it's a little late this year owing to a shortage of ash – that's the wood we use to make shinty sticks.'

'It all sounds very interesting,' said Vanessa. 'Is it like a hockey match only rougher?'

'Yes, it's not a game for the feeble-hearted.' Jock grinned. 'But Kathryn loves to watch it. You must come to the opening game with me,' Vanessa.

'I'd love that, Jock. Perhaps Kathryn will come as well, if she loves it that much.'

'Aye, perhaps she will,' he said with a disappointed look on his face. He had been looking forward to taking Vanessa out without the entire crowd around.

'Well, I'd better be getting back to the garage; will we see you tonight Vanessa?'

'No, not tonight, Jock. I want to be up bright and early in the morning. I have a living to earn.'

'Well, what about tomorrow, then?'

'I'll see. Perhaps I can let Kathryn know.'

'Bye then.'

'Bye, Jock' replied Vanessa.

Jock looked like a little boy who had just had his pocket money stopped. Vanessa watched his battered old MG until it was out of sight; he had christened it Mable. With a little pang she realised she couldn't drop in to the Boar quite as much. She liked Kathryn and would not like to see her hurt. It was obvious that Jock was getting too fond of her and she wanted to leave Kathryn a clear pitch. After all, I like him as a friend but that's all, she thought. The whole crowd were really good company and Vanessa was only too aware of unrequited love; vaguely she wondered if Carl missed her.

'Vanessa, do come in and shut the door. You are letting all the warmth out,' said her mother as she came down the stairs.

'Sorry, Mother,' Vanessa replied over her shoulder.

Vanessa helped her mother to tidy up and decided that an early night was in order. She placed her clothes in readiness for the next day and jumped into bed, where she lay thinking of Carl. Eventually she fell into an uneasy sleep. Instead of Carl, she dreamt of her rude man, and in her dream he was walking away from her yet all Vanessa wanted was for him to come back. Vanessa awoke with a troubled mind. Why was it that she couldn't forget the rude man? He was even spoiling her sleep.

CHAPTER 4

Vanessa found herself once more driving to Cleish House but this time she was drove her little red Mini to the back door. She was looking forward to the new job and felt as if she was going to enjoy it, especially with Kathryn working there. Suddenly Vanessa thought of her dream the previous night and looked around carefully, half-expecting her rude man to appear. There was no sign of him.

'Vanessa, I do believe you are disappointed,' she said to herself. 'Whenever you see him, he is only rude and unpleasant, so why care at all?'

The door of the house opened before she had time to knock and Aysha Collins was standing in the hall waiting for her. Guiltily Vanessa glanced at her watch. It was barely 9 o'clock. She was not late. Aysha's thin lips formed the semblance of a smile.

'Ah, there you are, Miss Broderick, I'll show you where you will work and then I will have to go and sort the laird's post. He's so punctual and is bound to be waiting for me.'

Vanessa spent a pleasant two hours cataloguing the beautiful books and arranging them on the empty shelves. Then, looking at the time, she scolded herself for not doing enough. It was already 11 o'clock and she had hardly started. She would have to refrain from examining them and reading paragraphs or poems out of them. I'm here to work, not enjoy myself, she scolded.

At that moment a maid entered with coffee and biscuits. Vanessa thanked her and stood at the window gazing at the well-kept gardens. Then her heart gave a queer little jump; there was her rude man. She watched his tall figure cross the lawn. His head was bent over a book he held in his hands. It must be his break, because he was not tending to the garden. Vanessa noticed the way he walked – proud and haughty, his dark hair gleaming in the September sunshine. He didn't look like a gardener, but his baggy tweeds and open-neck shirt suggested he was. Vanessa turned back to her work, vowing to press on to ensure she made up for lost time. In the next two hours she achieved quite a lot and was then interrupted by Aysha informing her that she may take her lunch break.

'Just one hour, of course.'

'Thank you,' replied Vanessa. 'Will it be all right if I walk to the stables to see Kathryn?'

She had brought sandwiches for lunch, hoping to seek out Kathryn and share them with her. Vanessa was not sure if she would be allowed to wander around the gardens, although they were certainly worth a close look.

'You can do as you please in your lunch hour, Miss Broderick. You will be supplied with coffee in the kitchen, but on no account must you wander around the house. Only the kitchen and this library, is that clear? The laird values his privacy, you do understand, Miss Broderick?'

'Yes, Miss Collins.'

Aysha gave Vanessa another one of those frosty smiles, left the room and closed the door after her.

Vanessa childishly stuck her tongue out at the closed door and was immediately ashamed. Whatever is coming over me, I never used to be like this.

She walked around the back of the house, through the vegetable garden, across the paddock and on to the stables, where she found Kathryn sitting outside on an upturned water barrel.

'Hi there, Kathryn,' Vanessa called out.

'Hi,' came the reply through what appeared to be a mouthful of chocolate cake. 'Why didn't you come to the Boar last night? We all missed you.'

'I washed my hair, and I don't like to leave my mother on her own every night. She's not always well; she suffers from asthma, sometimes quite badly.'

'That's a shame. Do you want some coffee?'

'Please. I forgot to call in at the kitchen on my way out.'

'Well, there's plenty here. Uncle always sends it out to me. He knows I'm terrible with time.'

'Your uncle?'

'Yes.' Kathryn blushed. 'Hamish McPherson is my uncle. He humours me. I love horses so he lets me work with them.'

'I don't think I have met him,' Vanessa replied, puzzled.

'You haven't met the laird?'

'Oh, you mean the laird is your uncle? But why do you have to work, Kathryn, when you have all this wealth?'

'I don't, silly. As I've told you, I love horses, and have done ever since I was a small child. Uncle only gives into my pet whims; he's a darling. I know you will think so when you meet him. Just because you're wealthy you don't have to give up the things you like, and I like horses. He believes that if you get pleasure from work you should work.'

'Just as he loves books, I suppose. I quite agree with him, but why didn't you tell me before, when I told you I intended to apply for the post here.'

'I really didn't think it mattered, Vanessa. I liked you and hoped that you liked me. Telling you that the laird was my uncle might have been a barrier to our friendship.'

The hour passed pleasantly with Vanessa and Kathryn promising to spend lunchtime together the next day. Vanessa saw no one on her way back to the house and when she reached the library shut the door and settled back down to work. She became so engrossed that she lost all track of time.

'Good heavens! Are you still here?' Aysha's sharp voice broke her concentration.

'Oh dear. I'm sorry, I had no idea it was that late,' Vanessa said, looking out of the window and seeing the shadows creeping in.

'You had better make haste then before it gets dark. You should have finished an hour ago. We don't like to keep our staff too late. Good night, Miss Broderick.'

'Good night, Miss Collins,' Vanessa answered, gathering her coat and bag. 'I can see myself out.' She walked out into the cool September evening and strolled to her car, enjoying the tranquillity and solitude of the grounds. On reaching the car, she paused and leant on the bonnet to watch the sunset. Suddenly Vanessa felt as if someone was watching her. She didn't turn as the person walked silently to her side. She had sensed who it was and was not afraid of him. Her heart was giving queer little leaps, however. Vanessa knew it was her rude man.

'Do you like it here?' he asked quietly.

'It's glorious,' she answered, 'simply glorious.'

'I'm glad you enjoy the sunset. It is beautiful.'

'Certainly in your world, I would have thought; other people's feelings don't seem to matter as long as you have your privacy.'

'Am I really all that bad?' he replied in a gentle tone.

'Perhaps you have spent too much time in the gardens and not enough with people. It's much nicer to share your experiences than look at them all alone, you know.'

'Do you think so, Vanessa?'

'How do you know my name?' she asked, looking into his deep blue eyes and finding it difficult to drag her gaze away. She realised how handsome he was – his dark looks and blue eyes, the muscles that seemed to ripple under his shirt. She tried to guess how old he was: perhaps late thirties. He looked good, especially when he wasn't frowning. Maybe he was younger than that. Vanessa broke the spell.

'What's your name? I can't go on calling you "the rude man" can I?'

'Is that how you think of me?'

'How else? I have come into contact with you four times and on three of those occasions you have been most objectionable, and seeing how we are both working at the same place, we could at least try to be civil to one another. I am sure the laird wouldn't like his staff to go around being unpleasant to one another.' Vanessa swung her blonde head.

'No, I'm sure he wouldn't.'

Vanessa looked at him again. Did she detect a note of humour?

'You may call me Mac, Vanessa, and I promise not to be rude again. Am I forgiven?' he smiled at her.

'Now you're laughing at me.' Vanessa stamped her foot in frustration. 'You are hateful,' she said childishly.

'Touché! Who's being rude now?'

For once Vanessa was speechless. The short magical moment had evaporated and she jumped into her car, started the engine with a roar and drove off down the lane a little too quickly.

Vanessa roared to a halt outside Briar Cottage and her mother opened the door before she could let herself in.

'There you are, Vanessa, I was beginning to get a little worried about you. Your tea is quite ruined.'

'That's okay, Mother, I ate too much at lunch. I'm really sorry, I quite forgot the time.'

'Never mind, you're here now, dear. Have you had a good day?'

'Yes, it's been great. He has some fabulous books, and some are quite rare. I just couldn't help reading a page or two.'

'By the way, Jock called to see if you would like to go to the amateur dramatics tonight. He said he would pick you up at 8 o'clock, if that's okay.'

'I really don't feel like going out tonight, Mother; I'm looking forward to a quite night with you.'

'Don't be silly, Vanessa, it will do you good.'

'But what about you, Mother; you don't want to be sitting here every night on your own.'

'I'm fine, Vanessa, and besides, Flora is coming around to visit me for a while.'

'Flora, Mother? Has she called?'

'Yes,' she wanted to check if we had settled in all right. When I asked her round she was quite reluctant. However, I persuaded her. Flora is really quite nice.'

Jock's words suddenly came flooding back to Vanessa. 'I wonder if Flora is Uncle Harry's Flora,' she said.

'What do you mean, Vanessa, Uncle Harry's Flora?'

'I'm not quite sure, Mother, I need to speak to Jock, but in the meantime could you forget about what I said.'

As Vanessa stepped into the shower she thought about the mystery that seemed to surround Flora and Uncle Harry. But where do Mother and I fit into it? Something had affected some of the villagers' attitudes towards them and Vanessa resolved to get to the bottom of it.

Jock arrived at 8 o'clock as promised, and when Vanessa came into the sitting room he let out a wolf-whistle.

'Do you know what a bonny sight you are, lass?' he said with a smile.

'Thank you very much, kind sir,' Vanessa quipped, bowing slightly. 'I really didn't know what to wear – slacks won't be out of place?'

'No, you look smashing, believe me. You'll be the belle of the ball.'

Vanessa felt quite pleased with her choice of purple slacks and sweater. She wore a chunky bohemian bracelet and matching earrings. Her hair was pulled off her face with a purple hair ribbon, and to finish the outfit she had chosen black patent ballerina pumps and a matching bag.

'Well, what are we waiting for?'

'Me!' said Jock. 'First, I have to have my cup of coffee and a slice of your mother's freshly made apple pie. Your mother has gone to get it'

'So, Jock McKenzie, that's all you have come for: you have designs on my mother's apple pie.'

His voice dropped an octave. 'Would you like to bet on that,' he said, moving towards her.

'No thank you,' said Vanessa moving to the other side of the room.

Why did life have to be so complicated, she thought, watching him wolf down his pie. People you want to take an interest in you don't, and really nice people like Jock, who you only want as a friend, have to spoil things by taking too much interest. Vanessa let her thoughts flit back to Carl once more. He hadn't even written to her, although he had asked for her address.

'Well, I'm ready now.'

Vanessa didn't respond.

'Hey, I said I'm ready,' Jock repeated, giving her a playful poke in the ribs.

'I'm sorry, I was just thinking.'

'A penny for them.'

'They're not worth a penny, believe me.' Vanessa laughed awkwardly.

'Goodbye, Mother, I won't be late. I hope you and Flora have a nice evening.'

'I'm sure we will, dear. Flora is going to share her recipe for orange cookies. It's a rather special one.'

'Will Kathryn be there, Jock?' asked Vanessa as she climbed into his car.

'Yes. Why do you ask?'

'I thought we might pick her up.'

'There's no need. She has the use of her uncle's Rover.'

'I see,' said Vanessa carefully. She could tell by his face that he realised she was pushing Kathryn at him.

'I'm sorry, Jock, I really didn't mean to...'

'That's all right. I forgive you.'

'Jock, would you mind telling me something?'

'It depends on what it is.'

'Who and what was Flora to Uncle Harry, and why does everyone know except Mother and me? Everyone who knows Uncle Harry tends to shun me. I'd hate for that to happen if I was out with Mother.'

'You really don't know about Flora?'

'No, silly, that's why I'm asking. Everyone seems so touchy, and somehow I feel that it's really important to Mother and I.'

Jock pulled up outside the local hall that was used for all manner of things. Tonight it was the amateur dramatic society.

'Well, where do I start. Flora was very friendly with Harry, and cleaned and cooked for him. And then Harry persuaded Flora to live with him; she gave up her home to look after him. They were as good as married but she was better than any wife would have been. His home was turned from a dull bachelor's house into a comfortable, elegant home.

'And all through his sickness, before he was admitted to hospital, she nursed him. Then finally, when he went into hospital, Flora was always there; she visited him daily, right to the end.

On the night he died Flora sat with him all through the night, never left his side until he took his last breath.' Jock paused before continuing. 'Pity they never married. It must have broken her heart to leave Briar Cottage. Everyone thought you must know. Let's face it, isn't it odd that your uncle never told you he was ill yet left you all his possessions?'

Vanessa looked aghast. 'Truly, we didn't know. My father and Uncle Harry fell out years ago. We hadn't seen him for years. Now I understand how it must look. How awful for Flora to be turned out of the home she had loved and looked after as her own. How could Uncle Harry have been so thoughtless? He must have realised when he left the place to me that Flora would be homeless. I just don't understand how he could do that; it's so unlike him. How she must hate Mother and I.'

'If you think that, you don't know Flora very well,' said Jock. 'Don't blame yourselves, Vanessa, you weren't to know. In any case, when Flora went to the reading of the will, the solicitor explained that Harry had made the will years before, a long time before Flora became his housekeeper. He had just neglected to provide for Flora by making a new will. I'm sure he would not have done it on purpose. It was probably just an oversight on his part. Besides, I know that now she has met you she thinks you and your mother are really nice.' Covering her hand with his, he added, 'Come to think of it, we all do, especially me.'

Vanessa blushed at the obvious meaning of his words.

'I must see her, Jock. Where is she living?'

'Well, she has a couple of rooms at Maggie McFarlene's; she's a widow, too.'

'It can't be the same as the home she left, Jock. It just can't be like Briar Cottage. It was obvious when we arrived that whoever had been taking care of it put a lot of love into making it a special home. That's what puzzled me when we arrived – even the sheets smelt of lavender. It certainly didn't look like a bachelor's home.'

'That's probably because she didn't leave the cottage until the day before you arrived.'

'But why didn't she tell us? We would have made sure she was looked after.'

'Flora's independent. She wanted it that way.'

'Still I'm sure we can come to some sort of compromise,' Vanessa said.

So engrossed in conversation were Jock and Vanessa that they were unaware of Kathryn approaching the car. Neither did they see the look of hurt on her face as she slowed and saw who was inside. With a wounded look, she quickly turned her car around and darted back the way she had come.

'Let's not dwell on the past, Vanessa, let's look to the future.' Jock smiled at her.

'And the present is the amateur dramatics, Jock,' Vanessa said to change the subject; it was getting a little too personal for her.

'Ok, I give in. Let's join the others,' replied Jock, this time not quite so jovially.

They were soon greeted by a crowd of friendly people, who Vanessa soon felt at home with. She watched with great interest as the actors took their places holding their scripts in their hands.

'Where's Kathryn,' a small girl with dark hair asked.

'She was here a minute ago,' someone answered. 'I saw her parking her uncle's car. She must have passed Jock and Vanessa.'

Vanessa suddenly had a flashback of Jock and herself, heads close, deep in conversation. How must it have looked to Kathryn? Vanessa realised she must do some explaining in the morning and vowed she would make doubly sure she got it right and did not give the wrong impression again. The hub of voices quietened down and the rehearsal for Shakespeare's *A Midsummer Night's Dream* began. Vanessa watched, enthralled. Later that night she said goodnight to Jock, firmly turning down an invitation to visit a relation of his the next day.

'I've been neglecting Mother far too much lately,' she insisted, 'and I intend to spend a little more time with her in the future.'

It was a disappointed Jock who left Vanessa to quietly let herself into the cottage, taking care not to disturb her mother.

Vanessa already loved her work in the library but today she was impatient to join Kathryn in the stables. Unwittingly she had hurt Kathryn and she had made up her mind that she must put it right.

More than anything, Vanessa liked Kathryn, and she was determined that Kathryn's suffering should not be prolonged. Her train of thought was interrupted when Aysha Collins popped her head around the library door, her vivid scarlet nails and dark coiled hair as immaculate as ever.

'I would like you to leave the cataloguing for a short while, Miss Broderick, the laird has rather a lot of personal mail and copy typing to do.'

'Of course, Miss Collins,' answered Vanessa with a coldness in her voice to match that of Aysha's.

Vanessa followed Aysha into her small office and settled down to a huge pile of letters and correspondence on various business contracts for the mysterious Hamish McPherson. Vanessa could not help noticing that she was getting through it far more quickly than Aysha, and soon it was almost lunchtime. The time had passed without a word from Aysha.

At last the stack of mail was completed and Vanessa straightened her aching back.

'That's all of them finished now, Miss Collins. May I take a break for lunch?'

'Oh, is it that time already?' Aysha said, checking her watch. 'Very well, but do try to catch up on the cataloguing this afternoon.'

Well! What an ungrateful beast, thought Vanessa. She really was the limit. Not a 'Thank you' or a word of praise. She did not like to blow her own trumpet but felt she had done well to clear that backlog of mail.

Vanessa made her way back to the library to collect her sandwiches. She would slip down to the stables to eat lunch, and if Kathryn was there she could sit and talk to her.

'What on earth are you doing in here?' Vanessa asked a little too sharply after opening the library door. The tall, arrogant figure of her rude man raised his head.

'I'm looking for a book, Miss Broderick, a book I can't find,' he replied icily. 'Oh, did the laird send you?' Vanessa had the good grace to blush. 'What was it he wanted?'

'It's a small book of verse by Robert Browning. I have tried to find it in the catalogue on your desk but you don't appear to have numbered it.'

'I know where it is,' Vanessa replied. 'I saw it with the books I intended to catalogue today. He writes such lovely poems.'

'You like Browning?'

'Yes. All those poets are good in completely different ways – Keats, Byron, Browning. Let me see now. It's here.' Vanessa picked up the book carefully. 'I meant to catalogue these this morning but Miss Collins asked me to help with the backlog of mail.'

'Really? 'I would have thought you would have enough to do in here.'

'Oh, I don't mind helping Miss Collins although I much prefer it in here on my own. I love these books. My father loved books, too, and I must take after him. Can you imagine owning all these books?'

His stern face relaxed into a smile.

'Just fancy,' Vanessa continued, 'being able to read Keats, Burns or Browning whenever you wanted too.' She turned to face him, realising that she had been prattling on, and saw that he was smiling. 'Now you are laughing at me again. Go on, you had better take the laird his book, you have kept him waiting long enough.' The look on his face confused her.

'Oh, the book,' he said, with a mysterious look on his face. If only she could have read his thoughts. He was curbing the desire to roar with laughter at her serious expression. 'Yes,' he said at last, 'I'd better be going so you can continue with your work.'

Vanessa collected her sandwiches with a strange feeling troubling her mind. She pictured Mac's face as he gently held the book. It was as if he, too, loved books. I know we got off to a bad start but he does seem to be making an effort not to be rude, she thought. I'll try to start again. Perhaps we can be friends. He must have a heart somewhere. Surely he doesn't make enemies of everyone he meets. Tomorrow she would go to the bookshop in the village and choose a book he could call his own, as a gesture of friendship.

Vanessa looked at her watch and quickly made her way to the stables. It would have to be a quick lunch if she was to get any work done on the books. Vanessa reached the stables quickly, only to be told by the stable hand that Kathryn had lunched in the house today and had not yet returned.

'She canna be well; it's not like Miss Kathryn. She looked a little peaky this morning and said that she hadn't slept well.'

Vanessa's heart went out to Kathryn; she really must make it clear that she had no interest in Jock. It distressed Vanessa to think that she had hurt Kathryn in any way. No longer feeling hungry, Vanessa wandered towards the orchard to the left of the stables and strolled among the trees. The ground beneath the trees was strewn with windfall apples. She bent and picked one up, looking guiltily around her. Surely they wouldn't mind her taking a fallen apple. Vanessa bit into the apple and continued to wander among the trees. A strange scent lingered in the air and delicately she sniffed as she strolled along. It was quite a pleasant smell and she tried to work out what it was.

'Well, hello there,' came Mac's voice from the foot of a tree. 'Are you enjoying your apple? They are Braeburns – quite the best in Scotland.'

Vanessa blushed. 'Yes, very much, but I didn't pick it from a tree,' she hastily replied. 'I wouldn't do that. It's a windfall. You don't think the laird will mind, do you?'

Mac took his pipe from his mouth and roared with laughter. I don't think he will. It'll be our little secret.'

'May I sit down?'

Mac patted the ground and Vanessa felt herself warming to him. Sitting beside him she opened her sandwiches and offered him one.

'My mother makes the best sandwiches in Scotland,' she said with a twinkle in her eye.

'Thanks,' Mac said, taking a sandwich and looking at her in a serious manner. Vanessa blushed under his scrutiny. What was it about this man that disturbed her? His dark arrogant looks seemed to make him more interesting but at the same time got under her skin. He reminded her of someone but she could not put her finger on whom. She glanced at her watch.

'Good heavens! I had better go and get some work done or it will be time to go home.'

'But you have only just arrived.'

'I know, but I have hardly touched the laird's collection today and he's bound to notice. I don't want him to think I've been slacking. Do you think he will?'

'You make him sound like an ogre.'

'I don't mean to. Anyway, I've never seen him so how can I judge? Anyone who loves books as much as he does can't be all that bad.'

At that moment, Vanessa saw the small book lying by Mac's side.

'Mac!' She was horrified. 'You still have the laird's book. They are too precious to be...'

Mac finished the sentence for her. 'Left with a gardener? I've never heard such utter snobbery.'

Vanessa was mortified. She had not meant it that way, but somehow she found it hard to explain. 'Let me be the judge of that,' he added icily.

'After all, I've known the laird a lot longer than you have, Miss Broderick.'

'I'm sorry,' stuttered Vanessa, for once completely lost for words. Quickly she sprang to her feet, confused and apologetic. Her usual cool and calm exterior had gone.

'I'm truly sorry,' she repeated, and turned to make her way back to the house.

She threw herself into sorting and cataloguing the crates of books as if her life depended on it. She bitterly regretted hurting Mac's feelings; the last thing she wanted was to be known as a snob. She would just have to make sure she did not give that impression again.

Later, standing by the library window, Vanessa watched the sunset throw a glorious gold and red hue across the fields. Even this gave her no joy, and a feeling of depression settled on her, just as it had when she had left Carl. She had been just another piece of office furniture to him. Vanessa left Cleish House feeling very much at odds with the world and was determined to stay out of Mac's way. It seemed she was destined to bring out the worst in that man, however hard she tried to be pleasant.

CHAPTER 5

'Are you sure, Vanessa dear, that we would be doing the right thing?'

'I'm positive, Mother. If Flora agrees to live with us, you'll never be lonely when I'm at work or when I have a night out. And besides, I like her and it will be good for her. She won't be lonely either.'

'I like her too and nothing would please me more than to have her living with us. I find her very good company and we have the same interests. And there is ample room. But will she think we are offering charity?'

'I don't think so, Mother. Once I have spoken to her she will realise that it's in both our interests. And she has a right to be here. I'm sure Uncle meant to provide for her, and he would have if he had known how ill he was. And Mother, if you keep on serving apple pie like that I'll be as fat as a pig. It was lovely.'

'Oh, Vanessa, I forgot to tell you that your laird from Cleish House sent us a huge basket of apples. They're in the kitchen. It will take us ages to use them up. I'll just have to bottle some for the winter. It's awfully kind of the laird; you must be making an impression on him.'

'Hardly, Mother, I've never met him.' A look of dismay crossed Vanessa's face. Surely Mac had not told the laird that she had eaten an apple from the orchard, even if it was a windfall.

'Vanessa, are you all right?' Her mother's concerned voice cut into her thoughts.

'Yes, Mother, just a little surprised. I must remember to thank the laird, if I ever get to see him. Come on, Mother, let's do the dishes. Then I can go and see Flora.'

Vanessa knocked on the shabby door of Maggie McFarlene's house and waited. It was opened by a very untidy woman and behind her was an equally untidy house.

'Is Flora in, please?' asked Vanessa.

'And whom shall I say is calling,' the woman replied, looking Vanessa up and down.

'Vanessa. Vanessa Broderick.' The woman's dull eyes flickered into life.

'Hmm. Step inside please.' Vanessa followed the woman, thinking how awful it must be for Flora, who was so house proud, to have to live in an untidy house like this. These thoughts strengthened her determination to persuade Flora to live with them in Briar Cottage.

Maggie practically thumped on the door at the top of the stairs.

'Visitor for you, Flora,' she shouted.

Flora emerged from her room.

'Why, Vanessa, what brings you here?' she asked, a flush creeping across her face.

'May I come in and talk to you please, Flora?'

'Why of course, please do.'

Vanessa followed Flora into the shabby but clean and tidy room.

'Would you like some tea?' Flora asked.

'I'd love a cup, thank you.'

Some minutes later Vanessa was sipping hot tea and eating homemade biscuits. She couldn't resist them, even though she had eaten a large evening meal.

'Well now, Vanessa, how may I be of help to you? Presumably you haven't just come to pass the time of day.'

'Well, Flora, I need your help. With me out at work all day Mother is on her own quite a lot and so needs a companion – someone she likes, perhaps someone who is a friend and almost family. We would want them to live with us. We couldn't afford to pay a salary but there would be free bed and board and as much free time as they wanted. Flora, we would like you to come and live with us.'

'I don't know what to say, Vanessa.' Tears appeared in Flora's eyes.

'Don't say anything, Flora, except that you will come back home.'

'You know, don't you, Vanessa? I never meant you to find out. You know how people make their own stories up. I loved Harry; he was my world. And underneath, he loved me. I knew about Harry falling out with your father. He always maintained it was his fault not your father's. But he was too proud to contact him. I never expected Harry to leave me the cottage, and he did leave me a small amount of money, so with that and my pension I'm fine.'

'Flora, all I know is that you belong at Briar Cottage and for as long as you want it as your home. It's not necessary for us to know any more. Please, do say you will come back.'

'I'd love to be back.' The tears spilled from Flora's pale blue eyes and her expression transformed into a watery smile.

'That's settled then. We will expect you tomorrow. I will get Mother to prepare your room and if you pack all your belongings I will pick you up in the car.' Vanessa picked up a biscuit from the table and impulsively kissed Flora on the cheek. 'And with biscuits like these, I think we are getting the best of the bargain!'

Vanessa felt better already. Tomorrow was Saturday and as well as choosing a book for Mac, she would try to see Kathryn and make sure they were still friends. Then she could feel completely happy again.

That night Vanessa studied her reflection in her dressing table mirror. Her cheeks had more colour these days and glowed rosily, and there was a sparkle in her large brown eyes. She realised she had left her teenage crush for Carl behind. He still occupied a corner of her heart but only a corner. He was her first unrequited love. It was strange: every time she thought of Carl, a mental picture of Mac appeared.

Her life here in Cleish was beginning to fall into a well-ordered pattern of friends and work, and what made it all seem worthwhile was that after only a short time her mother no longer lay awake struggling for breath. If only Jock would not read more into their friendship than there was life would be much less complicated. Slowly Vanessa crossed the room to switch out the light; perhaps tomorrow she could find the answer to her small problem. Climbing into the lavender-scented sheets she sighed with satisfaction.

The following day Vanessa took great pains to help her mother prepare the room for Flora. They made sure that everything sparkled for her return. If Vanessa felt at all apprehensive, there was no need; soon after Flora arrived, she and her mother were chatting over a cup of tea in the kitchen and planning how they would spend the coming winter.

'Mother!' Vanessa shouted from the stairs as she ran to pick up her coat. 'I'm just slipping into the village to do a little shopping. Is there anything you want?'

'Only some pickling spice, dear. Flora and I are going to preserve some onions and fruit for the winter.'

Closing the door behind her Vanessa was unaware of the attractive picture she made as she stood in the doorway of Briar Cottage. Her soft, moss-green sweater and tailored slacks hugged her figure perfectly, showing off her small, delicate breasts and slim hips. She had thrown her coat over one shoulder and rays of sun were playing with the tips of hair that curled around her face and ears, turning them to burnished gold. Neither was she aware of the tall figure with dark hair striding across the nearby fields towards her. He smiled as he caught sight of her. In his hand was a huge bunch of pink roses. But it was too late: Vanessa strode in the opposite direction not knowing that she had just missed the very person who was the subject of her errand.

CHAPTER 6

Vanessa studied the leather-bound books in the bookshop window, not wanting to buy one of the less expensive books. After a great deal of pondering she chose a blue-and-gold leather-bound volume of Shakespeare. It was a second-hand book but much nicer than the cheaper paperback volumes. Feeling quite pleased with her choice, Vanessa strolled around the shops for a small gift to give to her mother and Flora, not forgetting the pickling spice. It was while she was gazing into another shop window that she had an idea. It would be just the way to cool Jock's ardour. After entering the souvenir shop Vanessa purchased a small knife with the word 'Cleish' printed across the top. She would write to Carl and send him this small gift. She could also make sure that Jock knew about it, and with just a little embellishment, a white lie here and there, she could sort out the situation. Now to ring Kathryn and arrange to meet her at the pub. Perhaps, with a little luck, Jock and Kathryn would be there already.

Vanessa pushed open the pub's old oak door to find that her hunch was correct. Kathryn, Jock and a group of young people she knew were in the usual corner, their laughing camaraderie obvious for all to see. Vanessa joined them and was greeted by a chorus of friendly voices. At the same moment Kathryn turned and caught sight of Vanessa. A look of disappointment crossed Kathryn's face but, being naturally friendly and kind-hearted, she was quick to hide her feelings, put on a cheery smile and gave Vanessa a warm welcome.

I was just wondering where you were,' Jock broke in. 'I was going to call around to see you after this drink.' He moved quickly to her side.

Everything Vanessa had been taught as a child came crowding to the front of her mind. She hated telling lies, but for Kathryn's sake she was prepared to.

'You were, were you? Well you wouldn't have found me in. I have been neglecting Carl far too much since I arrived here, so I have been looking for a small gift to send to him. Mind you, I might even take it to him myself if I can get the time off work. Looking at all you couples I'm quite missing him. Look, Kathryn, do you like this knife?' she asked, turning her back on Jock. However wretched Vanessa felt it was worth it to see that hurt look on Kathryn's face disappear and after a short while Vanessa made her excuses and left.

Making her way along the country lanes Vanessa was deep in thought and did not notice the dark clouds gathering in the sky. She was too busy thinking of how she had hurt Jock, who had befriended her when she knew no one. a raindrop found its target and splashed onto her face, the first of the torrent to come. With a groan she realised too late that she had forgotten to pick up her raincoat as she left the pub. It was too far to go back for it, and it wouldn't help now that she was already soaking wet. I'll just have to make do with sheltering under the trees. Perhaps it will clear in a little while.

The wrapping around the book was beginning to rip. If she kept it in her hand it would be ruined. There was nothing for it but to tuck it under her sweater. She smiled, thinking of the funny side. Here she was, blonde hair plastered to her face, her slacks and sweater clinging to her body like a second skin, her hardened nipples forming a small ring at the top of her pert breasts. And to top she had a huge bulge protruding from her chest. She hoped to goodness no one came along and saw her.

Oh no! she thought, as she saw a figure running towards the tree. It only took a second to recognise the proud head of Mac, and for some reason she wished it was any one but him. She must look dreadful. She did not want anyone to see her looking like this, most of all him. Mac had already taken his jacket off by the time he reached her.

'Here, put this on,' he commanded. 'Why couldn't you be sensible and take a coat? You'll catch phenomena.'

'I did bring one,' she said defiantly, and as she turned to face him little rivulets of rain ran down her face and dripped from her chin. 'I forgot it when I left the pub. But Kathryn will know it's mine and look after it for me. Anyhow, I like the rain.'

'Yes, I've noticed. You are always wandering around country lanes getting wet, even if it's only your fingers. And to top it all, no one else is safe going out. You block the lanes and endanger motorists. You are the most irritating person I've met but you still get under my skin.' Reaching out he grasped her arms and pulled her close. 'What have you got to say to that?' He looked deep into her eyes.

Vanessa tried to think of a smart answer but failed, and instead pulled from under her jumper the sodden parcel.

'For you. It's a peace offering. It would be really nice if you would be my friend instead of my enemy.'

Mac took the book. 'Thank you,' he said. 'I will treasure it as long as I live.'

A shiver ran down her spine as she tried to understand the look in his eyes, and suddenly, for want of something to say, she answered, 'Well, I like that. Anyone would think you own the road.'

'Not quite,' he grinned. His face instantly looked years younger.

Mac continued to hold her and then swiftly bent his head and took her lips in a long passionate kiss. Vanessa responded with a passion she had never known before. As they both lifted their heads it struck her: every time she had come into contact with Mac they had clashed. But now, time seemed to have stopped and suddenly she realised what she had felt for Carl was puppy love, and that she, the cool Vanessa Broderick, had fallen madly in love with a man she found hard to get along with. It was a love so fierce it was almost suffocating. Vanessa stared into his dark eyes and began to tremble violently.

'Vanessa,' Mac said, his eyes full of concern, 'are you all right?' When she didn't answer and only stared stupidly at him, he swept her into his arms and began to make his way along the lane. Holding his head against hers to shield her face from the torrents of rain, he whispered, 'We'll soon be home, darling girl.' The only thought he had on his mind was the girl in his arms.

Vanessa's mother had been looking through the window, watching for Vanessa's return and when she saw them she ran to open the door.

'What's happened, Vanessa dear, are you all right?'

'Get her out of these wet clothes,' Mac commanded. 'Have you any brandy?'

Vanessa suddenly found her voice. 'I'm perfectly all right. If you would please put me down I can get out of my wet clothes myself.'

Mac dropped Vanessa to her feet as quickly as he had picked her up.

'Don't fuss, Mother.' A dull, red flush crept into Vanessa's cheeks. She fled the room, not least to escape Mac's penetrating gaze.

Once inside the safe haven of her bedroom she tried to collect her muddled thoughts. Why did he kiss me and call me his darling girl, why? How can I think I love him? It was only a few months ago when I thought I hated him. Still, they do say love is akin to hate, don't they?

Standing in front of the mirror, Vanessa was appalled to see what a sorry sight she looked. How could I expect him to fall in love with me looking as I do. I look an absolute wreck. My hair is plastered to my face and my clothes are dripping wet.

Yet still she could not dispel the magic she felt in her heart. Vanessa Broderick was actually in love. Had she dreamt that kiss, she wondered. Was it possible he could love her?

'Vanessa, do get out of your wet clothes. I've run you a nice hot bath.' Mrs Broderick was standing in the doorway watching her daughter with a puzzled look on her face. There was a different look about her daughter tonight, a glow around in her face. Vanessa turned to face her mother. She was flushed and her eyes were bright. She smiled and began to peel off her clothes and Mrs Broderick busied herself collecting the wet garments and carried them from the room. She told Vanessa to get into that hot bath quickly.

Vanessa felt calmer after her bath. Her hair was almost dry and she was calmer. She was ready to go downstairs. Would he still be there? She hoped so. She needed to reassure herself that she had not imagined that look in his eyes. She couldn't bear to think that he might have left. Putting on a dab of perfume she crept onto the landing. Yes, she could hear his voice. Her heart was beating a rapid tattoo on her ribs as she tried not to hurry down the last few stairs.

'There you are, Vanessa dear, I've just made some hot chocolate. It was so good of the laird to bring you home.'

'Who?' Vanessa couldn't keep the surprise out of her voice. She didn't seem to hear the rest of the conversation; she could only think what a fool she had made of herself. How he must have laughed at her expense, pretending to be the gardener and accepting a cheap book when he owned all those beautiful books in his library. Oh, what a fool she had been! Even Kathryn hadn't told her. Perhaps she had not been important enough for him to introduce himself properly in the beginning.

'I'm very tired, Mother,' Vanessa said. 'I think I'll go and lie down.' Her voice was dull and lifeless. Turning to Mac she was sure he was inwardly laughing at her. Yes, he *was* laughing at her; she could see it in his eyes. How could he make such a fool of her?

'Thank you very much for bringing me home, Mr McPherson.'

'Not at all, the pleasure is all mine.'

'Well of all the nerve.' Vanessa exploded and flounced out of the room. She was close to tears.

'Vanessa, come back,' her mother called. 'What on earth has come over you? I'm so sorry,' she said, turning to Mac. 'The soaking has turned her head. She wouldn't normally be so rude.'

'It's quite all right, Mrs Broderick, Vanessa and I have unfinished business. It can wait. I'll call again. Do kiss her good-night for me.'

'Well, what on earth did he mean by that?' Mrs Broderick said to herself. 'I wish I knew what was going on in this house.'

Then she walked to the bottom of the stairs and called Vanessa, but everything was quiet. Vanessa was not going to answer. She obviously was not in the mood for a heart-to-heart talk. She was busy building fences around her heart.

CHAPTER 7

Vanessa looked tired and heavy-eyed when she finally appeared the following morning. She hadn't come down for supper the night before and clearly hadn't slept well. Concern filled Mrs Broderick's heart when she saw her daughter's pale face.

'You don't look yourself. Is there anything wrong, dear?'

'No, I'm quite all right, Mother, although I have a couple of days' holiday owing to me and, if you don't mind, I think I will go to London for a long weekend. You will be okay with Flora to keep you company, won't you?'

'Of course I don't mind. It will do you good to get away. You can perhaps do a little shopping while you are there. I'll make a list of what I want; perhaps Flora will need something as well.'

Vanessa gave a low sigh. She hated the thought of going to work. If only she never had to go to Cleish House again. She was determined that she would now look for other employment and thought the situation was now impossible. She made a mental note to approach Aysha about the two days' leave and, gathering her coat and bag from the chair, let herself out into the damp air.

Arriving at Cleish House did strange things to Vanessa's heart and stomach. She was always cool and calm, and she hadn't thought it possible to feel like this. She dreaded bumping into Mac; somehow she couldn't think of her rude man as being the Laird of Cleish. How she wished he was just Mac.

'Miss Broderick,' Aysha's cold voice broke in. 'Is there a problem? You don't appear your normal self today. You are here to work and not to stare out of the window.'

Vanessa dragged her thoughts back to reality, hoping Aysha could not see the pain in her face.

'I'm sorry, Miss Collins, it is certainly quite wrong of me to waste the laird's time. I have rather a lot on my mind. I will stay a little longer tonight.

Actually, I was wondering if it might be possible for me to take the two days' leave owing to me next week? I would rather like to go to London for a long weekend. I'm really sorry to let you down but if you could get someone to replace me I would be very grateful. I have decided that this work is not quite what I was looking for.'

There, she had done it. Vanessa looked at Aysha and waited for her reaction. 'Well, let's not be too hasty, Miss Broderick. You most certainly can have the leave, and we are most satisfied with the work you do here. We certainly wouldn't like to lose you. Take your two days' leave, and if it's a question of money, I will speak to the laird.'

Aysha's mind worked quickly. If Vanessa left it would leave her a lot more work to do, and that was one thing Aysha did not like. Besides, she had her mind firmly set on ensnaring the laird. If she had more work to do, she would not have time to push her plans forward. This house, the laird's money and position was all she dreamt about. She had thought he might be attracted to Vanessa if he met her but Aysha had a way of keeping attractive women out of his path, although he never seemed to go near the library these days.

'What will you speak to the laird about?' came his stern voice from the open door.

'Why, Hamish.' Aysha's voice came out all treacly. 'Miss Broderick was just telling me that she wanted to leave and I was saying how sorry we would be to lose her. Her work is most satisfactory.' Mac looked at Vanessa, his eyes as cold as ice.

'If that is what Miss Broderick wants, we will just have to replace her. Just like a woman to start something she can't finish.' And with that he turned on his heel and left.

'Now look what you've done,' said Aysha, fluttering her scarlet-tipped hands.

'What I've done?' fumed Vanessa. 'If he had told me who he was in the beginning, instead of pretending to be the gardener...'

'Told you who he was? I thought you hadn't met him.'

'Well I did. I thought he was the gardener.'

'The gardener, Miss Broderick?'

'Now look here, Miss Collins, I'm tired of this conversation. May I get on with my work so that I can have my two days' leave.'

'I think you had better. I will do my best to replace you as soon as possible,' Aysha said disdainfully and quickly left the room.

CHAPTER 8

The shunting of the train taking Vanessa back to London had much the same effect on her heart as when she arrived at Cleish. Why had she been so foolish in allowing Hamish McPherson to capture her heart? Anything she had felt for Carl had been lukewarm compared to her feelings for Mac. How could she ever face going back to Cleish House, or even going back to Cleish, knowing that he was so near? What a fool he must have thought she was. Had he realised how she felt? Please God, she prayed, don't let him have noticed. Her cheeks went red at the thought of the blue leather volume of Shakespeare she had given him, a sopping-wet parcel she had pulled from under her sweater, and the deep look he had given her when he accepted it. It had meant more to her than she cared to admit. Bitterly she thought of what he might have done with it.

Vanessa's mind turned to her mother. She was so much better now they had moved to Cleish, and she and Flora got on really well. Vanessa toyed with the idea of asking for her old job back at Baldwin & Kent. After all, she no longer had to worry about her mother. Mother would be fine with Flora to keep her company. And I could still go back to Briar Cottage on my holidays.

It seemed as if she was destined to be unlucky in love. Never again would she be free: Vanessa's heart belonged to her rude man. Her thoughts went back to the day she had left home, and Carl, to live at Cleish. She still had an ache in her heart, for Mac not for Carl. You could not compare them. It wasn't the same pain, and the pain she had felt on leaving Carl was nothing to the longing she felt for Mac. Would she ever be happy? Her eyes suddenly filled with tears and her face pale had violet shadows beneath her eyes through lack of sleep. Vanessa felt as if her heart would break. She dabbed her eyes with a crisp white handkerchief from her pocket. Now, that's enough of that, she chided herself. Pull yourself together and have a cup of coffee. He won't care; he's still probably laughing at you. Sniffling, Vanessa went in search of the dining car.

The two days Vanessa spent in London dragged by; all she wanted was to go back to Cleish to be near Mac. But she forced herself not to run back to Scotland. Scotland where she had left her heart. Vanessa looked up her former friends at Baldwin & Kent and could not escape without seeing Carl. He insisted he was far from satisfied with his present secretary, hinting that he would soon have to dismiss her. He pleaded with Vanessa to return, going to great lengths to wine and dine her, using all his male charm to persuade her to return as his secretary. Before leaving to live in Cleish, Vanessa would have been flattered by his compliments and even promised to consider the option of returning to work for him. She would let him know within the month.

'I tell you what, Vanessa. I could do with a holiday so how about I come back with you to see this Cleish of yours?'

It was the last thing Vanessa wanted. He wouldn't fit in at Cleish. She now saw him for what he truly was: weak, selfish and self-centred. What on earth had she ever seen in him. However, she couldn't stop him coming to Cleish but told him he would have to stay in the local hotel. She could not bear to have him staying with them and decided to tell him at the end of his vacation that she would have to decline his offer. Anyway, Vanessa had come to love the quiet, gentle village of Cleish and felt Carl would not fit in with their lifestyle. She would somehow find another position in Cleish having burnt her boats with Mac.

Carl was to travel back with her. He had already reserved a room in the Boar's Head.

CHAPTER 9

Vanessa felt bored as she studied her pink-tinted nails. She was already regretting that she had let Carl back into her life and wished she had not called into Baldwin & Kent to see her old friends. All Vanessa wanted to do was go back to Cleish to sort out the misunderstanding and fix herself up with another job. That way she could get on with her life. Suddenly Carl's voice cut across her thoughts.

'Gosh, I'm hungry, shall we go for lunch?'

'I'm not very hungry, Carl. You go,' replied Vanessa, forcing a smile. Her head was beginning to ache and she thought she would scream if she had to listen to his bragging much longer.

'No, you must have something, old girl,' he protested.

Vanessa gritted her teeth. It was easier to agree than argue. She did not realise that her brown eyes looked over-large in her pale face and that Carl was genuinely concerned.

'Oh, all right. I'll just have coffee.' Seated in the dining carriage Vanessa thought back to the first time she had met Mac. It was in this very carriage. He had been rude, but looking back she recalled that he had been studying some papers. Perhaps she shouldn't have interrupted.

Vanessa jumped as she heard his deep rich tones once more.

'Would you mind?' He was standing next to their table with one eyebrow raised.

'It would be churlish of me if I said no,' answered Vanessa, her heart thudding against her ribs. Her face burnt pink as their eyes locked together. How she wished he would stop looking at her in that way.

'I say,' said Carl, 'do you two know each other?'

'Slightly,' Vanessa answered.

'Oh, I would say it was a little more than slightly,' Mac said, 'and soon we will know each other a lot more intimately than we have with Miss Broderick merely working for me.'

'You mean you are the Laird of Cleish?' Carl said with enthusiasm. He was revealing his utter snobbery. 'I say, how absolutely wonderful to meet you,' he enthused.

Vanessa thought she would go mad if she did not get away. One man she loved to distraction, the other was too full of himself for words. She excused herself, hoping to escape back to her seat in the reserved carriage. She did not get far; Mac's hand shot out and caught her wrist in an iron grasp.

'I think you and I have a little unfinished business,' he said. If your friend will excuse us.' He said giving Carl an icy stare. Keeping hold of Vanessa's wrist, he followed her down the aisle, leaving Carl staring open-mouthed after them. Vanessa slid her carriage door open and stepped in, turning her face to Mac as he snapped the door shut.

'Well?' Vanessa set her pink lips in a tight line.

'You are due back at work tomorrow.'

'Yes, on the undertaking that you will replace me as soon as possible.'

'I don't think I want to replace you, ever.' Mac's voice had become silky, almost seductive. 'You've nearly finished the books. Surely two more weeks won't make that much difference. If we can call a truce for that short time it should tie in nicely.'

Vanessa looked at him questioningly.

'I'm to be married very shortly,' he said, not taking his eyes from her face. 'Oh!' Vanessa's heart felt as if it would break. 'Is it anyone I know?' she asked looking at the floor. He grinned lopsidedly.

'Yes, you could say that.'

Vanessa hoped that he could not see how wretched she felt.

'Congratulations,' she forced out.

'Come, Vanessa, you can do better than that,' he replied and pulled her into his arms. Lifting her head he kissed her until her senses reeled. His hands roamed her body until they located her small breasts. There they stopped to explore the hard nipples that stood in tiny peaks. Until then Vanessa had responded kiss for kiss but suddenly pushed him away with all her might.

'How could you,' she shouted angrily. 'I wonder what your bride would think of you. Do you always try to seduce your workers?'

'No, only the ones that play havoc with my peace of mind and get under my skin. Especially a little blonde I know quite well.' He gave a throaty laugh, pulling her once more against his lean body. Vanessa gasped as she felt the hard maleness of him.

'Please,' was all she could say in between kisses and gasping for breath. Vanessa felt that if she did not try to keep a tight rein on her feelings she would let him make love to her right there.

'If that's what you want, I'll leave it for now. But that's not what I want.' Vanessa's heart cried out, but when she did not answer he added, 'However, we are going to have a lot of fun getting to know one another in the future. I'll let you go back to that boring young man, but not for long.' He traced her cheek with his finger, continuing down to the top of her small breasts. 'Shall we say another three weeks working, then? It will be just enough time for what I have in mind.

'Now, about that case of mistaken identity. It was your own fault, Vanessa. I never told you I was the gardener.'

'Quite,' Vanessa answered wretchedly, 'but you could have put me right. You made me look such a fool.'

Gripping her by the shoulders, he said, 'I've never been very good at making apologies, Vanessa. What I'm trying to say is that I'm sorry. Please meet me halfway.'

Vanessa gasped as she saw the strange look in his eyes.

'All right. Perhaps I was wrong. But you didn't have to kiss me to prove it.'

'I kissed you because I wanted to. Until tomorrow.' He smiled, kissing her once more on the lips. 'Oh, by the way, inform that baboon of a friend that you are still working for me and that you will not be leaving Cleish in the foreseeable future.' With that he turned to open the carriage door.

'I won't?' said Vanessa, staring at him open-mouthed.

'You won't,' he said brooking no argument. 'I will be in Paris for the next three weeks and when I come home we will talk.'

Vanessa stared at his retreating figure. The truth dawned on her: he expected her to have an affair with him after he was married!

The next two weeks passed quickly. Most of Mac's books had been catalogued and Vanessa guessed that his future wife was Aysha Collins. Every time Vanessa saw Aysha she wanted to congratulate her on her forthcoming marriage. However, she just could not manage to get it out. For some reason, Aysha began to treat Vanessa with more respect, making sure that she took proper lunch breaks, for example, and that she went home at the correct time. This puzzled Vanessa; she could tell that it didn't come easy to Aysha to change the habits of a lifetime. Vanessa moved over to the window. The pain in her heart was almost suffocating her. The approaching sunset was casting a vivid splash of colour on the horizon.

'Vanessa,' Kathryn shouted as she burst through the door. 'There you are. I haven't seen you for ages.'

'I'm sorry, Kathryn, I've been really busy.'

'Yes, I've heard,' smiled Kathryn, 'but your secret is safe with me!'

Vanessa looked puzzled.

'It's hardly a secret,' she said, thinking that Kathryn was referring to her impending departure from Mac's employment. Kathryn continued to babble on.

'Uncle Hamish is back from Paris and has sent me to tell you that you are dining here tonight. We have a local shinty match tomorrow and he wants you to attend. It will be the last one before Christmas and Hogmanay. Uncle Hamish and Jock are both playing.'

Vanessa looked at Kathryn in dismay. Her cheeks were burning red and were almost the colour of her sweater.

'I'm sorry, that's impossible. My mother is expecting me home.'

'Uncle Hamish has already gone to fetch your mother and Flora, so there's no problem. He's been gone a good half-hour. He asked me to tell you earlier but I went to the stables and took longer than I should. Am I forgiven?'

Vanessa held out her arms and the two girls hugged.

'You know you are, Kathryn. I'm just angry with the laird.' Vanessa hesitated over his title. It had been much easier to call him Mac. 'Please take no notice of me. But I can't see why he could not consult me first. I am a little tired and would have preferred to have gone home.'

Kathryn gave an impish smile. 'You'll just have to get used to that. Uncle likes his own way. You'll be fine when you freshen up. You can have a shower here and borrow one of my dressing gowns. Uncle said he was bringing back some clothes for you to change into tonight.'

Well, this was the limit. How dare he, she thought. Wait until I get him on his own. Who does he think he is? she fumed inwardly.

Vanessa looked around the room Kathryn had shown her to. It was decorated in silver grey and pink. The bedcover and the sham pillows were of pink satin. The furniture was Victorian and highly polished. On the dressing table was a huge bunch of red roses. Vanessa walked over to smell them. A small envelope poked out from among the leaves. She moved away quickly. Obviously they were meant for someone else and Vanessa felt as if she were intruding. Still feeling angry at the way Mac had organised her evening, she slipped into the sapphire blue silk dress that had been laid out on the bed with clean underclothes and a pair of matching shoes. The blue of the dress complimented her fairness and the fitted bodice moulded to her figure, showing her tiny waist.

A knock came on the door and Kathryn popped her head in.

'You look stunning,' she exclaimed. 'Uncle Hamish chose the dress himself. He said it was your colour.'

'He did, did he?' Vanessa said, angrily. 'And who chose the underwear. I hope for his sake it wasn't him.'

Kathryn laughed. 'That's a thought! Come on, it's time to go down.'

Vanessa and Kathryn entered the sitting room to find her mother sitting on one of the huge cream settees next to a very elegant woman of around her age. Flora and Aysha were both sitting on huge armchairs. Mac was towering above them, smiling and talking, and Jock was by the drinks' cabinet pouring drinks as if he was used to dining with Kathryn and Mac. Jock looked up and smiled in Kathryn's direction. The look he gave Kathryn said it all. Vanessa smiled; her subtle actions had worked and Jock now looked as if he only had eyes for Kathryn. Perhaps there would be two weddings, not one.

Vanessa's heart ached as Mac turned and bent towards Aysha to catch something that Aysha had said. He then threw back his head and laughed. He then noticed Vanessa and his look sent her heart racing. He looked magnificent in his dark green and navy kilt, white shirt complete with ruffles, and matching socks and sporran. He caught Vanessa by the arm.

'Did I select everything you needed,' he whispered. Vanessa drew her arm away and pulled it tight to her side, hoping that Mac would take the hint, but it had the opposite effect: he gripped it even tighter. She gritted her teeth to stop herself crying out in pain. Poor Aysha, she would have her work cut out being married to Mac.

'Would you like a drink before dinner?' His face was almost boyish tonight and he looked very happy. Gone was the stern, haughty look.

'No, thank you.'

'Jock, Vanessa will have a dry sherry,' Mac said, ignoring Vanessa's answer.

'Now, I have someone I would like you to meet. Mother, this is Vanessa who I was telling you about. Vanessa, this is my mother, Madeline McPherson.'

At that moment the tall, elegant woman stood up.

'Hello, Vanessa, I'm so pleased to meet you at last,' she said kissing Vanessa on the cheek. 'Anyone who can put up with my son and his musty books must be quite a person!' She smiled.

Vanessa smiled back. 'Pleased to meet you, Mrs McPherson.'

'Oh please call me Madeline. Everyone else does. But don't shorten it to "Mad". That I can't stand.'

'Your dress looks very nice,' Mac said to Vanessa in a mocking tone. She shot him an angry look.

'Thank you,' she replied in a stilted voice. Vanessa inwardly fumed. She would have really liked to have had a few choice words with him, but how could she make a scene. Why had he insisted on her being part of this dinner party. It was beyond comprehension.

'I think it's time to go in for dinner,' he said, keeping the same steely grip on Vanessa's arm and leading her into the dining room. The large dining table was made of yew and was set for eight people. The table centre was of Waterford crystal and had flowers trailing from its centrepiece. The table was set impeccably with white china and the pattern around the edge was Wedgwood Marquisette. A small blue flower was set in to match the blue flowers arranged in the centrepiece. Mac sat Vanessa on his right and his mother on his left. Flora and Mrs Broderick sat down next, then Jock and Kathryn. What surprised Vanessa was that Aysha sat at the other end of the table. She did not notice the smoked salmon starter, the duck a l'orange or the lemon lush, and neither did she touch the wine. In fact, she ate very little. Mac rubbed her arm where he had left his fingerprints, and whispered, 'I'm sorry.' Vanessa tried hard not to look at him. He was flirting with her and it really was unforgivable. Whatever must Aysha be thinking. Why was I so stupid? she thought. If I hadn't sent Carl back to London, Mac would have had to invite him as well, then this would never have happened; she could have pleaded a prior engagement. His company would have seen her through the approaching marriage. Vanessa knew now that it was impossible for her to stay in Cleish. She could not hold out against Mac's flirting, and she did not want to be his mistress. She glanced at Aysha's left hand and was acutely aware that Aysha was not wearing an engagement ring. How men took women for granted.

Sipping coffee Vanessa's spirits plummeted even further when Mac called for champagne with which to toast his forthcoming wedding. She felt sick with misery and wasn't aware of everyone smiling at her. She hadn't realised until Kathryn came to fetch her that everyone was staying at Cleish House; the room she had used to get ready was to be her bedroom for a week. Her mother had arranged it with Mac. Mac touched Vanessa on the cheek making her recoil like a spring, then looked at her with concern.

'Are you all right?'

'No, please excuse me,' she replied in a watery voice, her eyes suddenly filling with tears.

Kathryn stood up. 'I'll come with you.'

Mac waved her to sit down and followed Vanessa out of the room himself. Taking hold of her arm he said, 'A walk will calm you down and get rid of that headache.'

By this time Vanessa was past caring. She really did have a bad head.

He pulled an old coat out of the cloakroom, wrapped it around Vanessa and led her through the back door, whistling for his black Labrador to follow. I never even knew he had a dog, Vanessa thought.

With his arm around her shoulder he steered her towards the orchard. He was silent for some time. Then he stopped and reached into his pocket to take out his pipe.

'Do you mind,' he asked softly. Vanessa shook her head, not caring.

Mac took off his jacket and placed it on the ground. Then he pulled Vanessa down to sit next to him. Putting his arm about her shoulders he leant back and quietly smoked his pipe. Vanessa's head rested on his shoulder. By this time she was feeling much better. The fresh air had reduced her headache to a dull throb. Suddenly she recognised what it was she had smelt in the orchard the last time she was there – Mac's pipe. It was the Holland House aromatic tobacco her father had smoked when she was a little girl. She thought how easy it would be to forget his approaching marriage and a little sigh escaped her.

'A penny for them,' Mac said.

'They are not worth a penny,' she answered quietly, shivering.

'Are you cold?'

Vanessa shook her head. Getting up and pulling Vanessa to her feet, he said, 'It's getting damp. Let's go in.' Vanessa didn't answer. He lifted her face to look at him.

'Don't fight it, my bonny lass. It's meant to be,' and reaching down he claimed her mouth in a passionate kiss. His hands began to roam in a hungry manner, feathering lightly down her neck to slip inside her dress. He cupped the swell of the small breast in his large hand. With his other hand he pressed her slim body tight against his thighs, making her aware of his obvious desire. A broken cry escaped her lips.

'Don't. Please don't. I can't do this. Think how you will hurt Aysha if she finds out. It could cost you your marriage to her.'

'My dear girl, you are either very silly or very dense,' he said. 'I have no intention of marrying Aysha, although I know she would have liked that. I have made her very aware of my plans and of whom it is I will be marrying.'

'Who?' Vanessa shivered again.

'If you had concentrated at dinner you would have realised. As it is you can wait a little longer. We had better go in. You are cold.' He rubbed his hands up and down her arms.

Putting his arm protectively around her shoulder, he led her back to the house. They didn't see anyone as they climbed the stairs. He opened the door to her room and pushed her in and followed, gently closing the door behind him. He pulled her to him, slipped the coat from her shoulders and slowly appraised her figure. He gently slid the straps of her dress from her shoulders and his hand reached for the zip at the back and began to slide it down. Vanessa raised her hand in protest but Mac brushed it gently aside. Gently he let her dress drop to the floor, leaving her standing naked except for a flimsy pair of silk pants. With a groan he bent and began to nuzzle her ear and throat until his mouth closed over her rosy nipples. A gasp of sheer delight escaped from Vanessa. His hand began to trace a line down her flat stomach.

At that moment they heard Mrs Broderick's voice on the landing.

'Vanessa, dear, which room are you in. There are so many.'

A groan escaped from Mac's throat and he pulled Vanessa to the bed. Pulling the covers back he quickly urged her into the bed, covering her to the neck. He then sat on the side of the bed and shouted, 'In here.'

Mac was breathing a little heavily but by the time Mrs Broderick entered the room he was innocently sitting and looking at Vanessa's closed eyes.

'Poor dear,' exclaimed Mrs Broderick.

Mac rose from the bed and said, 'She's a little tired, Mrs Broderick. Let's leave her to sleep.'

As Mrs Broderick turned towards the door, Mac quickly bent over Vanessa and whispered, 'I'll be back, my sweet, we can't leave this unfinished.' Vanessa buried her burning face in the pillow. She could no longer look at him; her embarrassment was too acute. She knew she would have given herself to him unreservedly.

For a second Mac stood looking down at her blonde head. He loathed having to leave her. All he wanted to do was kiss her worries away and make love to her.

Vanessa lay awake for what seemed hours. The day had taken its toll on her nerves but sleep still evaded her. Lying in the darkness her body still ached from Mac's tender lovemaking. Suddenly there was a light tap and Mac opened the door. He was dressed in his pyjamas and a dressing gown.

'Can I come in?'

Vanessa nodded. She wanted to say no but was fully aware that she was now unable to. Mac took a key from his robe pocket and locked the door, and, walking slowly to the bed, he asked, 'Is there room for two?' Vanessa stared.

'Is there?' he repeated.

Vanessa nodded her head ever so slightly, and after pulling back the covers he slipped into the bed, pulled her to him and cradled her in his arms. He kissed her hair and took in the soft fragrance of her perfume. Then he lay still and held her for a while, willing her to make the first move. Vanessa moved restlessly in his arms. She wanted him and knew now that she would do anything he asked. Turning her face to him he read the answer in her eyes.

'My little angel,' he murmured.

Pulling her closer he took her mouth and softly kneaded and caressed her body. He murmured words of love, at the same time guiding her hands to his thighs. He let his hands slide to the inner part of her legs until he felt the velvet softness he was looking for. Raising himself above her he guided himself into her softness. His rhythm was soft and slow as he felt the resistance, until suddenly he slid unhampered into her softness. Their movements became stronger as she thrust her small hips to him, until they reached that ultimate goal of ecstasy. Spent and tired they lay and held each other tightly. Pulling the clothes over them Mac knew he would not leave her that night. They both fell into an exhausted sleep.

Mac was a creature of habit and his body clock always dragged him from sleep at around 6.30. However, this morning it was 7.15 before he was awake. Stretching his arms contentedly he looked at the sleeping Vanessa and felt the stirring of passion once more in his limbs. Stroking Vanessa gently he said, 'Come on, sleepy head, your lord and master needs you.'

Vanessa pulled herself from a heavy slumber to look into his passionate gaze.

'Come on,' he demanded, pulling her from the bed. 'A shower is what we need.'

Vanessa shyly averted her gaze, feeling sure he knew that she was aware of his rising passion. Following her into the shower he turned on the spray and gently soaped her young body. She did the same in return.

'You witch,' he groaned, and pulling her to him he lifted her onto his thighs. His lips never left hers until they were both spent and satisfied. Putting his finger to her lips he said, 'You must stop tempting me. We have an important match. I need my strength, woman.' There was a smile of sheer indulgence on his lips.

After towelling them both dry he put on the pyjamas that lay discarded on the floor, tied the belt to his dressing gown and said, 'You will find your clothes in the wardrobe. You look very sexy in that towel but I don't think it would be prudent if you went down to breakfast wearing just that.' He kissed her gently. 'I'll be back.'

Vanessa opened the wardrobe to find her clothes hanging neatly. She opened the drawers of the dressing table. It was obvious that he had packed and moved all her clothes to Cleish

House. How had he been so sure that she would become his mistress? Vanessa's heart was heavy. She had spent a wonderful night with Mac but she had no right to his love. Once she was dressed she would slip out of the house and hope that no one would see her leave.

She chose a pair of navy slacks and a warm, soft primrose sweater, navy sneakers and a short navy reefer jacket and was about to cross the room to leave when she heard a knock.

'Your breakfast, miss,' said a maid. Behind the maid was Mac, fully dressed in tan cords, a matching tan shirt and his tweed jacket with the worn cuffs.

Vanessa couldn't help saying, 'And you wonder why I thought you were the gardener.'

This time it did not anger him and he laughed.

'Keep your hands off. This is my favourite jacket.' Then, as an afterthought, he said with a cheeky grin, 'You can handle anything else, though.'

Turning to the maid he said, 'On a more serious note we can manage now.' He took the laden tray from her and placed it on a small table. He drew up two chairs.

'Now, you can't tell me you have no appetite today,' he said, passing her some toast. 'Would you like to pour or should I.'

Vanessa smiled and said, 'I will.'

'Did you look at the roses?'

Vanessa shook her head. He stopped chewing and looked at her, puzzled.

'You went to bed with me without looking at my note.' Once more Vanessa nodded her head.

'I had no idea it was for me.'

At that moment a knock came on the door.

'Vanessa, can I come in?' It was Kathryn. 'Oh, sorry. I came to see if you were ready for breakfast, but I see that Uncle Hamish has beaten me to it.'

'That's okay, Kathryn,' Mac answered. 'I've nearly finished. Come and eat some toast. Vanessa has the appetite of a bird but I'll soon change that. You can use my cup; you won't catch anything. Now I have to go but Kathryn, make sure you bring

Vanessa along with you.' Bending over Vanessa he said, 'We'll talk later. I think you might find you have misjudged me. However, you will be my mistress and a lot more for the rest of my life.' He swiftly kissed her on the lips. 'Wish me luck.'

Ruffling Kathryn's hair he strode out of the room. Kathryn was looking at the untouched bacon and eggs under the heated dish and was not interested in the intimate look that had passed between Vanessa and Mac.

Vanessa tried to make sense of what he had said. The roses had been for her. She walked over and pulled the envelope out just as Kathryn looked up. Vanessa hurriedly put the small envelope into her pocket, wanting to read it when she was on her own.

'This is great! Breakfast in your own room. Uncle Hamish makes me go to the dining room. I can see you have wrapped him around your little finger.'

CHAPTER 10

Later that morning Vanessa sat in a special area reserved for the laird and his family. The group included Aysha, Mac's mother, Kathryn, Flora, her mother and three people she had not met before. Vanessa was still feeling panicky, and the violet shadows under her eyes gave her skin a transparent look.

'Are you all right, Vanessa dear?' her mother asked. 'You did go to bed very early but you still look terribly tired.'

'Yes, Mother,' Vanessa answered, a blush covering her cheeks. She felt as if her mother was aware that Mac had stayed with her. What would she say if she knew that her tiredness today was the result of the long passionate night she had spent with Mac? How could she have fallen for the oldest trick in the book? But try as she might she was aware that she was putty in his hands.

Mac suddenly appeared and squeezed her arm as he passed. He took his place in the stand to open the game.

At the end of his short speech, he said, 'There will be the usual party at Cleish House tonight for both the victors and the losers. Anyone wishing to join us is welcome. However, tonight will be slightly different. We will also be celebrating my forthcoming marriage. The Reverend McCarthy will be asking my future bride to help present the cup.'

Vanessa looked at Aysha and wondered if she knew that Mac was to marry someone else. If Aysha felt half as bad as she did, then she pitied her. As Vanessa looked Aysha gave her a watery smile. At the same time Vanessa caught the eye of the young clergyman who was with their party and he gave her a brilliant smile.

The game was more exciting than Vanessa had thought. Watching Mac bully the ball up the pitch and pass it to Jock made her bite her lip. Suddenly Cleish were slightly ahead and Vanessa cheered loudly with the rest of the crowd. How hard the teams were fighting to win the cup. At the end, Vanessa could not look when the players lined up on the pitch. Her heart plummeted and she felt that she just could not watch his future wife. Vanessa loved Mac with all her heart but felt she could not live with the guilt of the previous night.

Suddenly, everyone was silent and Reverend McCarthy gently touched Vanessa sleeve, indicating that she should precede him. Vanessa stared at him and gently but insistently he urged her forward. Vanessa moved in a daze; Mac had asked her to be his mistress, not his wife. Reverend McCarthy said a few inspiring words to the players that Vanessa barely heard.

'Now, Vanessa, you present the cup,' he whispered.

Vanessa was so shocked that she trembled as she held the cup out to the waiting Mac and a player she did not recognise. There were tears in her eyes as she gazed at Mac. Suddenly there was a loud applause as Mac pulled Vanessa into his arms, pressing her against his muddy frame.

'I told you you would be my mistress,' he whispered, 'and the mistress of my heart, my wife and my lover all rolled in one. Don't refuse me in front of all these people.' He took a box out of his pocket. 'This was my grandmother's ring.' He slipped a huge aquamarine surrounded by diamonds onto her finger. 'It's a little large but we can soon remedy that.' Vanessa was too emotional to answer.

Mac then said, 'Remember last night. There's no going back. You're mine now, no one else's.'

Holding her by the waist he led her away to join the rest of the group. Mac's mother held her close.

'I'm so pleased, my dear. You are the first girl he has ever wanted and I guessed that you were special when he flew to Paris to bring me back. I'm sure you will make him very happy and he you. I hope the wedding will be soon.'

Mac laughed throatily and said, tongue in cheek, 'The banns have already been read and the wedding will be two in weeks.'

Vanessa looked at him. 'You were that sure of me?'

'Yes! I intended to keep you by my side until you agreed. That's why I packed all your clothes, even those flimsy things you had on last night,' he whispered, for only her to hear.

Her mother made her way to Vanessa's side and hugged and kissed her.

'I couldn't have picked you a better husband and I can tell he loves you, Vanessa. I could tell from the first night he called to see us.'

After the party that night Vanessa showered ready for bed and came out of the bathroom wearing only a towel. Mac was stretched out on the bed. He jumped up and led her to the window. The sun was just setting.

'You were right. The sunset is just glorious. We can watch it every night now, together.' Pulling gently at the end of the towel he said, 'You won't want that.'

Picking her up he carried her to the bed and said, 'I know we are not married yet but you fill my mind and my heart, and I just don't want to leave your side, ever.' Vanessa held out her arms and smiled, welcoming the passion that would be theirs.

Much later she said, 'Why did you not put me out of my misery sooner? I died a thousand deaths waiting to see who you were to marry.'

'Why it was you of course,' Mac said. 'I told you on the card I left with the roses. Have you still not read it?'

'No, I took it with me to the match intending to read it later.'

Mac groaned. 'I love you, Vanessa Broderick, and have done since the day I met you on the train. I'd had a heavy business meeting before boarding and at first I just thought you were another townie on holiday.'

'Well, I'm not. I'm here to stay. I love you, Hamish McPherson.'

He bent to take her in his arms once more and anything else she had to say was smothered by his mouth claiming hers.

*The Grass Is Greener
On The Other Side*

By Barbara Machin

CHAPTER ONE

Elizabeth stared into Stephen's eyes. They were to be married tomorrow and he had called around to tell her he had changed his mind. They had talked about moving to Australia and had agreed that they needed to concentrate on their careers first. Both Elizabeth and Stephen were junior doctors and worked at the same hospital. They had planned their wedding six months ago. Elizabeth looked at him with tears in her eyes.

'I thought we were going to talk about Australia once we had a couple of years' practical experience under our belts.'

'I'm so sorry, Elizabeth, I feel that it's something I need to do on my own. If we went through with the marriage, we could have children and it would never happen. I still love you, Elizabeth.'

'But not enough to marry me, Stephen, is that it?'

She stood up to face him and hair fell across her face.

'I've noticed I haven't seen you much over these last few weeks. Why couldn't you have told me before? We've sent all the invitations out. Now we'll have to ring everyone tonight to stop them turning up. When are you planning to go?'

'That's just it, Elizabeth. I accepted a position last month in Queensland, at the general hospital there, and I'm leaving for Heathrow tonight.'

'You knew last month and you continued to go along with this charade? Why? You've let both your parents and mine spend money that they can't get back or afford. How selfish is that? And now you're leaving me to clean up the mess myself.'

'Well, I can hardly stay and sort it out with you. I fly out soon.'

Her hazel eyes didn't leave his face and, moving her dark brown hair off her face, Elizabeth stared at him. She thought about all the times in the last two years she had helped him with his studying in the run-up to their exams.

'That's it, you go! I see you're a coward to the end. Don't worry about me. I'll be too busy to miss you.' Her usual calmness left her. 'Get out! Get out now!' Elizabeth's voice was reduced to an angry whisper. Stephen turned on his heel, leaving Elizabeth to slam the door after him.

Sitting there by the phone she knew she needed to ring her guests and her parents. However, she also needed to be in control of herself. Elizabeth didn't need sympathy. But she did need support and rang her best friend, who had been due to be bridesmaid. After a few seconds her friend Debbie answered. Elizabeth briefly told her what had happened.

'I'm on my way. I'll be there in 10 minutes.'

After opening the front door to Debbie, Elizabeth fell into her arms. She had controlled herself until then but she gave in to a storm of tears. Debbie held her until the tears subsided. Picking up the list of guests Debbie said, 'I'll start on this. You ring your mum and dad on your mobile. But before we do that, I'll make a strong cup of coffee. Don't worry, Elizabeth, it will just seem like a bad dream in a few weeks. Anyone who could do what Stephen has done is not worth a second thought. You're beautiful, Elizabeth, and intelligent, so let's get on with what needs doing and forget all about him. It's his loss not yours.'

Elizabeth felt much better when she had rung her parents and persuaded them not to visit there and then, but to come tomorrow as planned. Mum could help her return the wedding gifts. Over the next two hours Elizabeth and Debbie worked through the guest list crossing each one off as they did it. They rang the vicar and cancelled the service and the hotel where the reception was to be held. Once they had covered everything, Elizabeth and Debbie opened a bottle of wine. Just as they poured a glass the phone rang. It was Stephan's dad.

'Elizabeth, I've just had one or two phone calls to say that you've rung people to say the wedding's off. Why?'

'Has Stephen not told you?'

'Told us what, Elizabeth?'

'He came around about four hours ago to tell me that he couldn't marry me. He'd changed his mind.'

'He could just have been having pre-wedding nerves, Elizabeth.'

'No he wasn't. He was on his way to the airport. He flies to Australia tonight. He accepted a post in Queensland a month ago.'

'Why didn't you tell us before now?'

'Because the first I knew about it was four hours ago.'

'He wouldn't do that!'

'Look, I don't want to upset you but he has just done that. Believe me, I'm only glad that he did come and tell me or I could have turned up at the church none the wiser.'

'I'm so sorry, Elizabeth, it's not like Stephen.'

'Don't be. I'm glad he did. I've had a lucky escape.' With that Elizabeth gently put the phone down.

'Oh, Debbie, I can't believe that he didn't even tell his own mum and dad. How could he be so cruel?'

The next day Elizabeth's parents came down and her father Frank held her in his arms.

'It was probably for the best, lass. It could have been worse. He could have done it after you got married. Now let's get these wedding gifts returned and that's the end of it.'

When everything had been sorted her father cleared his throat and asked, 'What about your honeymoon? Have you done anything about that?'

'No, Dad, it hasn't entered my head.'

'Well, I'll nip to the travel agents and see if I can salvage anything from it. You stay here with your mum.'

'Okay, Dad.' Elizabeth sat drinking tea with her mum. She was much calmer now. She had brushed her hair and put it in a ponytail. Her hazel eyes had violet shadows beneath them but she still looked beautiful, her slim figure accentuated by her tight black jeans and black top.

'Are you sure you can't eat something, Elizabeth?' her mum asked.

'No, Mum, I'm not hungry yet.' At that moment her dad returned.

'They were very understanding under the circumstances and have given you a credit note for the money spent. Who paid for it, lass?'

'I did, Dad. Stephen promised he would transfer the money into my account but he never did. We had booked for three weeks so once I have cleared everything up I'll see if Debbie can get a couple of weeks off and we can go and have a break together.'

Debbie and Elizabeth had been friends since school and before Stephen came along they had always taken their holidays together.

'Right. Now, lass, do you think you would like to come home for a few days with us?'

'No, Mum, I'll be okay. There's life after Stephen. Running back home won't make it any better.'

Once her mum and dad had left, after insisting she ring if she needed help, Elizabeth went to the paper shop and picked up her medical magazine. Glancing through it she came across the hospital vacancies for doctors. Reading through them she came across an advert for a junior doctor at a general hospital in Scotland. It was around 50 miles away from her home near the Lake District. She didn't fancy going back to her current job and face the sympathetic looks of the rest of the staff. She rang the hospital in Scotland and they agreed to see her the next day. Elizabeth then rang Debbie and broached the subject of taking a short holiday. They arranged to meet later that afternoon and go to the travel agents together. That done, she began to feel more positive. They both decided that Jersey would be far enough for them and booked for the last two weeks of what would have been Elizabeth's honeymoon. Then, hardening her heart, she made sure she had all her credentials for the interview. Looking back on her study and training years, she realised that she had been the one who had found the exams easy, and she had been the one who had helped and pushed Stephen. Now she realised that she would have no problem with the interview; the result would be in the lap of the gods and depend on how many applicants there were.

CHAPTER TWO

Walking out of the hospital the next day Elizabeth was happy with her interview, They had told her there would be second interviews on the Tuesday afternoon of the next week and they would advise her by phone if she had got through. Driving back home she hoped she would be successful; if she was, she would rent a room until she could find something more permanent, It would be a fresh start.

On the Monday she decided she wouldn't leave her flat just in case the hospital rang. It was 3 o'clock and she had just about given up when the telephone rang. It was the secretary from the hospital advising her of her interview slot the next day.

She went to the bedroom to make sure her suit was immaculate the next day, then rang her mum and dad and told them she was feeling quite excited and had a good feeling about it.

The interview the next day was quite long and that was mostly a good sign. However, what would be, would be. The medical board promised that she would be advised of the outcome by phone over the next two days. The next day the hospital rang and offered her the position and she accepted. They said they had put a contract in the post and all she needed to do was sign it and post it back. Elizabeth arranged to start in six week, which would slot in nicely with her holiday plans. She then rang her superior at the hospital to explain that she was leaving and why, and they agreed that under the circumstances she needn't return. He said he was sorry to lose her and that she had a promising career ahead of her. He also said he didn't understand how, when Stephen had tendered his resignation, it was going to work for them after they were married, because he never mentioned calling off the wedding. Working it out she realised she would have three weeks after her holiday to find somewhere to live and put her flat up for sale. Her mum and dad would look after that for her.

CHAPTER THREE

The next day Elizabeth and Debbie went to the travel agents and managed to book into the Manor House Hotel in St Helier. Both of them were pleased. It was a very exclusive hotel.

'It will be just like old times,' Debbie said. 'Your dad used to call us the terrible twins.' Debbie even agreed to take a couple more days off to travel to Dumfries and help Elizabeth look for somewhere to rent and 24 hours later they jumped into Elizabeth's car and headed north, after booking into a bed and breakfast for one night. They were both very attractive girls, one, Elizabeth, tall and slim with hazel eyes and dark long curly hair; the other a typical blonde, with baby-blue eyes, a slightly fuller figure than Elizabeth but of the same height. As they toured the estate agents they attracted lots of admiring glances from passing men and those working in the estate agents. Debbie responded with a huge smile but Elizabeth stared coldly, vowing that no one would make a fool of her again. After visiting what seemed like every estate agent in Dumfries, they found a suitable flat and Elizabeth asked if it would be possible to view it there and then.

'I'm sure I can manage that if you give me a smile,' the young man said.

Elizabeth just stared and asked, 'Is your manager here?'

'Yes, but she is not available, and of course you can view the flat, miss.'

'Doctor Elizabeth Rubenstein,' she said without a smile.

'I'll just get someone to take you,' he said, somewhat red-faced.

The flat wasn't furnished but Elizabeth had her own furniture. It had two bedrooms and a large kitchen-diner. The lounge was also a good size. The bathroom did not have a bath, just a large shower. It was decorated throughout in magnolia and the carpet was a light gold. Looking at Debbie Elizabeth said, 'This will be great. I can introduce colour in my cushions and throws.' And looking at the estate agent she said, 'I'll take it. Can we go back and talk terms?'

'Yes, certainly.' He was careful not to be presumptuous with her as he had already been warned that she was a little touchy and to be careful.

After suppling him with her references and paying the surety and three months advance rent she signed the contract, leaving her present address with him in case he needed to contact her and advising him that she wouldn't be available for the next three weeks. She was feeling more positive when they left.

'Let's find somewhere to have something to eat, Debs,' she said, using her friend's pet name.

'Only if I can start calling you Beth again,' Debbie responded.

'Of course you can.' Elizabeth laughed, remembering that it was Stephen who had insisted it was more ladylike to use her full name. The returned to their B&B and changed, Debbie choosing a baby-blue dress, white sandals and a white clutch bag, and Elizabeth selecting a straight black fitted dress that she teamed with red strappy sandals and a red clutch bag. She put in her ears a pair of ruby and diamond earrings her mum and dad had given her for her 21st birthday. Ruby was her birth stone. After finding an exclusive Italian restaurant, the waiter at the front of the house escorted them to a table. Sitting and taking in the ambiance around her, Elizabeth gasped as a pair of steel grey eyes met hers. Whoever he was he was scrutinising her. He appeared to be looking at her from top to toe. Elizabeth returned his look with a cold stare and resumed her meal.

'Blimey, Beth, he seems to like the look of you.'

'How do you know it's me? It could be you, Debs. In any case, I'm not interested.'

At that moment he appeared next to their table.

'Good evening, ladies.'

'Hello,' said Debs, while Elizabeth returned his stare without smiling and once again concentrated on her meal.

Lifting an eyebrow, he commented, 'Well perhaps not,' and nodding to Debs, frowned and continued towards the desk at the front. Neither Debs nor Beth noticed him point to their table and handover his credit card. Five minutes later the waiter approached their table with a bottle of wine.

'With the compliments of Mr Le Revere.'

'Who?' said Debs.

'The gentleman who just left.'

'Oh come on, Beth, you're not going to let that scumbag Stephen spoil the rest of your life, are you?'

'He won't,' Elizabeth said. blushing.

'Did you look at him properly? He was tall and lean and had black hair and such lovely eyes.'

Elizabeth laughed. 'How did you notice all that?'

'Because he was looking at you all the time and never appeared to notice me, so I could.'

'Now he could do something for me,' Debs said.

'Be my guest.' Elizabeth laughed.

After finishing their meal they strolled back to the B&B. Elizabeth was deep in thought; she knew it was early days yet in the last three days she had been able to start squeezing Stephen out of her mind. She was also busy building a huge fence around her heart.

After arriving home she spoke to her parents and explained that she had found somewhere and hoped she could get her furniture and goods moved on the following Friday. She asked them if they could be there to let the furniture removers in. She rang the estate agents and put her flat on the market, and arranged for all of her possessions to be moved. The company she used would not only move it but pack everything for her. Her mum and dad would be there to receive it. After packing a case with her holiday clothes and taking it to Debbie's, they then spent Thursday filling boxes with her dishes and clothes and labelling the boxes with which room they were to be put in. Her mum and dad would go down early and, after the beds were put into the bedrooms, they would make one up for themselves and stay a few days until the flat was as it should be, giving Elizabeth time to get to know the area.

With those arrangements made, Elizabeth signed with relief. She could now have her holiday in peace; she certainly needed it. Sitting at Debbie's sipping a glass of wine she quietly reflected. Who would have thought that all this would happen to her? She had thought that her life was nicely mapped out. How wrong can you be? she thought. If she had learnt any lessons through this experience it was not to put all your eggs in one basket.

CHAPTER FOUR

After stepping off the plane at St Helier, Debs and Beth walked across the tarmac to the customs to get their luggage.

Suddenly a voice asked, 'Would you like some help, ladies?'

Looking up Elizabeth could not believe her eyes when she saw the man from the Italian restaurant. Well of all the nerve, she thought.

'No, thank you,' Elizabeth said a little sharply, giving him a cold look. Grabbing her case she wondered if he was following them. And later when she told Debs, she wondered how he could have been there when he had been in Dumfries so recently.

'It's just a coincidence,' Debs said.

'A strange one, you must admit.'

'Oh, Beth, what have I told you? Try and enjoy life while you can. If you keep treating everyone as if they are all like Stephen you will live a lonely life.'

'I'm sorry. I have to be cruel to be kind.'

'Do you think Stephen will be living the life of a monk? I don't think so. Look how you said he was always trying to get you to sleep with him while you were at university. Not everyone is like us. We both watched what we were doing. Remember most of us studying medicine were ducking and diving. There will be plenty of nurses in most hospitals who would be willing to put it about for a good looking doctor.'

'I suppose,' Elizabeth conceded.'

'Listen to Aunty Debs. He is one hell of a handsome man.'

The took a taxi to their hotel and as they got in Elizabeth saw the man from the restaurant climb into a black Jaguar behind them. He joined them at the hotel's reception desk and gave Elizabeth a puzzled look once more. When a receptionist approached him he asked, 'Is my mother upstairs?'

'Yes, sir. Here's your key.'

'Thanks, Helen.'

He nodded at Elizabeth then took the stairs two at a time, and while Beth and Debbie were changing into shorts he was at the reception desk checking which room they were in. He was certain he recognised the name Elizabeth Rubenstein, but he had not heard of Debbie Slater. He then wrote a card and asked for a bottle of champagne to be delivered to their room. On returning to their room Debbie noticed the champagne at once.

'Oh, look Beth, it looks as if they have made a mistake.' Debbie started to open the card.

'Debs, is that the action of a doctor?'

'Well, how will we know if it's a mistake if we don't read it?'

Quickly read the card and passed it to Elizabeth. Debbie had a huge grin on her face. The card read. 'Lose the attitude. You are spoiling yourself. And that's a shame because you are quite beautiful. I would very much prefer a smile. An admirer.'

'Well of all the cheek.'

'Come on, Beth, you must see the funny side.' Debbie was bent double with laughter. 'The most we can do is enjoy it.' The sight of Debbie sent Elizabeth into peals of laughter as well. She did see the funny side, even if it was only seeing Debbie laughing like that. In the hospital Debbie had always strived in to show her serious side but never quite managed it.

The next day Elizabeth and Debbie were handing their key in when Mr Le Revere walked down the stairs holding the arm of an older lady. Elizabeth was looking at him thinking that Debbie was right: he was devastatingly handsome. At that moment he looked up to see Elizabeth looking at him. He smiled slowly. This time she didn't give him a cold stare but blushed and turned away. Then both he and the lady disappeared through a door marked Private. Giving herself a sharp reminder she told herself that they were all the same; one man was no different from any other. But try as she might she could not get him out of her mind.

The next day they hired a car and drove around the island, returning quite late and ordering dinner from room service. Over the next few days Debbie and Elizabeth saw very little of Mr Le

Revere and by the end of the first week Elizabeth was more relaxed and less uptight. She realised that her dad was right: it was for the best that it had happened before they got married rather than finding out after the wedding. The grass would always have been greener on the other side for him; she wouldn't have been enough for him. She realised that now.

Both Elizabeth and Debbie already looked tanned and healthy although Debbie was a much lighter shade. Both girls looked very attractive. As they approached the reception desk and asked for their key, the receptionist said, 'Here's your key and a note from Mr Le Revere. You are the attractive young lady with dark hair in room 226,' she said, smiling.

Elizabeth stared open mouthed at the receptionist while Debbie smiled and said, 'Life after Stephen. What did I tell you?'

Elizabeth gave Debbie one of her stern looks.

'Come on, Beth, what's happened to your sense of fun?'

Elizabeth couldn't stay cross with Debbie for long. Her laughter was infectious and soon they were both in their room holding their sides through bouts of laughter.

'Come on, Beth, share your message. I would if it was me.'

Trying to keep a straight face she read the note.

'My beautiful stranger, I can't stop thinking of you. I've had to return home but I would like it very much if you would ring me on this number. My mother said she would look out for you. However, you have been coming back quite late and my mother would be sitting with my father by then, who isn't well. I hope you will ring me so that at least I can see you smile. Sebastian Le Revere.'

'Why couldn't it be me?' Debbie said, holding her chest above her heart.

'Stop fooling around, Debs, this holiday has really done me good. You know the hurt might not have gone altogether, but I am questioning whether I did really love Stephen. Yes, I am getting over it. The worst is the thought of having to face people and having to admit that he left me virtually at the altar. It has done nothing at all for my confidence, and it will be long time before I get involved with another man.' Looking at Debbie she added, 'But just think of the fun we can have while you are waiting for your Mr Right to turn up!'

'And what about our Sebastian?' Debbie said, tongue in cheek.

'What about him, cheeky?' Elizabeth retorted. 'He's a stranger, and my mum always told me not to talk to strangers.'

Arriving back home Debbie, for once, was quiet.

'What's the matter, Debs, you're quiet?'

'I know. It's just that I will miss you. We've worked at the same hospital since we finished medical school, and not only that you will be living 50 miles away. Don't tell me that's not far. It's too far to pop around and share a bottle of wine.'

Elizabeth hugged Debbie to her. 'I'll miss you too, Debs. Who will I ring the next time I'm dumped?'

'People won't make a habit of that, Beth, and certainly not the handsome Mr Le Revere.

'I probably won't set eyes on him again, Debs, and yes, he was very good looking, but I still feel that I'm better off making sure I have a rest from men for a while. I'd like to be in control of myself again. Thinking back, I did fall in with Stephen's wishes most of the time and he never appeared to be interested in what I wanted, so yes, I think I would like to be my own master. Look, Debs, we'll make time somehow to have a night out. We're likely to get a day off now and again that coincides.'

'Come to think of it, we didn't manage many when you were with Stephen,' Debs said.

CHAPTER FIVE

Elizabeth surveyed her little domain. Her mother was in the kitchen making sandwiches and her father was putting up the shelf in the bathroom. Elizabeth and Debbie had just finished putting the new cushion covers on and hanging the curtains. The cushions she had chosen were red velvet to match the curtains and there was a smaller cushion in a gold-figured design. Her suite was in a deep rich gold. A couple of good oil paintings were hung on the wall. A small Chinese rug in red and gold was on the hearth and her furniture had been set out to perfection. She favoured antique yew. Her precious crystal glasses gleamed after the cleaning her mother had given them before she came back from Jersey, and everywhere was neat and tidy. Elizabeth's parents were going to have a sandwich and a cup of tea and would then drive home. It was Debbie's weekend off so she was to stay with Elizabeth until Sunday afternoon when she would travel back. Elizabeth herself would start at her new appointment on Monday. Once her mum and dad had left she and Debbie settled down to a bottle of wine and a good natter. They talked about old times. It no longer hurt Elizabeth to talk of her college days; she had successfully put Stephen to the back of her mind and they had decided to stay in and enjoy their drink. Tomorrow they would explore the district. It was quite late when they turned in and because of this they slept late the next morning. Elizabeth awoke to the phone ringing. It was her mum and dad calling to see if she was okay.

'Yes of course I'm all right, Mum. Yes, I will let you know when my weekend off is and I will come home for Sunday lunch. I miss you, Mum. Bye.'

Elizabeth's hair hung down in unruly curls. Her hazel eyes looked like liquid pools of gold. Banging on Deb's door she shouted, 'I'm in the shower first, lazy bones.' She quickly showered and put on navy slacks and a short-sleeved cherry-red sweater. Debbie yawned as she made her way into the bathroom. They really had been late to bed last night taking. Elizabeth went into the bedroom to dry her hair, and put it into a chignon at the nape of her neck. Returning to the lounge she found Debbie eating toast and drinking coffee.

'I'll just have my coffee and fruit and we'll go and paint the town red.'

'Or maybe blue,' Debbie said. Come on, Beth, smile.' At this, Elizabeth began to smile. 'See, that's the Beth I know and love. Let's enjoy our day. Who knows who we'll meet.'

Elizabeth smiled once more. 'I feel a spending spree coming on,' and laughing they left the flat.

Walking down the street they were a picture of health and vitality. Elizabeth had regained some of her sparkle. They entered a large department store, and stopping at the cosmetic counter she chose some new lipstick and a bottle of her favourite perfume, Eternity. Laughing, they made their way to the ladieswear. They were unaware that Sebastian Le Revere had spotted them as he came out of the menswear department. He thought, I was right. She's not just beautiful, she really sparkles when she smiles. Her warmth is there for everyone to see. He had only seen her a couple of times however he knew he would not rest until he knew her a lot better.

He had fallen head over heels in love with a beautiful stranger. Stopping at the perfume counter he asked to see the perfume that the lady with the dark hair had just purchased. He then bought the largest bottle they had.

Glancing towards the ladieswear department he resisted the urge to follow. He didn't wish to appear to be stalking them. He had bumped into them three times, now, so he was sure she must live around this area. It felt as if he was destined to meet her again.

Elizabeth and Debbie left the department store overloaded with bags. Between them they had made quite a few purchases. Happy and relaxed they made their way back to Elizabeth's flat where, over a coffee and biscuit, they made plans to visit an Italian for their evening meal. Debbie's needed to go home the following day as she was on duty at the hospital on the Monday. It would be a couple of weeks before they could catch up again.

At around 6 o'clock they got changed. Debbie wore a darkly shaded blue dress which fitted around the waist and hips but flared out below the knee. Elizabeth wore a peacock-green suit with a slightly longer skirt, and black patent strappy kitten-heel sandals. As they entered the Italian, the young waiter recognised them at once and showed them both to the same table they had occupied previously. With a smile he held their chairs out for them to sit down, then handed them the menus. After ordering a bottle of white wine they chatted about next year's holiday, if they were both free.

'Well, I certainly will be,' said Elizabeth. 'I intend to have some me time before I look at another man, and then it will only be my dad. He's the only one I can trust.'

At that moment the door opened and in walked Sebastian Le Revere. Spotting the two girls at once he stopped at their table.

'Good evening, ladies, did you enjoy your holiday?'

Debbie smiled at once and replied, 'Yes.'

'And you, Elizabeth?' He looked into her eyes.

She could not drag her eyes from his and even though she didn't want to, she replied without smiling, 'Yes, thank you.'

'Well, that's an improvement,' he said. 'If you could try a small smile next time... Enjoy your meal.' He then walked to a reserved table for one. He could not help but watch Elizabeth under his slightly closed eyelids.

'Come on, Beth, give him a smile. He'll be putty in your hands.'

'Debs, that's what I thought about Stephen. It proves how wrong we can be. Look, don't worry about me, I just need a little time to adjust. Everything will be all right given time.'

'It better be, Beth, because trust me, I'll be on your case.'

Elizabeth had to smile. 'That's what worries me.' At that they both laughed.

Finishing their meal, they called for the account, and getting up to settle it Elizabeth could not help but steal a glance at her admirer. If she thought he would not be watching she was wrong. As she glanced up, she looked directly into his eyes and he gave her his slow smile. Despite trying to ignore him she smiled slightly and blushed deep red.

'Well, tell me, Beth, will you use this restaurant after I've gone back,' laughed Debbie. She was rewarded with a gentle punch on the arm by Elizabeth. Both girls walked back to the flat smiling.

Watching Debbie get into her small car the next day Elizabeth made her promise to ring and arrange to meet on their next available day off, and, after waving her off, she turned and went back into her flat. She closed the door and sat down. Until then she hadn't had time to think, particularly of Stephen, and as she tried to dissect what had happened, she could not focus her mind because she kept thinking about Sebastian Le Revere. Try as she might she kept thinking about the way he looked at her and how handsome he was. In fact, he must have thought her very rude. Oh well, she probably wouldn't see him again, as she would be working long hours.

CHAPTER SIX

Monday of the following week arrived and Elizabeth examined herself in the mirror, smoothing the skirt of her grey suit to ensure there were no creases and that she had no runs in her tights. Once satisfied she picked up her jacket, doctor's bag and handbag, then made her way outside to her car. At the hospital she slipped her jacket on and picked up her bag and strode towards the entrance. She spoke to the young woman behind the counter.

'I'm Doctor Elizabeth Rubenstein. I'm reporting for duty.'

'Hello, you're expected. I'll just ring the office and they'll send someone down to fetch you.'

Before she had time to think a young woman arrived and said, 'Hello, my name is Sally. Welcome aboard, Doctor Rubenstein. Follow me and I'll take you to the chief. He will show you around and explain your duties, as you will be attached to his team in cardiology.'

Elizabeth followed Sally along the corridor. Sally knocked on a door.

'Doctor Rubinstein, sir,' Sally announced. Elizabeth gasped. She was looking at Sebastian Le Revere.

'Thank you, Sally,' he said, not taking his eyes off Elizabeth's face and holding her gaze while giving her his slow puzzled smile. 'There is a God,' he breathed.

'Pardon,' Elizabeth said.

'I'll explain that some other time. I wondered where I had heard the name Elizabeth Rubenstein. Now I know – in my file. If we are to work together can we call a truce, Elizabeth, or do you prefer Beth?'

'Firstly, I wasn't aware we were at war. Secondly, I think Doctor Rubenstein would be a better title at work. However, I concede that I might have been a little rude.'

'Do you?' Sebastian gazed at her. 'Yes, I quite agree. Around the wards it needs to be formal, but out of earshot we can be normal work friends.'

Elizabeth gave a slight smile. 'Very well, sir.'

'Let's get on and do the ward rounds and then I'll show you your office. Then we can have a coffee and continue this conversation some other time. Tell me, Beth, don't you trust men?'

'Whether I trust men or not it shouldn't impact my work. I know I'm a good doctor, but I can say it would take a lot for me trust a man other than my dad.'

'Give it time,' he said. 'We might be able to change your mind on that. After all, we have all our life to do that.'

That comment sent her heart hammering against her ribs. The cool Elizabeth Rubenstein knew straight away that it would be very difficult to dislike this man.

They walked around the wards and discussed the different patients. He asked her opinion here and there, to gauge her knowledge. He was pleasantly impressed. He took her to the intensive care ward and high dependency wards were. They discussed each patient and checked their medication. As they walked through the corridors, he also introduced her to passing doctors who were going about their business. One or two of the male doctors openly showed great admiration, making Elizabeth visibly squirm and feel uncomfortable. This did not go unnoticed by Sebastian.

'Right, let's make our way to your office, shall we?'

'Yes, sir.' Sebastian seemed to be deep in thought. Opening the door to her office, he said, 'Sit down, Beth.' Elizabeth looked at him, blushing.

Picking up the phone, he said, 'Sebastian Le Revere speaking. I'm in Doctor Rubenstein's office. Could you send coffee for two and some plain biscuits, please.' He studied her face as she sat opposite and tried to meet his gaze. Once she had looked at him she couldn't drag her eyes away and could not believe how she was feeling. She felt like a silly teenager, despite stating that she was off men. She saw his eyes change from silver to stormy grey with emotion, until the spell was broken by a knock on the door.

'Your coffee, Mr Le Revere.'

'Thank you, Sally.' Looking at Elizabeth he asked, 'Cream?'

'Yes please,' she said quietly.

Passing her a cup and offering her a biscuit that she refused, he then poured himself a cup of black coffee.

'I think, Beth, that for the time being I'd like you to shadow me to give you a deeper knowledge of cardiology, and besides, I'll also be able to get to know you a little better.'

'Why?'

'Because it will give you a little more insight into how to work as part of the team and, as I said, selfishly I'd like to know you a little better myself.'

'You would?' whispered Elizabeth.

'I would, but it comes with a price.'

'What price?'

'Just a hint of a smile.' His gaze did not waver.

Smiling slightly, Elizabeth said, 'You are now sounding like Debbie.'

'Believe me, Beth, I'm not always so keen to know strange ladies, but something about you is playing havoc with my heart that I have yet to diagnose. And although I think Debbie seems quite a nice person, it's you that's making my heart palpitate. Tell me, is Debbie a relation?'

'No, she's my best friend. Has been since school.' Elizabeth blushed.

'I know we don't know each other very well but how about me being your friend as well? Btween the two of us, we might get you to smile all of the time and not just when you are with Debbie?'

'I'm not ready for that yet.'

'Why, Beth?' he said gently.

'I assure you I won't let it impact on my work sir. It's personal.'

'I see, but we will talk about it when you're ready. Is that a promise?' Elizabeth nodded. 'Now, look through your list of patients, try a walk around the wards yourself and I'll come and find you when its lunchtime – around 1.30.'

'Okay!'

Standing up he bent forward and gently squeezed her arm. 'Tomorrow will be soon enough to throw you in the deep end.'

She watched his tall figure stride away, thinking, I can't believe it. I do like him but no, I should not get involved with anyone else so soon.

Picking the files up one by one she began to read through the case notes. Once this was done she decided to familiarise herself with the wards. Yes, she had walked around with Sebastian but doing so herself and reading the treatment charts at the end of the bed gave her a better insight into the treatment given.

Meanwhile, Sebastian had made his way back to his office. He had decided to ring his friend and Elizabeth's former boss from the last hospital she worked at. Waiting for Josh to answer his phone he tapped a pencil on his desk.

'Hello,' said the voice at the other end.

'Josh, hi, it's Sebastian Le Revere here.'

'Why, Sebastian, how are you?'

'I'm fine, Josh. The reason I'm ringing is that we have recently had one of your doctors start on my team here, a Doctor Rubinstein. Could you tell me why she left her job there?'

'It was personal, Sebastian.'

'I gather that, but do you know why?'

'It was nothing to do with her work. She's a very promising young doctor and a hard worker.'

'Can you tell me what the problem was?'

'I could, but I wouldn't want her to be embarrassed about someone there knowing.'

'I wouldn't let her know we were aware, Josh.'

'Okay, as long as I have your word. Well, six weeks ago she about to get married but the night before her wedding day her intended went to her home and called it off. The awful part of it was that he had accepted another post in Australia a month before and hadn't told her. Why he left it until the last minute I'll never know. And to cap it all she had to sort everything out herself. Can you think of anything worse? Apparently he was on his way to the airport when he stopped off to tell her. It was a good job she had Debbie, her friend. She's a doctor here.'

'Do you think she still loves him, Josh, and were they a couple that lived together before marriage?'

'Why would you want to know that, Sebastian?'

'Humour me, Josh, you know I wouldn't ask if it wasn't important.'

'I know you wouldn't but now you intrigue me.'

'So what do I think?'

'Well, given time she will get over him and if she knew about the little nurse that went with him to Australia she certainly would, and no, Elizabeth was not that type of person to live with him. The two people that I would say have kept themselves decent are Debbie and Elizabeth. Now you tell me why this interests you, Sebastian. It won't impact her work, I can assure you of that. She is a very dedicated doctor.'

'Well, I met her around five weeks ago. I was on my rest days when she came for her interview so I didn't know who she was. I saw her in the restaurant I use here and fell in love with her, even though she was a complete stranger. At that point I was not aware of who she was. Do you think I'm quite mad? I don't very often fall for strangers and I couldn't understand why I felt as I did. Then I saw her again in the same place, and again in a department store. And I still felt the same. Then I had a week off to go and see Mum and Dad and I couldn't believe that she was there in Jersey. And to top it all she stayed at their hotel in and I realised I won't ever feel any different.

'But I knew there was something wrong because she never seems to smile. And when I went to work this morning, low and behold she was my junior doctor. I won't disclose that I know and I'm aware I need to tread carefully. I'm really grateful, Josh. I hope you are right and that I can earn her trust.'

'Well, if I know you, Sebastian, you will. But promise me you will let me know how you get on. I will expect an invitation to your wedding!'

'Thanks, Josh. Trust me, there will be a wedding if I have my way. But how long it will take me I just don't know. Do you think I've gone quite mad, Josh?'

'No, Sebastian, you have been waiting for the right person to come along and I would imagine it's Elizabeth. I hope it's because she's a lovely person. I happen to think you're a great guy. Go and get your girl but as you say, tread carefully.'

'Well, thanks again Josh I will be in touch.'

Sebastian put the phone back on its stand. It was understandable that she did not smile at him and it would take a while to earn her trust. He then sat staring at the files in front of him. Oh well, he thought, I'd better get something done. He checked his operations for the next few days and his workload. He then decided to go to intensive care and check the progress of patients. Once that was done he would check the rota and see what shifts had been allotted to Elizabeth.

When he went past a ward and saw Elizabeth discussing a patient's notes with one of the nurses. It certainly hadn't taken her long to involve herself with the patients, to get a feel for the running of the wards. She was certainly keen to get involved. Sebastian liked that. Carrying on past the ward he made his way to the office and asked to see the month's shift pattern. He could see that she was working on quite a few days when he was on. He wanted to see the quality of her work. He believed in being fair. However, he needed certain doctors to be in the operating theatre when he operated and to be satisfied that he could include her if needed.

It was nearing 1.30 so he strolled back to the wards to find Elizabeth. He found her talking to Mr Jones, who had had his bypass operation eight days earlier. If all was well he would have the two metal rods they had inserted into his chest, to restart the heart if needed, removed the next day. If this was successful and Mr Jones settled down he would be discharged the following day.

'Doctor Rubinstein, tell me your thoughts on Mr Jones's case.'

'Well, his prognosis is quite good and everything should go well in terms of removing the rods. However, he will need support set up beforehand. He was living on his own so he will need help and supervision. Without this, it might undo the good work the surgical team have done. He has obviously suffered with high cholesterol and had veins that were 70 per cent blocked. Perhaps he would benefit from sugar-coated Aspirin say 75mg. Then we should monitor the results to see if he needs any more medication.'

'And what about John Shepherd? He was admitted two days ago. His heartrate had dropped to 31 and the paramedics found it quite hard to raise it in the usual way.'

'We could do an infusion or give him a pacemaker but first of all I would try new medication. His heartbeat is a little too fast now, so how about Bisoprolol Fumarate 2.5mg and perhaps Eliquis Apixaban to thin the blood – 25mg. And a pravastatin in the evening – that might do the trick. And of course monitor the medication.'

'I think you will do very well in cardiology, Doctor Rubenstein. You will be one of the doctors attending surgery with me tomorrow. Do you think you will manage that?'

'I'm sure I will,' Elizabeth answered confidently.

'So now we can have lunch.'

Walking to the restaurant with her they kept up small talk. Elizabeth chose salad and water for her lunch, Sebastian a salad. He was just about to add a bowl of chips when he looked up at Elizabeth who shook her finger and said 'No.' She then pointed to a jacket potato and whispered, 'Think of your health.'

'As long as you smile I'll let you bully me.' Elizabeth had to smile. 'You look beautiful when you smile. It lights up your face. Thank you.' Elizabeth blushed, not knowing how to answer.

For the rest of the day Elizabeth familiarised herself with her surroundings. When it was time to go home, she found Sebastian loitering in the corridor near her office.

'Hi Beth, are you eating at our restaurant tonight?'

'No. Do you eat there all the time?'

'Most of the time. I have no one to take pity on me.'

'Is that a hint?'

'Could be.'

'All right. I concede that I haven't been very friendly so if you behave yourself you can come home with me and share my meal. I made a beef casserole yesterday. There is enough for two with some veg. You will have to follow me. I live in Charlton Court. I've rented a flat there, number 2.'

'I know where that is. I have a house a few streets away. I'll park my car at home and bring a bottle of wine. Okay?'

Elizabeth gave a slight smile and nodded her head. Her heart was beating a mad tattoo against her ribs. Where had all her good intentions gone? He only had to smile at her and her legs felt as if they had turned to jelly.

At her flat she went straight to the kitchen and turned the oven on. She slipped out of her coat and put some baby carrots on to cook. She seared some asparagus in a hot griddle pan. She then quickly set the table and, putting on an apron, returned to the kitchen. The doorbell rang. She let Sebastian in and he gave her that slow smile that was playing havoc with her heart.

'Make yourself comfortable,' she said, 'and take your jacket off.' he did as he was told and followed her into the kitchen.

'Is there anything I can do?'

'No, it's all under control.'

'I didn't expect anything else, Beth. How about a glass of wine while you cook?'

Turning to him she nodded her assent and rewarded him with a slight smile.

He looked around the kitchen until he found the cutlery drawer and located the corkscrew. He filled the two glasses on the table and took them into the kitchen. He gave Elizabeth a glass and stood behind her. His closeness was playing havoc with her senses. Elizabeth turned around to send him back into the lounge and their eyes locked. She had to drag her eyes away.

Pointing to the lounge she said, 'Go and sit down. The kitchen is my domain. It will be yours later, when you wash up.'

'I don't like the sound of that.'

'You'll be all right. I have marigolds. She put the veg in covered dishes and placed the dishes on heat- resistant pads on the table. She then filled two plates with casserole, making sure he had a large helping, and carried them to the table.

'Thank you, Beth.'

Sitting and eating together seemed a natural thing for them to do. 'This is good, Beth. I'm not sure that when I cook you a meal it will be this good, but I will try.'

'You will cook me a meal?'

'I will! I did cook when I was a student doctor.'

'We all had to,' Elizabeth said. 'It made it fun. The most exciting bit as a student, though, is when you have achieved your goal. My mum and dad were so proud of me.'

'Where do they live?' he asked.

'About 50 miles away, just outside the Lake District. It's not too far. It will take me about 30 minutes to get there. Would you like some more casserole?'

'Are we having a desert?'

'Yes.'

'Well in that case I'll wait.'

She took the dishes into the kitchen and cut two slices of lemon lush, carrying them in with a jug of fresh cream.

Smiling at Elizabeth, he said, 'I'd happily eat in this restaurant every night, if you'd let me.'

'I thought you were going to cook for me next?'

'I will, I promise you. You're good company, Beth.'

At this, Elizabeth blushed. 'I'll put the coffee on.'

'How about another glass of wine?'

'Just half a glass. I don't often drink when I'm working the next day, but I'll treat this as an exception.'

Popping the dishes into the dishwasher and putting the coffee back on she noticed he was standing watching. She sat down on the settee and he immediately came and sat beside her. Lifting his glass, he said, 'Here's to many more comfortable nights together.'

Elizabeth looked at him and once again she could not drag her gaze away. This time it was the phone ringing that broke the spell.

'Hi Debs, yes fine but can I ring you back later? I'm entertaining. Yes, I am. I'll ring you back, cheeky.'

Sebastian had closed his eyes.

'Are you okay?' Elizabeth asked.

He opened an eye. 'No, I'd like to stay all night because I'm so comfortable.'

'Well we are both working so we'll have coffee and another half hour to an hour and then you will have to go home to your bed.'

'Must I?'

'Yes, you must. After all, you said yourself you are operating tomorrow and if I'm to watch you I need my beauty sleep.'

'Believe me, your beauty takes my breath away now.'

'Do you say that to all the girls?'

'No, not at all. Only the ones I can't get out of my mind.'

'Well, in that case, you can go home after your coffee and dream about me, but don't blame me if you can't cut a straight line on the patient's chest tomorrow.'

'Coffee, then, and I'll try to drag myself away.'

She poured coffee. 'You're not having black, it will keep you awake.'

'I agree. Tonight I will need my sleep. However, I'm sure there will be some nights when I won't want to sleep, depending on if you change your mind about me and on how you feel about me in the future.'

'Why are you bothered about me liking you?'

'Because my business is mending people's hearts, and a certain person might break my heart and I won't be able to put it back together without help.'

'Come on. I think you need your bed.'

'Okay, I'll go on one condition.'

'What's that?'

'That I pick you up for work in the morning and after work we go to our restaurant for our evening meal. My treat.'

'But's that's blackmail,' Elizabeth said, trying to look offended.

'Now you know you want to, no strings.'

'If it gets you home and in bed, okay, I give in. What time in the morning?'

'Eight-thirty.'

'Right,' Elizabeth said, standing to get his jacket. Sebastian had fought the urge to kiss her all night, and still felt the need to touch her. He drew her to him gently kissing her on the lips. He searched her eyes and they told him everything he wanted to know. Bending once more to kiss her again. 'That's on account. Eight-thirty.'

Elizabeth nodded and smiled, and on impulse kissed him on the cheek. 'Goodnight, Sebastian.'

After closing the door behind him she sat on the settee, her heart doing somersaults in her chest. This couldn't be possible. How could she feel this way? It had been only five weeks since Stephen had left. She needed to be careful. She 29 now and not long out of medical school. Stephen had always been there. She realised that she had drifted into her relationship with him. He had leant on her throughout their study and exams. He had dropped her as soon as she was no further use to him. But if he hadn't she would never have met Sebastian. She dared not analyse her feelings. What if he was just leading her on? She couldn't stand rejection again, and besides, if he did reject her it would be far worse than when she was dumped by Stephen.

The phone rang. It was Debbie again.

'I thought you were going to ring me back.'

'I was. My visitor has only just left.'

'Well, spill. Who was it? Male or female?'

'It's a long story.'

'Come on then. I'm waiting. I need something to brighten my day. Tell Aunty Debs. How was your day?'

'Very enlightening. I reported to the hospital and a member of the office staff took me to my superior. I then walked into the office and guess what! This will please you – guess who it was.'

'Who? I don't know anyone there.'

'Yes you do. Sebastian Le Revere.'

'You're kidding!'

'No, I'm not. I'm telling the truth I've just had him over for our evening meal.'

'How come, Miss Misery?'

'He waited in the corridor after my shift was over and asked me if I was going to dine at the Italian. I said no and asked him if he dined there every night. He said mostly, but because no one took pity on him. I blurted out was that a hint, he said might be and I found myself saying I'd made a casserole yesterday and that he could share it. We've just spent a very platonic evening together.'

'You lucky so and so. What I'd give. Something tells me you'll be glad that Stephen did dump you.'

'I think I am, Debs, but I've only seen him three times as well as today and he's not putty in my hands. I think it's going to be the other way around – I'll be putty in his. I've got to be careful. I couldn't stand rejection by him, Debs. And he kissed me before he went and I let him.'

'Now listen here, Beth, I'd swop places in a heartbeat. He's fantastic. Grab him with both hands! Have you any plans to see him again other than work?'

'He's picking me up in the morning and I'm having a meal at the Italian tomorrow night with him.'

'Now I've got to start thinking about our nights out, Beth. You're not going to dump me again are you?'

'No, I'm not. You will always be part of my life, Debs. We have been friends too long to lose contact. We will have nights out. That's something that Stephen taught me – we all need other people as well as partners, and Debs, I'm so glad I kept to the rule. No sex before marriage. It's not good to sleep around.'

'If I had a date with Sebastian Le Revere I might slacken my rules,' Debs said with a laugh.

'No, you wouldn't. You're like me so stop being cheeky, you cheeky pup. Right, I'm in theatre with him tomorrow so I need my beauty sleep.'

'Well keep me informed. I want to know every detail, understand?'

CHAPTER SEVEN

The next morning Elizabeth was eating her cereal when the doorbell rang. It was 7.50. It was Sebastian.

'Goodness, you're early.'

'I felt the need to see you. When we get into the operating theatre all my concentration will on my patient so I won't have the luxury of looking at you, so I selfishly thought I would have a cup of coffee with you before we go in.'

'Come in, then, do you want some cereal?'

'No, I've had breakfast.'

She made some coffee and brought it into the lounge. He took in her fitted grey dress which had three-quarter sleeves edged with a lighter-grey silk. It would be fine under her white overall. He also noticed a matching jacket on a coat hanger and her cherry-red strappy shoes. Elizabeth already had black flat heeled shoes on and her briefcase was ready. A short black jacket lay next to it. She was quite organised – a casual jacket for work and the matching one for the meal after work. He liked that. He patted the seat beside him.

'Are you going to sit by me for five minutes?' Their eyes locked and all her good intentions went through the window as she sat down beside him. 'That wasn't so hard was it?' Shaking her head she continued to return his gaze. After placing his mug on the coffee table he placed his arm around her, gently pulled her towards him and claimed her lips in a lingering kiss. He then traced his lips across her eyes and moving away said, 'That was just what the doctor ordered.'

'Which doctor?' Elizabeth asked.

'Both of us, I hope,' was his smooth response. 'I'd like ten minutes holding you quietly before we go to work. Is that okay by you?' Elizabeth nodded and let him draw her close. She laid her head on his shoulder and they sat there quietly for the next 15 minutes. 'I could stay here holding you forever. I think you've bewitched me, Beth. I haven't been able to think straight since I first set eyes on you.'

'Well, doctor, you will have to pull yourself together. You have work to do. It won't help the poor man who's waiting for you to mend his heart so we better stop being silly and get ready to go.'

'All right, but can we continue later?'

'We'll see!'

Letting go of her he stood and took his cup and her cereal bowl into the kitchen, washed them and stacked them on the drainer.

When he returned Beth had put her jacket on and picked up her shoes and was about to pick up her briefcase when Sebastian said, 'I'll take that and your jacket. Have you got your key?'

'Yes.' She smiled back at him without thinking.

He looked at her and said, 'Thank you, once again, sweetheart.'

They were wrapped up in their thoughts as they walked together to Sebastian's car. Elizabeth was concerned that she was getting involved too soon and thinking, Will it end in tears? I hope not because I really like him. I couldn't possibly have loved Stephen. Meanwhile Sebastian was thinking, I know I can't live without her. I've not seen that much of her but I know she is the only one I want. However, I can't mention the marriage word. That must be taboo and all I want is to have her in my bed every night, and in my life forever. But will she trust me?

He opened the boot of his car and laid her jacket flat. He put her shoes in as well then opened the door for her and got in himself.

'One for the road?'

'Excuse me?'

'Just one more kiss to see me through the day? Elizabeth answered by turning her face to him to receive his kiss.

Arriving at work together could cause gossip. Would he mind, she thought. She had to ask.

'Do you mind us arriving at work together?'

Looking into her eyes he said, 'Why should I? I'm very proud to have you by my side. In fact I think I'm going to kiss you again, right now. You had better get used to it because you are driving me crazy. Tell me you can feel it too.'

'Yes,' she whispered, and with a groan he leant forward and kissed her once more.

'Well that definitely will have to last me until tonight.'

'Is that a promise?'

'I wish we had longer so I could show you,' he said, giving her that slow smile. His eyes promised more to come.

Elizabeth thought, I need to pull myself together. Her heart was racing and she knew she needed to compose herself before she went into theatre with him.

They walked through reception together and Sebastian stopped long enough to say, 'Scrubs at 9.30, Doctor Rubenstein.' And with a quick smile he went to his office while Elizabeth made her way to her office, a gentle smile playing on her lips.

After checking a new patient in and quickly checking any work to be completed she made her way towards the theatre at 9.20. There, she joined Sebastian, a theatre nurse, another junior doctor and the anaesthetist. The theatre nurse pointed her in the direction of the sinks.

'Roll your sleeves up and scrub up to the elbows.'

She allowed the nurse to help her on with the green uniform and to place a mask at her neck. She caught Sebastian's eye and his quick smile.

'Right, ladies and gentlemen, let's get on with the task in hand.'

The patient was already prepped and from then on was all concentration. Elizabeth watched carefully as Sebastian asked for a scalpel. He made the incision in the chest to expose the ribs and quickly parted the ribs to expose the heart. He soon had the blockages cleared and the vein they had already taken from the leg was put in place to complete the bypass. The chest bone was soon wired back in place and rods inserted, and the chest incision sewn up. Still on a life support the patient was taken to intensive care.

Looking at the clock on the wall she realised that it had taken between six and seven hours to complete the operation and her admiration for Sebastian increased 10-fold. He was obviously a very talented surgeon.

'Shall we wash up and break for lunch?' he said.

'Well done, sir,' the other junior doctor said.

Thank you, Conor. I'll be asking both you and Doctor Rubenstein for any thoughts you had during the operation. Now, Beth, are you going to the restaurant?'

'Yes, sir.'

'And you, Conor?'

'Thank you, sir. I have someone to see today but some other time.'

'Right, come along, Beth, let's get out of these scrubs and wash up. I think we have earnt a short rest. Are you okay, sweetheart?' he whispered as they walked towards the restaurant.

'Fine, sir,' she answered.

'It's Sebastian when we are on our own.'

Looking around, she replied, 'Okay, Sebastian,' and smiled.

Elizabeth picked a salad and water again, while Sebastian had a steak salad and black coffee.

'Well done,' she said, pointing to the salad and smiling.

After lunch he suggested she accompany him on his rounds and once this was done he said, 'I'd better check my messages, and then I'll go to my office and check my workload. I'll come and find you around 7 o'clock so don't try and go home without me. I'll come and find you.' Looking up and down the corridor he quickly kissed her on the lips and was gone.

Elizabeth wanted to hug herself. She felt happy yet it was only six and a half weeks ago when she had thought she would never smile again. She couldn't wait for 7 o'clock to come around.

It was 7.30 before Sebastian came to find her.

'I'm sorry, Beth, everything has taken longer than I thought. But it won't take a few minutes to get to the restaurant and can I say, Doctor Rubenstein, you can smooth my fevered brow any day.'

'Are you sure you want to go out? You must be tired.'

'I am, and I know we will have a great meal. Then afterwards perhaps we can sit on your settee and you'll let me hold you for a while?'

'Why, doctor, what are you suggesting? It might not be good for your blood pressure.'

'I'm sure it will be the best medicine you can give me. In time, I will be looking for stronger medicine.'

'You will?'

'I will.'

'I think we had better go, don't you,' Elizabeth said, looking into his eyes and melting.

He took her jacket and shoes from the car, helped her to change her jacket and held her arm while she slipped her sandals on. Inside the Italian the young waiter smiled a welcome.

'Your table, Mr Le Revere.'

'You booked in advance?'

'Just in case. If they hadn't had a table I might have had to cook for you and I'm not sure you would like that experience,' he said with a smile.

'But you promised you would cook for me and I will hold you too that.'

Elizabeth chose salad and spaghetti bolognese, with tiramisu and coffee to follow. She suggested they left the wine alone as they needed to work the next day.

'You know you are sensible and beautiful and I love you. There, I've said it. I wasn't going to say that yet because it's only been a short time you've known me. Please don't feel you have to say anything before you're ready, but please think about it. I don't think I will ever love anyone else.'

Reaching across the table he covered her fingers with his strong hand. Elizabeth laced her fingers through his. Her smile told him everything.

'You know, this will always be our special place. I fell in love with you the moment I set eyes on you, and you just wouldn't smile at me.'

'There was a reason. It was personal and I'm not ready to talk about it yet, but I will tell you about it sometime.'

'But please tell me you love me back. I need to hear it.'

'Sebastian Le Revere, I love you. Is that enough for now?'

'Yes, but I warn you, I want to own every part of you, as you will own me forever.'

They made their way back to Elizabeth's flat and as soon as they were inside Sebastian had her in his arms. Passion flared between them. He kissed her eyes and her neck, and Elizabeth found herself responding to his love-making.

'I think you had better make me a coffee before we get carried away, don't you.' Elizabeth nodded her head although all she wanted to do was to remain in his arms. She felt shameless. She hoped he didn't realise that she would have given herself to him in a heartbeat, something she would never have done with Stephen. She was shocked at her own thoughts.

She brought in coffee and sat down beside him, this time adding cream to his cup.

'Black will keep you awake.'

'There you go again, bossy boots!'

'I'm speaking as a doctor, sir.'

'Well, I will feel relaxed if I hold you tightly. I can't stop thinking how lucky I am.' Putting his arm around her he then relaxed back into the comfort of the settee. 'Have I told you in the last five minutes how much I love you?'

'No, but you can tell me now if you want.'

Snuggling up to her he began to kiss her neck and trail kisses up to her eyes.

'By the way, there is a conference in London in eight weeks. Will you accompany me?'

'I'd love to,' Elizabeth replied.

'Then I think we will have to talk about where we go from here. Will that give you enough time, sweetheart, because I know I need you in my bed forever and I'm trying hard not to gather you up now and make love to you? I'm willing to wait for a short time to do it properly but I don't want to wait for too long.'

Blushing, Elizabeth buried her head in his jacket, and kissing her once more on her head and laying his cheek on her hair they sat in silence for around half an hour.

'I think you had better make your way home, Sebastian, it's almost 10.30 and we have work tomorrow.'

'If I must. But I will be here at 8.30 to pick you up, or I could stay here?'

'That would be defeating the object, Sebastian. We were coming very near to doing what we shouldn't and besides, my mum says I have to be a good girl.'

'Yes, but she didn't tell me I'd got to be a good boy.'

'No, but you will be, won't you?'

'Okay, I'm going make sure you are ready in the morning. Shall we eat here tomorrow or my place?'

'If we eat here then we can have something healthy, agreed?'

'Yes, doctor,' he whispered, nibbling her ear.

Pulling him up from the settee she said, 'You will have to go or I won't be responsible for the consequences.'

CHAPTER EIGHT

The next seven weeks past in a whirl of working at Sebastian's side. It was a pleasure to watch and listen, and to learn many of his skills. He was so dedicated and caring with his patients, and if he did not finish until late then Elizabeth stayed late as well. On these occasions they either went to the Italian or back to Elizabeth's to raid the fridge or eat what Elizabeth had prepared the night before. Tonight they had finished late and Elizabeth said she would make an omelette and salad, and sugar-free jelly with fruit.

'You are marvellous. I can't think of anything better. I can't wait until we get back. Kiss me now, woman,' he said, pulling her to him and pressing his body against hers just as three nurses walked past.

'Whoops,' Elizabeth said. 'Now you've caused gossip.'

'Does it matter, my love? 'It's time they knew you were mine and it's time we talked about our next move, which I hope will be in my bed.'

'You're not trying to compromise me, doctor, are you?'

Looking into her hazel eyes he said, 'You should by now be able to work out what I want with you,' his grey eyes changing from silver to a stormy grey. Kissing her once more and threading his fingers through her long dark hair, he added, 'I love you, Beth, and I need you.'

'And I love you, Sebastian,' she breathed.

'Come on, sweetheart, let's go back to your flat and get something to eat.'

The phone rang as they arrived at Elizabeth's flat.

'Mum, hi. As it happens, Mum, I'm off this weekend. Just hang on.'

Putting her hand over the mouthpiece she said to Sebastian, 'You have this weekend off as well, don't you?'

'Yes, I do, sweetheart.'

'I haven't been home to see my parents since coming here because a certain man has kept me busy. Do you fancy Sunday lunch at Mum's with me or would that be too presumptuous?'

Flashing her a brilliant smile, he said, 'If Mum cooks like you, I can't think of anything better.' Elizabeth gave him a grateful smile.

'Yes, Mum, I'd love that but can I bring a guest with me? Thanks, Mum, perhaps you could invite Debs over too. Thanks again, Mum. Is Dad okay? Good. Love you, Mum, see you Sunday.'

Elizabeth wound her arms around Sebastian's neck and kissed him with such passion that they stood holding each other close. He was the first to break the spell.

'If you carry on, Beth, I'll either have to have a cold shower or take you to the bedroom. So you had better get our meal. I've already told you I want to do it properly but I don't know how long I can hold out against your charms. Next week at the conference we will have to talk.'

They worked side by side in the kitchen. Elizabeth made the salad and Sebastian the omelettes. This was safe for him – he was used to making them. After the meal Elizabeth put the coffee on and slipped the dishes into the dishwasher.

Patting the seat by his side, Sebastian said, 'This is my favourite time of the day. Just you and me sitting close.' He put his arms around her, kissed her brow and then rested his head against hers. Suddenly Elizabeth realised that Sebastian was breathing heavily. He had fallen asleep. She was glad that she had insisted that he had water with their meal. She also realised that he would be too tired to drive home, even if it was just a couple of streets away.

'Here goes, Sebastian,' she whispered. 'You are not going home tonight. Let's get you into bed.'

'Your bed,' he mumbled, looking into her eyes.

'Yes, my spare bed.' Holding him up, she walked to the spare room and started to undo his shirt, saying, 'Don't get your hopes up, doctor. I'm a doctor too and I've seen everything you've got many times before.'

'That's a shame,' he said, yawning. 'I'd have had fun explaining my body parts to you.'

She threw his shirt over a chair. 'Trousers next.' He held his hands in the air.

'Have you no shame?' she said, carefully undoing his trousers for him and in one movement pushing him down on the bed, slipping his shoes off and removing his trousers. She lifted his legs onto the bed and covered him up. 'Would you like me to tell you a bedtime story?'

'It's a good job I'm so tired,' he said.

With a smile she walked to the other side of the bed and climbed on top of the covers. 'I'll lie here until you fall asleep, in case you're frightened.' '

You could get under the covers with me,.'

'Don't push it,' Elizabeth said, kissing him.

Opening her eyes sometime later Elizabeth realised that she too must have been tired. It was dark in the bedroom and the lounge light was still on. After gently kissing Sebastian on the lips she carefully got up and put her pyjamas on. She fetched a blanket from her linen cupboard, set an alarm clock and gently climbed back onto the bed beside Sebastian, lying on top of the covers. She pulled the spare blanket over her, placing her arm around Sebastian, and very quickly drifted off to sleep.

Waking to the rattle of dishes, it took Elizabeth a few moments to realise who was in her kitchen. Putting her head around the kitchen door she said, 'Did you sleep well, doctor?'

'I'd have slept better if you had been under the covers with me,' he said, walking over and holding her close to him. He kissed her neck and her lips, then held her body as close as he could.

Elizabeth could feel his desire and gently pulling away, said, 'I'd better have a shower.'

'Would you like me to come and wash your back?'

'If you did, we might not make it to work and you look as if you have had a shower.'

'I have, but we'll have to leave a little earlier so I can nip home and change my clothes. It won't take five minutes. We have time for a slice of toast and some coffee, then we'd better head for my place, which I hope will soon be our place.' Elizabeth smiled, showered and slipped into her own room, quickly dressing in a black fitted dress. She dried her hair and put it into a chignon at the nape of her head. She would put her lipstick on while she was waiting for Sebastian to change. They still had plenty of time and sat at the kitchen table drinking the coffee he had made and nibbling toast.

Elizabeth was amazed at the size of Sebastian's large Georgian house. The hall walls still had wood panels to halfway up and the hall itself was huge. But it lacked a woman's touch. The lounge also needed light colours to brighten it up. The paintings on the wall were expensive but needed a lighter background behind them, to show them up at their best. Most of the furniture was antique and even that needed to be shown at its best with a lighter background, and perhaps a lighter suite and carpet along with some bright cushions and curtains. Elizabeth would felt that she would love to give it a makeover and breathe life into it. Sebastian came in behind her and put his arms around her.

'I know what you're thinking. It's unloved. I've been so busy since I bought it that I've never got around to renovating it. That's something we can do together.' Kissing her he said, 'We better make tracks.'

As they walked into work together Elizabeth could almost feel her colleagues talking about them. Squeezing her hand, Sebastian whispered, 'We'll only be a seven-day wonder. They will soon find something else to gossip about. I'll see you later for coffee, okay?' Elizabeth nodded and remembered that all-important smile he liked.

She could not help wondering where they would go from here. She realised that whatever she had had with Stephen was nothing. However, she knew she loved Sebastian with all her heart and that if he asked, she would sleep with him in a heartbeat. Elizabeth also knew she could not live without him. She hoped when they talked next week at the conference he would ask her to marry him rather than to live with him. He had said he wanted to do it properly and marriage was what she wanted. She felt that Sebastian did, too. Elizabeth was looking forward to her parents meeting Sebastian.

CHAPTER NINE

Sebastian had agreed to stay the night at her mum's and Elizabeth had assured him that her parents wouldn't mind. They had plenty of room, even if that cheeky pup Debbie also stayed. Sebastian had on a pair of grey slacks and a pale blue shirt and grey Gucci pullover. He looked casual but smart. Elizabeth was wearing her black slacks with a gold blouse. Her hair had been in a ponytail but Sebastian had pulled the clips out before they left the flat and asked her to wear it loose, because that's how she had it the first time he set eyes on her.

Once in the car he leant over for a kiss, saying, 'I love you so much it almost hurts.'

Elizabeth gave him a cheeky smile. 'Let Doctor Rubinstein kiss you better.' It was some time before he put the car in motion.

It was now three and a half months since she met Sebastian and she could not believe how deliriously happy she was. She felt that nothing would burst her bubble. It was known in the hospital that they were now an item and neither Elizabeth nor Sebastian minded that. They stopped at a flower shop on the way.

'Wait here, I won't be a minute,' Sebastian said, and returned with a huge bouquet of yellow and white roses, sunflowers and mixed foliage. 'It's for one of the other ladies in my life.'

'Oh, tell me, doctor, who is the other one?'

'Well, if your mum is to welcome me into the family, I have to make sure she learns to love me as well. I know you didn't really meet my mum when we were in Jersey but I thought when we have a couple of weeks off perhaps your mum and the two of us, along with Debbie of course, could travel to Jersey for a holiday. I could introduce Debbie to my cousin Bruce. We'd stay at Mum's, of course.'

'Where does your mum live, Sebastian, at the hotel?'

'Yes, I was born there. It was our home before Mum and Dad turned it into a hotel. It had become too large for them and of course the running costs were high, and not wanting to move they changed its use. I still have a suite of rooms, and if I let Mum know in advance she'll make sure two rooms are kept for your parents and Debbie.'

'What about me?'

'I could arrange for you to share my room. We could arrange it this weekend. I have my diary in the glove compartment.' He reached over and opened the glove compartment. 'Heavens, I forgot about that.' He pulled out a gift bag. 'For you.'

It's Eternity, my favourite perfume. How did you know?'

'Do you remember going into a department store with Debbie when you came back from Jersey? You went to the cosmetic counter and bought some lipstick and perfume and then you went to ladieswear. I was coming out of the men's department and I wanted you so much that I went to the perfume counter and asked for a bottle of whatever you had just bought. I put it in there to give you if I could get you to speak to me. First of all, you ignored me, then my natural charm won you over. And I was so busy trying to make you mine I forgot all about it.'

Squeezing his knee as he drove, Elizabeth said, 'I'll thank you properly later.'

'I can even remember what you wore.'

'What did I wear?'

'If I'm not mistaken, the slacks you have on today and a short-sleeved, red sweater, and may I say you looked radiant.'

A few minutes later they turned towards Elizabeth's parents' house.

'It's the detached house with a black door. There will be room for you to park on the drive.'

The got out and Sebastian opened the boot for the overnight bags. Elizabeth took hers while lacing her fingers between his. At that moment her dad opened the door.

'There you are, poppet,' and holding his hand out to Sebastian, he said. 'I'm Frank Rubenstein. Elizabeth's father.' They shook hands and as they did so Sebastian made sure he did not let go of Elizabeth's hand.

'Sebastian Le Revere.'

Elizabeth's parents needed to know that he was part of their daughter's life.

'Come in, come in,' Elizabeth said as she walked through the door pulling Sebastian behind her, still hanging on to his hand. 'We are going to stay overnight, Dad.'

'Great. Your mother will be pleased. You know how she worries about you. Maureen, love,' he called, 'Elizabeth is here.'

Elizabeth's mother appeared through an open door. Sebastian would have known her anywhere: she was an older version of her daughter. Her hair was thick and cut in a slightly shorter style, and there were signs of Elizabeth's rich hair colour, plus a few grey streaks here and there. Her eyes were startlingly similar to Elizabeth's. Her face lit up when she smiled at her daughter who let go of Sebastian's hand to hug her.

'Mum, this is Sebastian, my... ' She stopped to look up at Sebastian.

'Boyfriend,' he said, raising his eyebrows at Elizabeth and giving her that special smile. 'And with your permission, sir,' he added, turning to Elizabeth's father, 'I hope to become more.' There was a short pause.

'I'll make some tea,' Elizabeth's mother said. 'Sit down, Sebastian, and make yourself comfortable.'

'I'll help you, Mum.' Elizabeth followed her mother into the kitchen. Her father sat down opposite Sebastian

'When did you two meet each other?'

'I first saw Beth around six weeks before she started her job at the Dumfries general. She came into a restaurant I use with her friend Debbie and I couldn't take my eyes off her. In fact, it amazes me that she is the double of her mother. She is beautiful.

'The only thing that worried me was she didn't seem to want to smile, and I needed her to smile at me. Believe me, sir, I've always been too busy to notice people. However, your daughter's beauty blinded me. The next time I saw her I was visiting my mother and father in Jersey and both Beth and Debbie were staying at my mother's hotel. I then had to come home to work and still hadn't managed to get Beth to smile at me. And shortly afterwards I went for a fitting for a new suit in a department store and she was there once more with Debbie. That same night they were in the restaurant and finally she smiled back. But then they left and the following week she started to work at the hospital I work at.'

'And what do you do at the hospital?'

'I'm a doctor.'

Suddenly Beth spoke from the doorway. She was carrying the tray for her mum.

'Now come on, don't be so modest. Sebastian is not only a heart surgeon but my boss, and I can say he is an excellent surgeon. Dad. I've watched him operate, so I know.'

'Well, we'll have to keep him in the family just in case I ever need him!'

Hugging her dad Elizabeth said, 'You are a long way from needing either of us but I'm sure, when the time comes, both I and Sebastian will be here for you.'

Sebastian stood up. 'I need to go to my car. I won't be a second. I'll have milk.'

'And no sugar,' Elizabeth added.

'Okay, bossy boots.' He smiled and nipped to his car for the flowers, and as he straitened up, Debbie arrived. Sebastian waited for her to climb out of the car.

'Hello there,' he said.

'Hello,' Debbie answered. 'Beth's mum said she was bringing a guest. I guessed it would be you. Before we go in I will tell you that you'd better not hurt my best friend or you'll have me to contend with.' She smiled to take the sting out of her words.

'Debbie, I will never hurt Beth and I hope she will never hurt me. I think you might have guessed I love her and I think she loves me, so relax.'

He stepped aside so that Debbie could walk in front of him, and chuckled when they walked in as Elizabeth's father said, 'Oh goodness, we're in for a rough ride now. I don't know if I can put up with the terrible twins for the weekend.'

'Calm down, Dad, and have your tea.'

'Here you are, Mrs Rubenstein. These are for you.'

'Thank you, both of you. They are lovely. I think I'm going to like having you around, young man.'

'That's good, because I plan on being in your lives for a long time to come.' Sebastian gave Elizabeth a serious look.'

Frank looked at his wife. 'We have an offer on your flat, Elizabeth, and we brought your post back.' He opened a draw. 'That's the offer, lass.'

'That's good, Dad. Everyone likes to knock a little off. I'll ring and accept. The sooner I get rid of it the better.'

'And here's your post.'

Most of it was junk mail but there was also a white envelope. Elizabeth scowled and ripped it up. 'You going to the kitchen, Dad? Will you put that in the bin where it belongs?'

Sebastian was now sitting on the settee and Elizabeth joined him and reached for his hand. She now felt safe, and knew that this was where she belonged.

The weekend was a roaring success and Elizabeth's parents could see that what had happened had, in the end, given Elizabeth real happiness. Before they left to go back to Scotland, Sebastian broached the subject of the holiday. Elizabeth's parents could also manage the end of July.

'But,' he said, 'Elizabeth and I don't want to go without Debbie.'

'Even if you are a cheeky pup,' Elizabeth added. Debbie dissolved in a fit of laughter, which set Elizabeth off as well. Once they had recovered, Sebastian asked Debbie to check whether she could get the time off for the trip.

'Will do, boss,'

'And if you're not careful I'll have a word with your senior, Josh,' Sebastian said.

'You know Josh?' asked Elizabeth.

'Yes, we were at university together. He's a great guy and a good friend.'

The next day they waved Debbie off.

'Stay happy, you two,' she called through her car window. 'And thank you, Mum and Dad, for inviting me. It's been great. Bye.'

It was also time for Elizabeth and Sebastian to leave. 'I've had a great weekend and I can tell Elizabeth has, too,' he said. 'I hope I can visit again. Don't worry about Elizabeth. I'll take care of her.' He opened the car door for Elizabeth and settled her in the passenger seat, and waving once more climbed into the driver's seat and pulled out of the drive. Elizabeth leaned back and rested her hand on his leg. Reaching down, he rubbed his thumb along her hand.

'I love you, sweetheart,' he said.

'That's good, because I love you more.'

CHAPTER TEN

Elizabeth spent the next week in a dream. Her days at work were spent working on her own or shadowing Sebastian. Always they had their coffee break together and it was the same at lunchtime. Nights were spent together in her flat and sometimes taking a walk after tea, or eating at the Italian. Elizabeth had never been happier; Stephen was a distant memory. Her only regret was that she had not seen through him and broken the engagement off herself.

Sunday arrived and Elizabeth and Sebastian had to get ready to leave for the conference early the following day. Sebastian had packed his case and put his dress suit in a carrying bag, along with Elizabeth's sapphire blue cocktail dress, which fitted to the hips and flared out in a cloud of chiffon. She had teamed it with silver strappy sandals, a silver stole and a small silver clutch bag. She had also packed essential daytime clothing. They were working that day and after work would eat at the Italian. Sebastian would stay over at Elizabeth's so that they could be ready to travel early.

Holding hands, they entered the restaurant and were instantly ushered to a vacant table for two. They were now favourites of the waiters. Just as they finished their main course Sebastian's phone rang. He looked at the number.

'I'll just have to take this. I won't be a minute.' Then Beth heard him say, 'Margo, how lovely to hear from you.'

When he returned he didn't tell Elizabeth who it had been and she didn't ask. However, she thought he seemed pleased to have heard from Margo and that his voice had taken on a very caring tone. He looked quite pleased with himself.

'Do you want afters, sweetheart?'

'No, I'm quite full. I'll just have a coffee.'

Reaching for her hand he said, 'In that case, the sooner we have coffee the sooner I can hold you in my arms.' The worried frown immediately left her face. She was just being over-sensitive. She knew inside that Sebastian was not like Stephen. She loved Sebastian and he loved her.

The next day they were up bright and early and, holding her tightly in his arms before they went, he said, 'It's a long drive to London. I'll have to get my fill before I go. But you know, sweetheart, I'll never be satisfied until you are sleeping by my side.' Holding her tightly he kissed her and Elizabeth responded. All she wanted was for Sebastian to love her. 'We had better go before we do something that wouldn't make our parents proud of us.'

As they drove to London Elizabeth found herself thinking of the unknown Margo and wondering who she was.

'Are you okay?' Sebastian suddenly asked.

Forcing a smile, Elizabeth answered, 'I'm fine. I was just wondering when Debbie will let us know about our holiday.'

'Oh, I forget to tell you. She already has. I needed to speak to Josh about something and I asked to speak to Debbie while I was on the phone. It's all arranged. I spoke to your father last week as well. So let's enjoy this weekend and see what happens while we are there.' Elizabeth smiled and relaxed back into the leather upholstery of his Jaguar.

Sebastian quickly booked them into their rooms at the Hilton. They were opposite each other. Hers was decorated in cream and gold. The cream settee was large and had green and gold cushions. Sebastian whispered, 'There would have been enough room for both of us on here.' The bed was huge and had gold covers and a green silk throw. Sebastian's room was much the same, comfortable and large. Once the attendant had gone Sebastian pulled her on to the settee and kissed her, and, taking her left hand, said, 'Beth, I love you so much. Will you marry me?' He took from his pocket a small blue box and opened it to reveal a large solitaire diamond ring. It fitted her finger perfectly.

'Yes, yes I will marry you,' Elizabeth replied, throwing her arms around Sebastian and kissing him with so much passion he had to pull her arms from his neck.

'You nearly strangled me,' he said with a laugh.

'How did you know what sized ring to get?'

'The plastic cracker ring you were playing with in the children's ward – remember you tried it on for the little girl? She lent it to me. Now, woman, get me my coffee. And while you make it I'll fetch your dress. It's still with my suit and needs hanging up for tonight. The conference is tomorrow but there's a dinner tonight with a speaker and dancing after.' Elizabeth looked at the ring sparkling on her finger. Sebastian loved her.

Later, as they sat together on the settee, Sebastian started to kiss her. 'I can't wait to make love to you,' he murmured. Elizabeth pressed herself to him and they were both carried away with passion. Sebastian began to explore her small breasts, stroking and kneading until he could feel the small peaks. Groaning he gently moved her away. 'We'll have to control ourselves or we'll be visiting maternity sooner than we want. Then your mum will be after me. Shall we go for a walk or do you think we can manage to sit quietly for an hour and hold each other?'

Elizabeth smiled and moved back into his arms. She had never known such happiness. She adored Sebastian.

At around 6 o'clock Sebastian said, 'Time for a shower. Make yourself beautiful, sweetheart. I'll be back around 7 o'clock, then we'll go down and have a drink and mingle.'

As they walked into the conference centre they were unaware of what a striking couple they made, Sebastian tall with dark hair, startling grey eyes and in his perfect dinner suit, and Elizabeth beside him, slender in her blue cocktail dress, her dark hair hanging loose and her hazel eyes shining with happiness. They ordered drinks and found their table. He then saw a colleague and introduced Elizabeth as his fiancée. After sitting down he whispered, 'Are you okay?'

'As long as I'm by your side, I'll always be okay,' she said, smiling into his eyes.

The speaker soon finished his speech and assured them that the following day's talk would be would cover heart transplants in depth, a subject of great interest to most of the surgeons and consultants present.

The band struck up a waltz and Sebastian held out his hand to Elizabeth, and, holding her close, they began to circle the floor. As the music ended Elizabeth said, 'I'm just going to powder my nose.' Sebastian waited patiently for her to return but as she walked back he was amazed to see a man grab her hands. It was obvious to Sebastian that she was trying to pull away. He quickly walked over.

'Excuse me, sweetheart, it's our dance,' he said, turning his flint-grey eyes towards the stranger and giving him a withering look. Putting his arm around her he led her back onto the floor. 'Are you okay?' Not daring to speak she nodded her head and moved as close to him as she could. The man was Stephen. What was he doing back here? He had implored her to forgive him saying that he had made a massive mistake. As she had struggled to free her hands she wondered what she had ever seen in him. He was weak and spineless and she wished he had stayed in Australia. She was so thankful that she had Sebastian at her side. How could she have thought that all men were like Stephen?

Brushing his lips against her hair he held her tightly to assure her that she was safe with him. Sebastian did not ask her who the man was. He was waiting for her to tell him and was certain that, given time, she would. Eventually they gathered their belongings and Sebastian held her close as they left.

Reaching the door to her room, she said, 'Sebastian, will you stay with me tonight?'

He knew he would always look after her and kissing her gently on the lips, he said, 'Go inside. I'll just get my pyjamas and toothbrush and I'll be back.' Once back in her room, he said 'I'm sure they will have a spare blanket in the wardrobe. You get under the covers and I'll lie on top under the blanket. I would very much prefer to be under the covers with you but I think I'm capable of controlling myself for a short while longer.'

Elizabeth gave him a loving smile. Seeing Stephen had unnerved her but could not diminish what she felt for Sebastian. She felt the need to be near him and instead of getting under the covers held them open for him.

'I know we have the strength to wait. We can be close and can hold each other.'

'You do know this will be torture, don't you?'

'If it is for you, it's the same for me, but we both have the strength and that's because we can control ourselves, so get in.'

'All right, bossy boots, but don't blame me if it turns into a party.'

Getting under the blankets he sighed and pulled her into his arms, kissing her with a yearning. 'Just ignore my body.'

'Don't worry. In our line of work we see it every day.'

Despite the fact she could tell he wanted her they both managed to snuggle up and fall asleep and when she opened her eyes in the morning Sebastian was still holding her tightly and had his legs wound tightly around hers. She gently stroked his face and tried to kiss him.

Sebastian opened one eye and said, 'I should think so, woman. If you knew the control I had to have last night.... I'm to have a wash and shave and then you can have the bathroom while I get dressed. Then we can have breakfast and go for a walk.' He then remembered that his clean clothes were in his room.

'You will just have to put one of the hotel dressing gowns on, and I'll get dressed and check if the corridor is clear. Then you can nip back and get dressed.'

'Right, it's a plan.' He found his key and she went to the door. 'The coast is clear.'

He quickly nipped out and into his room while she closed her door went into the bathroom to wash and dress. She wore a pair grey slacks and a grey blouse, and placed a red cashmere V-necked sweater with her clutch bag. She slipped on her red strappy sandals and sat down to wait for Sebastian. Gazing down at her ring she realised how happy she was. When Sebastian returned, he was dressed in grey slacks, a light blue shirt and was carrying a grey sweater. He pressed her body to his and reaching to the back of her head pulled the clips out and let her hair cascade onto her shoulders.

'That's better. My beautiful Beth.' In a rush of love she reached out and hugged him.

Strolling into the restaurant hand in hand they did not see Stephen sitting in a corner. Looking at Elizabeth he realised how stupid he had been. She had always helped when he had been in a jam and now he had nobody. Jane, the nurse who had gone to Australia with him, and soon lost patience with his selfish ways and had decided to go her own way. His move to Australia had not been a great experience for him.

After breakfast Elizabeth and Sebastian wandered in and out of shops hand in hand. They bought a gift for Sebastian's mum and dad. Elizabeth was looking forward to meeting his parents and spending some time with them. She was hoping that she and Sebastian would soon set the date for their marriage. The rest of the day and evening went smoothly and once again Sebastian spent the night with Elizabeth. The next they had breakfast and left for home.

CHAPTER ELEVEN

The next three months passed in a whirl of work and spending their free time together, and still they resisted the temptation to make love. Elizabeth wanted Sebastian as much or even more than he wanted her. However, she loved the fact that he respected her. And in any case, she hoped that it would not be long before they were spending every night together as man and wife. It was only a couple of days before they were to go to Jersey on holiday as a family. Sebastian had already taken his clothes to Elizabeth's flat but had said he needed to stay at home that evening as he had some last-minute business to clear up. He would be around the following morning to pick her up before they collected her parents and Debbie.

'I'll ring you tonight to say goodnight, my love. I know it's only one night but I'll miss you, sweetheart.'

'Shall I come and stay at yours?' she said, looking into his eyes.

'No, not tonight, sweetheart, it might take me longer than I think to sort out what I have to do. We will be together all the time soon. I love you and can't wait for tomorrow.' He held her tight. 'I'll have to go now, love.'

'Don't forget to bring my blue dress with you. It's still at your house with your dress suit.'

'Okay, sweet, I'll ring you tonight.' After kissing her once more he went to his car and drove off.

Elizabeth spent most of the next day ensuring that her flat sparkled and that she had packed everything. Sebastian had only packed a small case as he had clothes at his mother's hotel. In the afternoon she began to miss Sebastian. It would be a long day without him. It was around 6 o'clock when Elizabeth decided she would walk around to Sebastian's to surprise him. Surely he would have finished whatever he was doing and be able to spend half an hour with her. She picked up a cardigan and left the flat to walk the short distance to Sebastian's house but as she reached the driveway she heard Sebastian's voice say, 'You don't know how grateful I am, Margo. You are a sweetheart. Have you got everything? Good. I'll drive you to the airport.'

Elizabeth watched from behind the hedge. She was mortified. Sebastian had had a woman visitor stay overnight. It was definitely a suitcase he had put in her car. If it was nothing he would have explained. Why had he kept it a secret? She watched him pull off the drive. He was smiling. Was he cheating on her? Perhaps he had tired of her and couldn't tell her. Elizabeth loved Sebastian with all her heart and did not want to think of life without him; she knew she would never love anyone else. What she had had with Stephen was lukewarm compared to what she felt for Sebastian.

Almost in tears she made her way back to her flat. She pictured Sebastian spending the night with a very attractive woman, who had been tall with dark tanned skin as if she had been on holiday. Sebastian and the woman seemed quite close. Back in her flat Elizabeth crouched on the settee like a wounded animal and silent tears poured down her cheeks. How long she sat there she had no Idea. The phone rang repeatedly and she ignored it. She did not turn the lights on even though it was now was quite dark outside. Suddenly she heard a key in the lock. It was Sebastian.

'Beth, why are you sitting in the dark?' He flicked on the light and saw her tear-stained face. 'Whatever is the matter?'

'You ask that? I thought you of all people I could trust. You couldn't come last night because you had business to conclude so where did the woman come into it who slept at your house last night?'

'You mean Margo?'

'Oh, should that mean something to me? I saw you drive off with her in your car after spending the day and night with her. Why?'

'You're jealous.' He smiled. 'I love you, Beth, and expected you to trust me.'

'Well explain why you didn't tell me that you had a woman visitor to stay overnight.'

'Don't be silly, Beth.' Sebastian was getting angry. 'The business I concluded today was very important to both of us and I won't be telling you yet what it entailed.'

Glaring at him she spat out, 'All I know is you preferred someone else's company to mine. You could at least have told me you were getting tired of me. Perhaps you would like to take her on holiday tomorrow because I won't be coming with you.'

'Damn you, Beth. Yes you will.' He grabbed her shoulders and shook her. 'I won't let you spoil your mum and dad's holiday. That's selfish. You will come and you will enjoy it.'

Elizabeth looked at him and burst into a fresh bout of tears. Sebastian pulled her into his arms.

'Please don't cry, Beth, I love you and always will. It will all become clear when we reach Jersey, my love. Please try and trust me. And if you don't like what we have planned then you will be free to come home. But I'll never love anyone else and you will break my heart if you don't come. Do you realise we are having our first row?'

'I don't care,' she shouted.

'I'm not going home, Beth, I'm staying with you. You will come with me tomorrow and you will be nice because of your mum and dad. I happen to know they are looking forward to this holiday more than any. Don't struggle, Beth, because you'll only hurt yourself. I am not letting go of you.' Sebastian carried her into the bedroom and dumped her on the bed.

'Get undressed.'

'No!'

'If you don't, I'll undress you. I've seen lots of ladies' bodies so it'll be nothing new to me either.' He pulled off his shoes and began to undress himself.

Standing up Elizabeth said, 'I'll sleep in the other room.'

'No you won't. You'll sleep here where you belong, by my side, and don't get any ideas that you can slip off because I will be holding you so tightly for you to slip away.'

In the morning he quickly silenced his alarm. Elizabeth was still sleeping soundly. He resisted the urge to kiss her. He needed to dress before she woke up so gently got out of bed and quietly went into the bathroom to shower and shave. He put on a pair of blue denim jeans and a matching denim shirt, and slipped a black Gucci sweater over his head. After checking that Elizabeth was still asleep he went to the kitchen to put the coffee on, and once it was ready he poured a cup and took it into the bedroom. He placed it on the bedside cabinet. Gently kissing her he whispered, 'Coffee, my love.'

Elizabeth was in a state of half-awareness. She put her arm around his neck, whispered his name and kissed him. Suddenly she opened her eyes and pushed him away. 'Don't,' she said.

'Now stop that,' Sebastian said. 'I know you love me as much as I love you so drink your coffee and stop being silly.'

'I'm not silly at all. Yes, I will go on this holiday but only for my mum and dad's sake. When we get back, we're through and I'll get another position in another hospital or as a GP. Then you'll be able to spend as many nights as you want with your beautiful Margo. In the meantime we can try and be civil in front of my mum and dad but while we're on our own leave me alone.'

'You don't mean that. Tonight you will know why this has happened. I told you I could arrange for you to share my rooms and I'm glad I have. You need to be taken in hand.'

'Well, if I do, it won't be by you.'

'Beth, go and have a shower and calm down. This is getting us nowhere. We need to be off soon and your mum will know there is something wrong. I thought you didn't want to upset your mum and dad. They're looking forward to today more than anything. So please tell me you trust me. By not trusting me you are more than hurting me. Please, Beth. However much you hurt me I'll always need and love you. Please give me the benefit of the doubt.'

'Okay, but I thought it was too good to be true. It's as good as over. You should have confided in me and said you were having a visitor. At least then I would have trusted you.'

Sebastian stood and turned Beth to face him. 'Tell me the truth. Do you love me?'

Beth looked into his silver grey eyes and saw hurt and could not help but whisper, 'You know I love you more than life. This hurts me more than you will ever know but I won't let you make a fool of me.'

Pulling Elizabeth to him he plundered her mouth until she responded to his kisses, and trembling, he said thickly, 'You had better go and have a shower or we'll spoil tonight.'

'Why?' Elizabeth asked.

'Just go.' he replied. 'We need to leave soon. I'll have some breakfast ready for you as soon as you're ready.'

He checked that he had everything they needed – passports and plane tickets for everyone in his hand luggage – and placed it by the door with their cases. He just hoped things would go smoothly once they reached Jersey. He hoped Elizabeth would understand why he had done things the way he had.

It was a more controlled Elizabeth sitting in the car beside him as they arrived to pick up her parents. Debbie was already there and seemed really excited.

'I'm really looking forward to this holiday, aren't you, Beth.'

'Yes,' Elizabeth said, 'the sooner we get there the sooner you and I can have some fun.'

Sebastian suggested that the three women should sit in the back of the car because they were smaller and would have a little more room, while Beth's dad join him in the front.

CHAPTER TWELVE

It was around 12 o'clock when the plane touched down in Jersey. Sebastian pushed their baggage cart to the two waiting black Jaguars and introduced Elizabeth, his fiancée, her parents and Debbie to Bruce, one of the drivers. Elizabeth looked with interest at him. He looked to be around the same age as Sebastian and had the same dark looks and features. The other driver also had the same features but his hair was a light brown. He was introduced as Sebastian's cousin Jonathan. Passing the keys to Sebastian he said, 'Who's going to travel back with us?'

'You can take Debbie. I thought she and Bruce would get on well. Mind you, he will have to watch her because she's quite a cheeky pup.' He smiled, then drawing Beth forward, he said, 'This one belongs to me, so she stays by my side. And she definitely is not a cheeky pup, just a little feisty.'

'Then you should have a good time taming her,' said Bruce.' He then turned to Debbie. 'Right, my little cheeky pup, are you coming with me?'

'It looks as if I am.' Debbie smiled at him.

At the hotel the receptionist said, 'Welcome home, sir.'

'Is my mum in, Helen?'

She's right there, sir.'

Sebastian let go of Elizabeth's hand to hug the elderly lady.

'Mum you look well. How's Dad?'

'He's a lot better. He's just resting because he wants to be okay for the service.'

Sebastian's mother was tall and straight and had Sebastian's steel grey eyes. She wore a dark green dress with a brooch.

'Now, son, where is this young lady who has stolen your heart. I'm no longer your favourite lady.'

'You are still my favourite lady, Mum, but Beth is my favourite as well, only in a different way. I love her as well as you.'

'I know, son. Now where is she?'

Sebastian quickly reached for Beth's hand and put his arm around her waist.

'Mum, meet the only women other than you to capture my heart. It belongs to Beth for the rest of my life.'

Sebastian's mother hugged Elizabeth. 'It's lovely to meet you. I've heard a lot about you, Beth. You certainly must be special. My son has never shown any interest in anyone else but when he rings me now he spends all the time telling me how wonderful you are.'

'Mum, this is Beth's mum and dad.'

'Welcome to our home. And who's this young lady with our Bruce?'

'This is Debbie. She's Beth's best friend.'

Sebastian's mother said, 'My name's Sofia and if we don't get this show on the road we won't be ready. My husband James will join us at the ceremony. Now if Mr and Mrs Rubenstein and Debbie will come along with me I'll get you settled in your rooms. Then Mrs Rubenstein and Debbie can come back down and join you here. If your two don't mind waiting for a few minutes you can have a coffee but don't have a snack. It will spoil your appetite for the meal we have planned.'

Sofia turned to Helen. 'Could you order coffee for Sebastian and Beth, please.' And giving Elizabeth a hug and a huge smile said, 'I'll see you later, my dear.'

Elizabeth said, 'What about my room? My face is aching with trying to smile.'

'I told you I was arranging for you to share my room.'

'No, we can't do that. What do you think our parents would think? That's if we still cared about each other.'

'Beth, you know we still care about each other. Now here's your mum and Debbie.'

At that moment a little girl ran up to Sebastian and clutched his leg.

'Sebastian, you're here!'

Her hair hung down to her waist. It was dark and curly and her eyes were a silver grey.

'Why hello, Chantelle,' he replied. 'Where's your mummy?'

'She's coming, and Daddy too. He's talking to her.' Then looking up at Elizabeth, Chantelle said, 'Hello, are you Beth?'

'Yes, I am, how do you know my name?'

'Because Mummy and Daddy have been talking about you for ages and ages. Here's Mummy now.'

Beth turned, and found herself looking at Margo, the young woman who had stayed at Sebastian's. Quickly putting his arm around Elizabeth, Sebastian said, 'Beth, this is my cousin Margo. You have already met her husband Johnathon. Now give me a kiss to keep me going, then you need to go with Margo, Debbie and your mother, and of course not forgetting our Chantelle here. We will see you at 3 o'clock.'

'But I don't understand,' Elizabeth said.

'You will, my darling,' he whispered. 'And I hope you will find it in your heart to say sorry for questioning me. I hope against hope this is what you want, because if you don't, you'll break my heart. Now go.'

Come on, Beth, we have a lot to do,' her mother said, 'although Margo has worked hard already, let's get on.'

Elizabeth felt Chantelle take her hand, and looked down at the small girl who gave her a trusting smile and skipped happily alongside her. They took lift upstairs and entered a comfortable lounge, where, hanging on a rail, were 10 wedding dresses. Next to them hung Elizabeth's blue cocktail dress. There were also white bridesmaid dresses with dark red sashes.

'Mum, Debbie, what are these?'

'It's your wedding day, Elizabeth!' her mum said. 'Sebastian thought you might worry about him not turning up if you arranged it together so he asked us to help. We have known for weeks. Margo has stayed with us and helped find and fit my outfit and your dad's dress suit, and also Debbie's bridesmaid's dress and Sebastian's dress suit. All you need to do is choose which dress you want to wear.'

Elizabeth turned to Margo. 'I think I owe you an apology.'

'Whatever for?'

'Can I explain later?' Elizabeth had tears in her eyes.

'Yes, of course but first of all can we choose which dress you want to wear or we'll be here all day.' She gave Elizabeth a huge smile.

Elizabeth chose a dress of tulle with an overlay of lace across the top. It had a straight neckline and short sleeves; it was long and flared out at the bottom. After taking it off she was urged to have a shower, as time was short, and on coming back into the room she allowed Margo to dry her hair. Margo then helped Elizabeth to put on her dress and said.

'Sit there. The hairdresser will be up in a moment. Now Mrs Rubenstein, let's get you ready.'

The hairdresser came up and soon had Elizabeth's hair piled up on her head in curls. The veil was held in place with clips. Her hair had small red roses dotted between the curls. Margo gave her a glass of champagne.

'Just relax, Beth, and sip this.'

Soon, everyone was ready, including Margo, who was also to be a bridesmaid, 'mainly to keep Chantelle in order'. Elizabeth's mother was dressed in soft cream and had a small red hat and red shoes. Margo handed Beth a bouquet of red roses.

'How did you manage all of this, Margo?'

'Sebastian gave me your dress as a pattern. It was easy from there. I am a wedding planner and it is your birthday tomorrow. You have the family earrings your mother gave you and we have sewn a small bow of blue into the hem of your dress.' Then she took a slim case from a drawer and from it took a small gold cross fashioned in diamonds. 'Sebastian's mother wants you to wear this.' Debbie held the veil while Margo fastened it.

Beth's mother had already gone downstairs to join her dad, and Chantelle was becoming slightly boisterous.

'Are you ready?' Debbie asked. 'I think it's time.'

Beth looked at Debbie and hugged her. 'You are my very best friend, Debs, but now you will have to share me with Margo. Do you mind?'

'I don't mind at all except I want to be godmother to your first child.'

'Cheeky pup!' replied, with a huge grin on her face.

Her dad was waiting for her in the lounge and watched Elizabeth walk towards him with her three bridesmaids. She looked enchanting. The ballroom that had been turned into a chapel for the day and as Elizabeth walked in her eyes met Sebastian's. He gave her his slow smile, and with it the promise of good things to come. Standing at his side was Josh, his best man.

Elizabeth said her vows in a dream and Josh handed Sebastian the ring. Sebastian lifted her veil kissing her with such passion she was trembling when he let go.

'See. We made it. And tonight I have arranged for you to sleep in my room.'

'I love you, Sebastian, and I'm so sorry for not trusting you.'

'I love you, Mrs Le Revere,' Sebastian said, kissing her once more. 'But don't do that again. I've been on pins for two days.'

Much later in Sebastian's room's Elizabeth lay in his arms.

'That was worth waiting for, my darling. But I'm still hungry. I need a second helping. Do you mind, doctor, dear?'

'No, doctor, dear, you can have thirds if you want.'

'Now who is a cheeky pup? He laughed. 'I can't wait to get back and for you to change your name at work to Doctor Le Revere. That will upset them. They won't know who they want – you or me!'

'Ah but you forget. I'm a mere doctor whereas you are a consultant surgeon and are addressed as Mr Le Revere. But it will give them something else to talk about for another seven days and I will be the envy of all the nurses who I've seen eying you up.'

'Come here,' he said. 'Were wasting time.'

Two weeks later they walked into the hospital foyer.

'Good morning,' Sebastian said to the receptionist behind the desk. And turning to Beth, he said, 'Scrubs at 10.30, Doctor Le Revere.'

This would certainly give them more than seven days of gossip.

Wherever The Road Ends

By Barbara Machin

CHAPTER 1

Lissette sat in her flat ignoring the doorbell. She knew who was at the door and why, and had no intention of answering. She didn't want to give Nathan the satisfaction of wriggling out of his responsibilities. Her copper coloured hair hung down in thick waves, covering her eyes. She was tall and slim and had a pale peach complexion and green eyes. She was very striking. However, today her eyes were swollen and red, and she felt as if she hadn't any more tears to shed.

Lissette had met Nathan when he joined the firm of solicitors as a junior partner. She had been employed as a PA to the senior partner. He was of medium height and had blonde hair and blue eyes, and from the beginning had made a play for her attentions. Whenever he had come into contact with her he had made it his business to chat and flirt. At first Lissette was polite and pleasant but avoided making any arrangement to meet after work. He was not deterred, however, and he kept asking until she gave in and agreed. After that it soon became obvious that they were an item. For the last year Lissette and Nathan had been engaged. The plan was to move into his house and put their savings into a joint account. Nathan had already given her a key and in just one month's time she was to become his wife.

Lissette had sold her mother's house after she passed away and had been renting a flat since then. Her brother, John, lived in Australia and had flown over at the time to help complete the final details. John had asked her to consider moving to Australia to live with them but she liked her job and assured him that she was fine. Then Nathan had come on the scene and for the last few months she had been happy.

Her mind went back to that fateful day when she had gone to work and Nathan had been out of town working on a case. Lissette had received a call to say her going-away outfit was ready and would she go for a fitting. She had asked for a longer lunch break, promising to make up the time.

Grabbing her coat and bag she had left and driven the short distance to the boutique. The cream linen suit was Ideal for this time of the year and had looked cool and chic. The kitten-heel tan shoes, handbag and gloves completed the ensemble. After purchasing a few other items she had left the shop, put her hand in her pocket and realised she had Nathan's door key. She had decided to drop the outfit off and, humming to herself had driven to his house where she had noticed a small car parked outside. She thought it must be someone visiting a neighbour.

She had silently entered, slipping off her shoes because all the carpets were wall-to-wall cream. Padding up the stairs Lissette had stopped dead in her tracks, having heard the tinkling laugh of another woman saying. not again, and just as Lissette thought who's that. Then she had heard Nathan's laugh, pushed open his bedroom door and had seen him in bed with a blonde, whose laughter had changed to a scream.

'Lissette,' Nathan had gasped, trying to cover himself and the woman.

Speechless at first, Lissette had dragged the ring from her finger and, after recovering her senses, had said, 'You had better give her this as well.' She had thrown the ring and the key at him and run from the room and out of his house, tears streaming down her cheeks. What a fool she had been.

Once back at her flat Lissette had rung Rob to tell him she would not be back that day. Nathan had rung shortly after, so she had taken the handset off its cradle and turned off her mobile. There was no way she could speak to him. Two days later, she had rung Rob to give in her notice, for personal reasons, she had said. She had apologised for letting him down. The lease on her flat had been up in three weeks' time but she had already packed all her clothes and had realised she could not stay for the full three weeks;

she had needed to get away. Nathan had been knocking on the door night and day and she had needed to put him behind her. This was why she was sitting on the settee with her belongings packed and beside her.

All she needed now was to make sure he was not outside when she left. Waiting until almost midnight she locked the door to her flat and went down the back staircase to where her car was parked within the gated courtyard. She walked to her car and stowed her cases in the boot. She would drive as far away as she could and see where the road took her. After a while she noticed a signpost to Bristol and by that time had been driving for more than two hours. She decided to stop at the next services.

Lissette knew she needed to eat but left her sandwich untouched. She did manage two cups of strong coffee to help her carry on driving. Looking at her watch later she realised she had been driving for five hours. Oh well, I'll carry on a little longer to see where I end up, she thought.

After driving for another two hours Lissette left the motorway and continued to Brixham. She parked and strolled down the road to look for a café, and to calm her chaotic thoughts. I must have driven far enough now, she thought. The hurt in her heart was still there but she felt as if she was now detached from herself, but sitting quietly in a little greasy spoon drinking coffee she realised she needed to find a room – somewhere to stay for a couple of weeks to get her bearings before looking for a more permanent home. Lissette now felt hungry but did not want to eat there, so, picking up her bag, decided to take a quiet walk along the front. Making her way along by the harbour wall, mulling over what she would do about employment, she noticed the road was rich in fish and chip shops but it lacked a really good tea room. Then she spotted an empty double-fronted shop with a flat above. She pondered how much money she had in the bank and was glad she hadn't spent any of the money from the sale of her mum's home. Both she and John had been surprised at how much it had sold for – £800,000. Together with the money her parents had saved she had a considerable amount.

Lissette's mother and father had always encouraged her to save and by the age of 26 she had accumulated a modest sum herself. How glad she was that she had not placed her money into a joint account with Nathan, as he had been urging her to do. Their plan had been for him open his own office with her as his PA. Looking back she remembered counselling, One step at a time, and that the plan would keep until after they were married. She noted down the phone number and address of the estate agent selling the empty shop. She had forgotten all about the furniture she had put in storage; she had not been able to bear parting with all her parents' furniture and was glad now. I just need to find a room for a couple of weeks and when I've done that and had a shower I will find the estate agent and see if my funds will stretch to buying the shop, she thought. It was 9 o'clock in the morning and Lissette made her way back to her car, which, by chance, she had left outside a bungalow which turned out to be a bed and breakfast. It was long, low and clean looking, and it would do, she mused. She made her way to the door and rang the bell.

A young lady came out who was a similar in age to Lissette.

'Can I help you?'

'Yes, do you have any rooms?'

'Just one, miss, are you on your own?'

'Yes.'

'Good. It's just a single, you see.'

'That will be fine,' said Lissette, smiling.

'If you follow me I'll show you the room before you make up your mind. This way. My name is Gill.'

Gill was pretty and had light brown hair and brown eyes. She was clad in blue jeans and a white shirt. 'Are you here on holiday?' she asked.

'No, I'm thinking of moving here.'

'That's great. I'm sure you will like it here. This is the room.'

It was basic but clean. There was a bed with a pretty blue flowered bedcover, a small chair, a dressing table and a small television.

'This is fine,' Lissette said, placing her case on the floor.

'Shall we get you booked in then? How long will you be staying?'

'Could I book for a month with the option of making it longer if I need to?'

'Of course.'

Have you finished serving breakfast?' Lissette enquired. 'I've had a long drive and I could do with a drink and perhaps some toast.

'That won't be a problem,' Gill replied.

'Right, I'll just take a shower and I'll be ready in about 20 minutes.

Lissette put on a blue iced-cotton fitted dress and slipped on white flat pumps. After brushing her hair and putting it into a ponytail she looked fresh and pretty. She was eager to visit the estate agent, and after breakfast she assured Gill that she didn't need anything else.

CHAPTER 2

While standing outside the estate agent Lissette saw the advert for the shop. It was priced at £300,000 or the nearest offer. She could afford that and would have money left with which to decorate and stock the business, and she might still have some leftover. She asked for a viewing.

'I'm sure I can manage that,' a young man said, and told his colleague where he was going. After taking the keys out of the drawer he led Lissette outside into the sunshine, noticing how pretty she was.

He first showed her the shop, which was quite large but in need of decoration. The kitchen was also quite spacious but with outdated appliances. The upstairs was large enough and had two bedrooms, a shower, a lounge-cum-diner and a small compact kitchen. She would not need much furniture, just a couple of beds and a television, but also a new shower and cooker.

'Right,' she said to the young man who had said his name was Dan, 'I'd like to make an offer of £280,000, obviously subject to a survey. This is my mobile number. Could you get back to me as soon as possible. I will be a cash buyer.'

'Great. It could make quite a nice place with a little work.'

'Yes, I think so, too.'

Suddenly feeling drained she decided to go back to the bed and breakfast. She could have a nap and then walk down to the harbour again. She unpacked, took off her dress and climbed between the sweet-smelling sheets. She was later awoken by the ringing of her phone. It was the young man from the estate agent who told her that her offer had been accepted. She could not believe it, and asked him where she could find a solicitor. There was one practice in Brixham which had several partners. Lissette took the number and said she would send a surveyor and speak to the solicitor directly.

One month later the papers were signed and the funds transferred. At the solicitors she asked for Mr Peake.

'Of course, Miss Darcy, I'll ring to say you're here,' the receptionist said. 'You won't see the solicitor you saw last time – he's on holiday. You will see James Garner.'

Lissette entered his office to find a tall man standing by the cabinet. He had dark wavy hair and blue eyes. She put his age at about 30. He smiled at her but she did not smile back. She was off men.

'I won't be a minute. It's not my office and I'm not quite sure of Ken's filing system.'

'May I?' Lissette said, peering into the open cabinet. 'It's quite easy. Area, alphabetical order of surname.' She took out her file and gave it to him.

'That was very professional. Have you worked in an office?'

'In another life.'

'Right, it's Lissette, I see,' he said, looking at the file. 'That's a very pretty name. Now, if you would just sign here, please.' He gave her an assortment of keys. 'You are new here, aren't you?' His voice was deep and cultured. 'If there is anything else I can do for you don't hesitate to contact me.'

'I'm sure I won't need to,' she answered not smiling back and adding as an afterthought, 'but thank you. It's very kind of you to offer.'

She made for the door and closed it quietly behind her, leaving James Garner with a frown on his face. The lovely Lissette obviously didn't like men. He could quite easily have lost himself in those eyes. He made a mental note to get to know her better, whether she liked men or not. The look in her eyes told him someone had hurt her badly.

CHAPTER 3

At the bed and breakfast Lissette asked Gill if she could pay for the month she owed and book for another month.

'Of course you can.' By this time they had become good friends.

'I need a good decorator and a handy man,' she told Gill. 'I could do with getting the upstairs flat in the shop shipshape, then I can move in.' She added quickly, 'I have loved being with you but it makes sense to move in as quickly as possible.'

'My brother Ron is a painter and handy man and our David is a plumber. Would you like me to ask them? And sometimes our James lends a hand if he has a spare weekend when they're busy.'

'Yes please,' said Lissette.

'Of course, and when all the decorating is complete I'll help you move in and hang curtains, and put your dishes and pans away. Many hands make light work.'

Just one week later Lissette was stripping wallpaper and scrubbing floors while she waited for Ron and David to start. David would help her choose appliances and store cupboards for both the flat and the tea room. Lissette picked up some carpet samples for upstairs and chose tiles for the bathroom and a new shower cubicle. There was so much to choose from and she still had to fit in her mum and dad's treasured pieces. She wanted to make sure that the style she chose was sympathetic to the items she already had, to ensure the new pieces complemented the old.

Ron and David were very good and soon they had the upstairs fully renovated. Lissette bought two single beds for one room and a double bed for her room, and arranged for her parents' furniture to be delivered to the flat. Ron and David would carry it upstairs. Lissette and Gill went in search of tables and chairs for the café, and a dresser and shelves. In her college days Lissette had taken a hygiene course, which left one less thing to worry about. All she needed to do was update it. She had the flat carpeted in plain gold and bought rich soft-green velvet curtains

'I don't know what I would have done without your help, Gill,' Lissette said. 'You have been so kind, and if I felt unhappy when I arrived I certainly don't now. I have the whole future in front of me. This is a new start.'

Lissette and Gill were giggling like school girls as they returned to the shop. Gill shouted upstairs, 'Do you want a cup of tea?' and a chorus of voices answered, 'Three mugs, no sugar. We are sweet enough.' This was odd – they had expected just Ron and David.

Lissette put the kettle on and put cups, saucers and a pot of tea along and assortment of biscuits on a tray. They took the tray into the lounge where they found three men, two of whom were moving the small dresser towards the wall. One had his back to Lissette but he was familiar, and turning, he said, 'Our beautiful, professional Lissette. It seemed that there was something I could help with.' It was James Garner.

'I didn't know you had time to help, our James,' Gill said.

'I made time for you and Lissette,' he replied, looking at Lissette. She felt like a rabbit caught in headlights and couldn't look away.

'You will have to tell me what I owe,' she said. 'You have all been so kind.'

'Not at all,' Ron answered, relieving the tension. 'You already have our quote and I think it will come in at slightly less.' He motioned towards James. 'But his account will come in at lot more!'

'I won't be giving you my charges yet but I'm sure I'll think of something suitable,' James said, once more raising an eyebrow and looking directly at Lissette.

The talk turned to the downstairs tea room. Ron had already tiled the floor in block wood tiles and said he would start the decorating the following day. David would fit the appliances in the kitchen where the floor had already been laid with dark red ceramic tiles. For some reason James Garner was beginning to unnerve Lissette; he appeared to be scrutinising her.

'If you don't mind, Lissette, we will work tomorrow, then if all goes well we'll be finished within another week and a half,' Ron said.

'Of course I don't mind. The sooner it's finished the sooner I will be able to open.' Lissette smiled back at Ron. She had already met Ron's and David's wives and was more comfortable with them. But James Garner was a different cup of tea. Rob had been a great boss and she had never worried that he would be inappropriate with her. Now she didn't trust men in general.

Over the next week Lissette didn't see James but on the Saturday she arrived to find him helping with the delivery of table and chairs. They were putting the finishing touches to the tea room kitchen. James's easy manner with her made her a little more comfortable, but still she could not return his smile and refused to meet his quizzical gaze.

Monday morning arrived and Gill had found time to help put the tables in place. Inside the dresser were packets of biscuits and specialty teas ready for sale. The counter across the back had doors so that in the summer the cakes could be seen but were also always covered.

'Are you sure everything at the bed and breakfast is taken care of, Gill?'

'Yes, James arranged for a pair of extra hands to cover for me. He knew I wanted to help you and be involved right to the end.'

Lissette had planned on opening the following week and said to Gill, 'I need a couple of extra people – one to help wait on and someone to help in the kitchen.'

'Well,' Gill started to say, but Lissette held up her hand to stop her.

'You have a sister?'

'No, you silly goose,' Gill laughed, 'I wish! I'm outnumbered with brothers. I would have loved one. You, Lissette, are my adopted sister for the time being. Perhaps we can make it permanent!'

Lissette looked at her, puzzled, and, quickly changing the conversation, Gill said, 'What time will you open, Lissette?'

'Around 10.30.'

'Well, breakfast at the b and b ends at 9.30 and Sue, the girl who helps me, is after another job to top up what we pay her. I can recommend her. I'm sure she could be here for 10.30.'

'You're a lifesaver, Gill.'

'I could get my cousin to come as well. She's quite good at baking and cooking.'

Lissette threw her arms around Gill. 'You are the best friend anyone could wish for,' she said with tears in eyes.

'It's almost becoming a family business,' Gill said, cheekily.

'I wish you were my family. You are lucky. My brother is in Australia. How I wish he was here.'

'Well, who knows, perhaps he will have something to come over for,' said Gill, kissing Lissette on the cheek. 'I must dash. I'll send Sue and Beth to see you.'

CHAPTER 4

Lissette surveyed her little kingdom. Everywhere gleamed, from the menus at the back of the counter to the large copper kettle outside and the sign newly painted 'The Copper Kettle'. It was 10 o'clock and in another 30 minutes she would open her tea room.

She checked the lounge upstairs, with its gold carpet and her mother's corner cabinet holding the crown derby that had been her pride and joy. It also contained her grandmother's small French gilded figures and a small bookcase holding a selection of her much-loved classic books. The dresser that James and David had placed by the wall, a small French settee, her father's leather chair and her mother's smaller lady's Chesterfield chair were also there. She had also purchased a small cream marble surround that housed an electric log fire and a small dining table with two chairs. The kitchen sported cream cabinets with a glass display cupboard housing her selection of crystal glasses, the bedroom was pink and gold, and the second bedroom was blue and gold. Lissette sighed with contentment. Nathan had not ruined her life, just destroyed her faith in men.

She heard the door open. That would be Beth letting in Sue. She went down and was impressed with how they looked in their black skirts with white blouses and white frilly aprons. From 10.30 on they were all quite busy with a steady stream of tourists coming in and wanting the cake that Beth and Lissette had baked, which was rapidly disappearing. Both Ron and David came with their wives and at one point Ron's wife Sheila helped out. Beth and Lissette took it in turns to bake scones and more cakes. When 5.30 came around Lissette gratefully turned the sign to 'Closed'.

'Beth, Sue, sit down and I'll make us a cup of tea. We've earned it.'

Lissette couldn't help but feel disappointed that James had not been in. For some reason she had missed him. Gill called her that night to see how she was and they chatted about different things.

'By the way, James said he was sorry to have missed your opening day but he will be back next week. He had to go to London. He had a case at crown court – he's a barrister as well. He said he'd be in to extract payment for time given!' She laughed.

Later, Lissette started to dissect her feelings. She no longer felt hurt and realised she had become engaged to Nathan because she felt alone, and because he was persistent. The only thing she had insisted on was that she didn't live with him before they were married. He had tried to steer her to the bedroom a couple of times but she had stuck to her no-sex-before-marriage rule. She was glad now, because she realised that their marriage wouldn't have lasted; she hadn't loved him. Lissette now sensed her future stretching before her and went to bed tired and happy, falling asleep the moment her head touched the pillow. Her dreams were laced with James standing and smiling down at her, holding his hand out to her.

For the next few days her eyes always went to the door when it opened. She knew she was looking for James but a week passed and she still hadn't seen him. Lissette was also missing Gill, who probably couldn't get away because it was the busy season. They had become best friends; Lissette was amazed at how her life had changed over the last three and a half months: she now owned her own flat and café and had some very good friends. She did not get much free time but would do in the winter. Around 11 o'clock the door opened and this time Lissette didn't look up until she sensed someone standing in front of her. Her eyes locked with his and she had trouble speaking. He broke the silence.

'Don't I get a welcome home kiss?' James asked.

Lissette looked at him, speechless.

'Oh well, I'll just have to help myself.' And before she knew it he had brushed her lips with his.

'Well of all the cheek,' Lissette exploded. 'Don't think I'm an easy target.'

'Now why would you think that, my lovely Lissette?' He looked into her eyes in a quizzical manner. 'That was the first instalment of your payment,' he joked, wagging a finger at her. 'And I'll have a slice of that apple pie with cream and a black coffee, and five minutes of your time, please.'

Lissette was about to say no when he put his finger to her lips. 'Sue and Beth can manage. It's not too busy.'

She carried the tray to a table, her brain saying one thing, her heart another.

'Now, about the rest of the payment. By my reckoning you owe me four days of your time.'

'Time?' Lissette repeated.

'Yes, time, my dear Lissette. I gave mine and the least you can do is give me yours in return.' He raised that eyebrow.

Lissette persuaded herself that yes, he had helped, so the most she could do was help him. But she still parried. 'We are quite busy at the moment.'

'Well, that's too bad. In one month's time I'm to attend a function and I need you to come with me. We can get another member of staff from an agency to help Beth. She is quite capable of taking charge while you're not here.'

'If I do that are we quits?'

'Might be, but as I helped at a weekend it should be double time. And you will need an overnight bag, of course.'

It was Lissette's turn to wag her finger. James held his hand up with a smile.

'I understand. It's too soon for any of that. I promise I'm quite trustworthy. Ask our Gill. Now, although I'd love to stay chatting all day I have a solicitor to interview who would like to join the practice.' And quickly, taking her by surprise, he leant forward and brushed his lips across hers, leaving Lissette breathless and bemused. 'Until tomorrow.'

That night Lissette could only think of James. She felt restless. Nathan had been a solicitor. Were they all the same? Lissette was no longer upset about Nathan but she wouldn't like to go through that hurt again, and she couldn't understand why James had suddenly become important to her. She was looking forward to seeing him tomorrow but why did he want her to go to the function with him? He was quite handsome and could have easily found someone else to go. She didn't dare to hope; now where had that thought come from?

The next day James came in with a smart blonde lady and, after seeing her to a table, strolled over to Lissette.

'Oh, you have found someone to go to the function with, after all.'

'Yes, you. Sandra is just a solicitor at the practice.'

'Is she going?'

'Yes, Lissette, with her boyfriend. You're not getting out of it that easily. A bargain is a bargain.'

'I'm sorry, I just thought... '

James broke in. 'Are you jealous?'

'No, not at all.'

'The lady doth protest too much.' He smiled. 'Now, to business. Sandra has come to sample your wears and I've come for a completely different reason, which I'll explain some other time, when we are alone. For now I'd like two coffees, two slices of that delectable pie, and tea for you. I've chosen a table with ample room.'

'But... '

'No buts, Lissette, this is your tea break with me. Now get to it, my lovely Lissette.' It was a bemused Lissette who joined them at the table.

'Sandra, this is Lissette. Lissette, this is Sandra.'

'What a pretty name,' Sandra said, 'so unusual.'

'Yes, my mother was French. She met my father when he was in the army.'

'Do you still have family in France?'

'Yes, my cousins. My mother and father are dead but I also have a brother who lives in Australia.'

'It's good that you have met James, then.'

It was Lissette's turn to raise her eyebrows. 'It is?'

Sipping her tea she realised that she liked Sandra and that she had made some good friends, but where did James fit in, friend or.... It hit her like lightening: she was doing exactly what she didn't want to do; she was falling in love with him.

'A penny for them, Lissette,' James said.

'They are not worth a penny, believe me.'

'Well in that case I will need to earn a few more pennies to learn what you are thinking, so Sandra and I had better get back to the office but I'll see you later. We can have a drink.'

'We can?' said Lissette, staring at him.

'Yes,' he replied, getting up and quickly kissing her. 'I'll be here at 7.30. Make sure you are ready.' His ready smile was there for her as he left. She could not, and would not, make the same mistake. She didn't wish to complicate her life again. She needed to stop this before it got out of hand.

CHAPTER 5

It was now cool in the evenings and Lissette chose a pair of cream slacks and a matching cream blouse. She slipped her feet into a pair of tan peep-toe flat shoes, placing a matching tan sweater ready. She still didn't know why she was obeying James. He hadn't asked her; he had told her. He appeared to expect her to agree. She looked at her hair and brushed it until it shone, then twisted it round to form a chignon at the nape of her neck. Slipping amber ear rings into her ears Lissette studied herself. She was happy with the results. At last, her green eyes had regained their sparkle.

Sitting in her mother's leather chair she felt happier than she had in a long time and began to look forward to the night ahead. She realised there was life after Nathan. True to his word, James rang the bell at 7.30 and Lissette felt a frisson of excitement as she crossed the tea room floor. James looked relaxed and happy.

Tucking her arm through his he said, 'It's a nice night. Shall we walk first?', and dumbly, Lissette nodded. After finding an empty bench facing the sea he spread his navy sweater across it and sat her down next to him, placing his arm around her. 'Payment,' he said, adding, 'But if the price is too high I won't pay.'

Then he said, 'Tell me about yourself. Did you have a tea room before coming to Brixham?'

'No I didn't.'

'What did you do, then?'

'You ask a lot of questions.'

'That's because I like you. Do you like me?'

'Yes, in a way,' she answered shortly.

'That first time I set eyes on you in my office you looked lonely and unhappy. I wanted to know more about you.'

'I was a PA,' she suddenly said trying to change the subject. 'Gill has become a good friend so I'm not lonely now. All I know is that I'm glad this is where the road ended.'

'That's a strange statement.'

'Well, perhaps sometime I will explain but at the moment I don't want to think about it.'

'I can wait,' he said looking into her eyes. He kissed her on the mouth.

'Will you stop doing that?'

'For now. Let's have coffee back at your place and we can make arrangements for the function we're going to later in the month. I have employed a lady for a week to cover for you.'

'A week? It's only two days and I could have employed someone myself.'

'But it's double time,' he said wagging his finger again.

'I'd say it was more like treble time you are charging.'

'Come on, let's go back to your place and talk about it over coffee.'

He put his arm around her shoulder and by this time she was enjoying his company too much to object. All she knew was that she felt safe with this man. She didn't think he would be like Nathan but even now she couldn't be sure. Will it be what you see is what you get? she thought.

At her flat he made himself comfortable on the couch. Lissette realised he was tired.

'Brandy,' she asked. He nodded. 'Do you want your coffee black?'

'No, I'll have a little milk in it.' When she returned he had fallen asleep. She picked up a book and began to read, and at 12.30 fetched a blanket and covered him up. His eyes flickered open and he pulled her down beside him, and kissed her eyes and her neck before reaching her lips. Lissette responded with passion.

When they came up for breath, he said, 'We had better go to bed. Can I stay?' Lissette stared at him. 'Spare room, unless.... '

'Spare room,' said Lissette before he could suggest anything else.

She leant on the inside of her door and heard him turn off his light. It seemed the most natural thing in the world for him to be there. She couldn't sleep and knew that if he had suggested it she would have allowed him to share her bed. That was something she had never allowed Nathan to do.

Lissette woke to the smell of cooking bacon. There was a light knock on her door and James walked in carrying a cup of tea.

'Have that. The shower is free. Do you want some bacon after your shower?' Lissette shook her head.

'I'll have some cornflakes.'

Bending and kissing her he said, 'We need talk about where we go from here.' Lissette nodded dumbly. 'When you get up and have had your shower I will have to go. I have an early meeting and I need to go home and change.'

When Lissette entered the kitchen he was standing by the sink deep in thought. He asked, 'Do you mind if I leave my dishes?'

'No.' She smiled at him and realised this was the first time she had felt completely comfortable.

'I can't get you out my mind. I will be busy over the next two weeks but I will be here on the following Friday at 11 o'clock to pick you up. You need your overnight things, a spare day outfit and something pretty for the evening. I'm missing you already. Oh, and the lady from the agency will call at around 3 o'clock.' He left, blowing her a kiss.

A week later Lissette was surprised to see him walk in. 'I thought it would be another week before you called.'

'I missed you,' he answered. 'The solicitor I interviewed is meeting me here, although we have some concerns about him and I won't be offering him the job.'

The bell jingled again. Lissette was about to serve coffee and the complimentary biscuits but when she saw who it was the tray fell from her hands. In a heartbeat James was on his feet.

'Lissette, are you okay?'

Not answering, she stared at the new arrival. Nathan was walking towards them.

'Lissette, at last I know where you are, darling,' he said in a smooth voice.

'And now that you do, you can leave and don't come back.' She began to tremble. James had his arm around her.

'Go upstairs, Lissette, now,' he ordered. 'I will sort this. Beth, go up and look after Lissette for me. Sue, can you manage to clear up this mess? I don't think this meeting will take long.'

He invited Nathan to sit down. 'This won't take long. You worked for Rob Peake in the Midlands and on checking your records I've a found a few flaws in your references. Is there an explanation?'

'I only applied for the position of junior partner. My private life is no one's business but my own.'

'Should your private life be in doubt as well? I was talking about your professional life. I don't think we need to discuss this any further. I'm afraid we are unable to offer you the position. But tell me, do you know Lissette?'

'Of course I do; she's my fiancée.'

'I don't think so. Lissette and I are engaged to be married so I will take a dim view if you try and carry on in this vein. I must also warn you to stay away from here.'

'You can't do that,' Nathan said, trying to call James's bluff.

'Yes I can and my word as a barrister will carry more weight, so stay away. Is that clear?'

Without another word Nathan stood up and left, slamming the door behind him.

For a good hour James sat at the table fighting the urge to go upstairs and hold Lissette in his arms. He needed to think. Beth had come back down and had said that Lissette had taken a sleeping pill and was now soundly sleeping. She assured James that she would stay at the tea room with Lissette for as long as she needed her.

'No, Beth, I want you to stay until I say it's okay to leave her. Will you promise that?'

Beth agreed. She was fond of Lissette as well, and she could tell that her cousin was in love. He was the glue that had kept their family together when her dad had died. At that time he had just started as a junior partner at a practice in Torquay. He had helped Ron and David to train in their trades and had funded them when they started their businesses. He had even used what money he had from the sale of his mother's home to start the bed and breakfast, which meant that all of them were making a living. Now he deserved some happiness himself. She hoped and prayed that he would find it in Lissette.

CHAPTER 6

The next week passed in a daze for Lissette. She jumped every time the door chimes sounded, looking half-fearful and then half-relieved when it wasn't Nathan. Gill rang her to remind her that James would be picking her up at 11 o'clock on the Friday.

'Lissette, I know something has happened and we want you to know we all love you. Me, Ron, David, and it goes without saying, James, more than any of us. You must know how he feels about you. He would walk through fire for you.'

'Gill, I don't want to talk about it now. Someday I will explain. I thought I would never trust anyone again before I met James.'

Meanwhile, James had concluded his business a day earlier than he expected, and after arriving home sat in his lounge, overlooking Goodrington Sands, and watched the sun set. He was still struggling with the thought that Lissette had something to do with Nathan – that excuse for a man. He loved her and knew that, whatever had happened, he needed her. He would just have to get over the thought that Nathan had touched her in some way. Staring at the sunset he told himself what had happened in her past was none of his business. It was their future that mattered. With that, he felt better.

Friday arrived and Lissette opened the tea room at 10.30 as usual. She had spent the last two days baking and preparing enough food for them to be going on with. The lady that James had employed was here and Beth had agreed to stay in the flat while Lissette was away. Lissette's bag was behind the counter ready. She had dressed in a moss green trouser suit teamed with a gold-coloured blouse. Her copper hair was once more hanging in loose waves around her face.

The door opened and James walked in, and the women sitting at the tables looked at him admiringly. He walked over and whispered, 'You look lovely, Lissette.'

She was sure he could hear her heart pounding and knew she had fallen hook, line and sinker for him; she was his and would do anything he asked. Who would have thought that four months ago she had sworn she would never look at another man as long as she lived?

After opening the door of his Volvo James helped her in and stowed her bag in the back. He lay her evening dress flat on top of the bags. His dress suit was hanging on a hook in the back of the car.

'Are you all right?' he asked.

'Yes, never better.' She smiled.

'That's my girl.'

Despite himself, he couldn't resist asking about the incident in the shop.

'Are you over what happened with Nathan at the tea room?'

'Yes,' she whispered.

'He said you were engaged to him; do you still love him?'

'No.'

'Can you tell me about it?'

'No, not yet.'

After arriving at the Hilton two hours later James carried the bags. Their rooms were next to each other.

'Go and freshen up and then we can go and have something to eat,' he said. He kissed and hugged her close. 'Don't be long.'

Fifteen minutes later Lissette was sitting on the end of her bed when she heard a tap on the door. James did not wait for a reply and opened the door, smiling at her. They went down to the restaurant and the waiter showed them to a table.

'Something light?' he asked.

'Yes please,' James replied. 'We'll have our main meal tonight.'

They scanned the menu.

'Will lobster salad do?' James asked Lissette, who nodded. 'Any afters?'

'No thanks.'

James ordered the salad, and coffee and brandy to follow. Lissette suddenly laughed.

'What are you laughing at?'

'Are you going to fall asleep?'

Smiling, James replied, 'That's puts my charges up.'

'Now I don't mind paying,' she said, smiling back at him. 'It's becoming quite enjoyable.'

'I'll hold that thought. What would you like to do now? Go for a walk before we get ready?'

'Yes, I'd love that.'

'Good, now eat up.'

Later, as they walked along the street holding hands, he stopped outside a jewellers.

'It's Gill's birthday soon. Let's go in and you can give me some ideas as to what to get her. Will you try on some rings? Gill's hands are about the same size as yours.'

'Can I help you, sir?' the assistant asked.

'Yes, we want a present for my sister. My friend's hands are about her size.'

'But, sir, for a ring the lady really needs to try it on herself.'

'Well, let's try a few anyway while we're here.'

The assistant took a ring from a tray and gave it to Lissette, but it was a little tight. The second one she tried fitted well and the assistant told them it was a size N.

'Perhaps you're right,' James said. 'It would be better if my sister came in herself. Can we see some earrings instead?'

'That's a better idea, sir.'

He returned with two trays of earrings and, after looking at several pairs, James chose two – one sapphire and diamond, the other emerald and diamond.

They left the shop and walked for another half hour. Then, turning to her, James asked, 'Are you happy?'

'Yes, I think I am,' Lissette replied.

'Are you sure?'

'Yes I'm sure.'

'You don't know how happy that makes me. I'd like to make love to you right now, but somehow I think that you are not that kind of girl. I can wait, but not too long, my lovely Lissette.' His eyes were full of promise. 'Come on, let's get back now. I'll give you a knock at around 7 o'clock. You can shower and will still have plenty of time to make yourself beautiful.'

As soon as Lissette closed her bedroom door James quickly made his way back to the jewellers. He wondered if he was doing the right thing; should he wait a little longer? His heart said no, and that he needed to trust her. The assistant spotted him straight away and made his way over.

'Was there something you forgot, sir?'

'Yes, in a way, an engagement ring.'

'Ah, that explains it, sir. It's unusual to ask a lady friend to try on a ring for someone else.'

'It was the only way I could find out what size she needed. Emerald and diamond, please.'

The assistant quickly fetched a tray of rings and set it down in front of James, who selected a twist of three large emeralds surrounded by large diamonds.

'Size N, please,' James said.

'That's quite an expensive one, sir.'

'The lady is worth it,' he replied.

The assistant wrapped the box. 'Congratulations, sir.'

'I haven't asked her yet!' James said with a smile.

'Well, good luck then, sir.'

CHAPTER 7

James looked at himself in the mirror. His dress suit was impeccable. Here goes, he thought, and smiling, he knocked on Lissette's door and went straight in. She was wearing a strappy black cocktail dress with silver shoestring straps, and a silver stole and silver sandals.

'You never cease to amaze me, Lissette. Once more you look beautiful. Sit down a minute, would you.' He pulled over a chair, then bent down on one knee and took the box from his pocket.

'I've never done this before. It's the most important moment of my life. I know its quick and that you haven't known me long, but I've loved you from the first time I set eyes on you in the office. Please will you be my wife?'

Lissette couldn't speak.

'Please don't say no,' he pleaded. Tears welled in her eyes.

'Yes, I will. I love you, too.'

James slipped the ring on her finger. 'These are to match,' he said, holding out the emerald earrings. 'We will have to get married soon; I want you so much.' Lissette responded to his kisses with passion. James groaned. 'We had better get out of here before we start something we can't finish.'

Holding her hand they left the room to join the party downstairs, and as they walked in, several people joined them and spoke to James, who introduced Lissette as his fiancée.

'You lucky fellow, James,' one man said, particularly loudly. 'And we meet again, my lovely, runaway bride. Playing games again?'

It was Nathan.

'Is that what you think,' James said. 'Excuse us.' He put his arm around Lissette and led her to a table.

221

'Lissette, tell me again. Are you sure everything is over between you and that despicable man?'

'Not now,' she said in a small voice.

'Why did he call you his runaway bride?'

'Because we were to be married four months ago.'

'You got over that quickly.'

'Yes,' was all she could say.

'As you know I interviewed him a couple of months ago. We were looking to take on a junior partner but his poor reputation went before him, so I declined to offer him the position. You must have known what he was like and yet you were going to marry him.'

'Please, James, I will explain, but it's too raw at the moment.'

'Very well. We will try to enjoy tonight and we'll talk about it when we get home. Would you like a drink?' He did not look at her.

'Yes, just a tonic water with ice and lemon, please.'

Why had he turned up? She had been so happy but now that horrible episode came flooding back.

James went to the bar. Had she allowed Nathan to make love to her? he wondered. She did not appear to be that sort of woman. Nathan walked across and stood alongside him.

'You'll have to watch her with your wallet,' old man.'

'You think so?' James said, giving him a withering look. He walked away.

Nathan now wanted to spoil Lissette's life. Her sudden departure had ruined his position as junior partner at the practice: Rob had guessed why she had left. Nathan had been banking on using Lissette's money to open his own practice, so the least he could do was wreck her plans with her new love. He blamed Lissette for what had happened but he had already been warned about his behaviour. It had only been a matter of time before he was sacked.

The night went from bad to worse. Lissette felt as if the bottom of her world had dropped out.

'I'm tired,' James said eventually. 'Shall we turn in?'

They went upstairs and he opened her door for her without looking up, then went to his own room. Until now he had always given her a kiss when he left her but he had just left her without even a goodnight. She felt far worse than when she had found Nathan in bed with the blonde. She should have known that James would be the same.

Packing her bag and squashing in her cocktail dress she scribbled a note for James:

'I understand that for some reason you think badly of me. I thought I did not trust men but you changed my mind. However, I must be wrong. It is possible not to know someone properly. You obviously don't trust me. Don't be so quick to judge. You, of all people, should have checked your facts. Where there is no trust there is no love. Now I see that you are not the person I thought you were. This must have been the shortest engagement in history.'

Putting the ring and earrings into the envelope she slipped down to reception and asked for the bill for her room. She left the envelope at reception, marking it for James. She then took a taxi to the station. This was becoming a habit, she thought sadly. But she couldn't up sticks this time. She had invested too much in her business. But she did need to get away for a while, so booked a ticket to Scotland. She would ring Beth first thing in the morning and ask to take over for a while and to stay in the flat.

Beth lived at the bed and breakfast with Gill but said she would hold the fort but to please come back soon because they all worked so well together.

'I will, Lissette replied, 'but I need a little time. Please tell Gill I will be in touch.'

Lissette then changed the sim card on her phone. She needed to get over this and become strong again. Nathan was now in the past, and James as well. She would go back, but only when she had the strength to keep him at a distance. She vowed to stay single and never to get involved with a man again.

After her long journey to Scotland she found a leaflet highlighting places of interest. One place particularly stuck her: Lochgoilhead. There, there was a hotel called The Drumsine; she hoped its peace and quiet would ease her hurt.

After a month of long walks and exploring the village she realised she would have to sell her tea room and get another job.

Her dream of having a happy life in Brixham was over. James simply didn't love her. She knew she would never stop loving him but it would be too hard to see him with someone else. It would not be possible to return; she wanted to vanish again.

Suddenly she felt very alone and was desperate to hear a familiar voice, someone who would always be there for her. She thought of John, her brother, and his wife Jane. She dialled his number and as they spoke something in her voice made him think that something was wrong. Lissette poured her heart out, telling John about Gill and James and the rest of their family.

'Why have you left your tea room if, as you say, they have looked after you as good friends?'

'It was Nathan. He turned up to meet James and took me by surprise.' Her voice began to quiver. 'A couple of weeks later I went to a function with James and he was there again. He said something to James that made him angry. I know now that I didn't love Nathan. I missed Mum and he took advantage of my loneliness. I just drifted into the engagement. I'm glad that he showed me what sort of a man he was in the end. But I've still lost the only man I'll ever love.'

'Who? Nathan? John asked, confused. 'I never liked him but he was your choice.'

'No, James. We were engaged and I'll never get over losing him. I love him. Whatever Nathan said to James upset him. Then I left the hotel and left a note and the ring. It's such a mess. I don't want him to know how much he hurt me or that I still love him.' Lissette started to cry.

'Give me your address. I'm getting the next flight over. I'll have something to say to Nathan, and this James won't be getting off lightly either.'

'Please, John, there's no need,' Lissette was sobbing. 'Lissette, I'll be on my way tonight. No arguments.'

CHAPTER 8

After lying wide awake for several hours James felt he could not stand feeling this way any longer. He knew Lissette couldn't possibly have known what Nathan was like. He needed to tell her he loved her and that, whatever Nathan said, he always would. After putting on his dressing gown he slipped out of his room and knocked on Lissette's door, calling her softly. When Lissette didn't answer he thought she must have fallen asleep. He knocked again, a little more loudly, but still there was no response. Perhaps she had gone down for an early breakfast.

He dressed quickly and took the stairs two at a time, composed himself and calmly walked into the dining room.

'Has Miss Darcy been down yet?' he asked a waiter.

'No, sir, not yet.'

James watched the door as he drank his coffee. Where on earth was she? He had not taken her for someone who sulked. Grimly, he made his way to reception and asked if Lissette had gone out.

'I'll just check for her room key, sir,' the receptionist said, and a moment later added, 'She appears to have checked out, sir.'

'Has she left any message for me? James Garner, I'm in the next room.' The receptionist found the envelope and gave it to him. He knew before opening it that his ring was inside.

Reading her words his heart sank. Why had he reacted so badly? It had been the thought of that man mauling her. He intended to get to the bottom of this. He had an important business meeting in the Midlands that he couldn't miss it, but he had wanted Lissette to go with him. Now he would have to go on his own. Perhaps, while he was there, he would call at the solicitors Nathan had worked for. He had been at university with the senior partner there.

He rang Lissette's mobile and realised she had switched it off. It was nearing 10 o'clock. If he rang after 10.30 he would get one of them and at least he would know she was home safe. He called his friend Rob who, unknown to him, was Lissette's old boss, explained that he would be nearby and asked if they could meet for lunch. He then rang The Copper Kettle. Beth answered.

'Did Lissette arrive home safely, Beth? Is she there?'

'No, I'm afraid she's not. She rang early this morning, asking me to get someone to help out. She said to take wages out of the takings and she put me in charge. She said she'd be back soon. I'm to stay in her flat to make sure I'm on hand.'

'Damn,' said James. He returned to reception to pay their account. Only then did he discover that Lissette had already paid her own.

Half of him wanted to rush back to Brixham to see if there were any clues as to her whereabouts. However, he needed to get to Peake and Freeman to see Rob Peake. He was soon sitting down and explaining to Rob why he was there.

'I know that Nathan's last position was here. I chose not to offer him a job with us but I have a personal interest in him.'

'I'm not surprised he didn't get it,' Rob replied. 'We terminated his employment because he made a couple of underhand transactions. He was already on a slippery slope and I only retained him as long as I did because he had become engaged to Lissette, my PA.'

'Lissette Darcy worked here?'

'Yes, you know her, James?'

'Yes I do. We're engaged.'

'You are? I'm so pleased! She worked here from school age. She is one of the most lovely people you could know – kind and considerate. Why she never saw through Nathan I will never know.'

'So I don't have to watch my wallet, as he suggested?'

'You didn't believe that, did you? Lissette is too straight for that to be a concern.'

'Well, she certainly seemed to have enough money – definitely enough to buy a property.'

'Of course she did. Nathan probably saw the file for her parents' estate. It was quite sizeable and we think that was why he asked her to marry him. In fact, he boasted about it to one of my colleagues. He took advantage of her when she was low.'

'What did he do to make her to run away, if she didn't know what he was like?'

'Has she not told you? I'm really not sure I should tell you, James. If she wanted you to know, would she not have told you already?'

'You know I wouldn't divulge who had told me. But I need to know for myself.'

'Okay, but you understand that this is in strict confidence? After they were married Lissette was to move into Nathan's flat until they bought a house. But shortly before the wedding, when he was supposed to be at a business meeting, she decided to drop off a new outfit at his place. He didn't hear her and she found him in bed with a prostitute. None of us heard from Lissette after that, other than to say she would not be coming back because of personal reasons. It sickened me when he made excuses, saying she was like an ice maiden with her old-fashioned no-sex-before-marriage rule. He would have been a very lucky man if she had married him.'

'You don't know how pleased I am, Rob,' said a relieved James. 'I just needed to know whether she still had feelings for him. Do you mind if we skip lunch? I need to get back. But we'll be inviting you to our wedding.'

'Of course, James, you must go. I'll hold you to the wedding invitation, though!'

James strode out of the office. All he needed to do was conclude the business he was there for and get back and find Lissette.

CHAPTER 9

James arrived back home the next day and went straight to The Copper Kettle to see if Beth or Sue had heard anything from Lissette. They had not.

James felt sick not knowing where to look. However, Beth insisted that Lissette was coming back. He would just have to be patient. Summer turned into autumn, and then winter arrived. Beth kept the tea room open for the locals; it had become a favourite meeting place, but everyone seemed to ask about Lissette.

Early in the new year Lissette called Beth and told her she was selling up. It would be the best thing for all of them if she didn't return, she said.

'But what about James?' Beth said. 'He's going frantic waiting for you.'

All Lissette could manage to say was, 'I have put the property into the estate agent's hands. I wondered if you could pack up my belongings ready for the storage company to collect. My mum's furniture will go into storage until I can buy somewhere else. I'm sorry I have to sell. I have a new job now and I need some of my capital to get a flat. Please tell James I hope he will find the happiness he craves, and give my love to Gill.' Lissette's voice began to break with emotion. 'And try not to think badly of me, Beth. I love you all – James as well, more than he'll ever know.'

'But surely, Lissette, you and James can get over this. It can't be that bad, can it?'

'Believe me, Beth, I wish we could.'

How was she going to forget him? She longed for him to turn up, hold her in his arms and make everything right. But somehow, she felt that this would never happen.

'She has to come back.' James stared at Beth. 'I will find her and bring her back.' A plan was beginning to form in his mind. 'Beth, as soon as the estate agent arrives, ring me. You and Sue will continue working here. I will buy the tea room under our portfolio and will ensure that Lissette will not be given my name. She won't know who has purchased it. We can't do anything about her furniture going into storage, but need to know when it will be collected. You understand, don't you, Beth?'

'Of course I understand.'

'I promise, Beth, I will trace her and when I do she will never get away from me again. I love her, Beth.'

'We all do, James.'

With a nod of the head and a promise to call in the next day James went home to await developments.

Two days later the phone rang. Beth had the details of the estate agent and James rang straight away and offered the full asking price, ensuring that no one else could buy it. He insisted that his name was not to be divulged. He had a small property development company and the purchase would be in the firm's name. He waited for Lissette's solicitors to contact him and sure enough, within a few days, he knew where Lissette was. Now to await the collection of her furniture. He was confident he would find her and his spirits began to rise; hopefully he would soon be with his beautiful Lissette. He had lost weight and his hair now had a few grey streaks. The sooner he found her the sooner he would have peace of mind.

Three days later he was discreetly sitting outside the tea room awaiting the arrival of the storage company, and when the men arrived he took down the firm's phone number and address which was printed on the side of their van. Immediately, he started his car and headed for Dunoon, where he booked into a hotel. Lissette was not the only person who could take time off.

After a coffee and salad he felt fortified, and ready to scour the town for Lissette, and searched until late evening to no avail. He was determined to try again the next day.

Gill rang that night to say that a copy of the contract from the vendor's solicitor had arrived. Everything was falling into place.

'Okay, Gill, read the address and phone number out to me, please. Great, I will be calling there tomorrow. I hope I will have some news for you when we next speak. Goodnight.'

That night James had a better sleep than he had had in months and after completing some business the next morning he took a leisurely walk to the solicitors. As he approached he was shocked to see Lissette walk out of the building arm in arm with a tall man. They seemed deep in conversation and appeared to be very close. He wanted to drag her away and it was a confused James who made his way back to the hotel. Perhaps, somehow, Lissette had managed to hide her true self. Granted, she had returned the ring so was free to see anyone she wanted. However, she seemed to get over her love affairs very quickly.

He arranged to sign the contract, sent it back to the solicitor and transferred the money from his account. Deflated and unhappy, he packed for his return to Brixham.

James threw himself into his work, which sometimes took him away for several weeks. After one trip he returned to find that Rob Peake had rung. He thought he had better return his call.

'I was wondering what had transpired with you and Lissette, as I hadn't heard from you? I was so happy that you were engaged but then found out recently that you had split up. Believe me, Lissette is one of the best. She must have been in touch with John, her brother in Australia, because he flew over. He must have been very worried about her. John called in while he was here and asked me to ring her. He said she had lost weight and was beginning to look unwell.'

'Her brother?' James gasped. 'Is he tall with sandy-coloured hair?'

'Yes, how did you know?'

'I've been one hell of a fool, again.' James told Rob what had happened.

'You are one hell of a fool, James. I could bang your heads together. She is suffering because of you.'

'Do you know her address, Rob, please,' he begged.

'It's a good job I know your intentions are honourable.' Rob gave James Lissette's address.

James swiftly asked Rachel, his receptionist, to reschedule his appointments for the following week. 'That should give me just about time to sort myself, I hope.'

He started out for Dunoon immediately and walked to the flat in which he understood Lissette to live. There was no response so he settled down to wait for her to return. Sure enough, at 6.30, Lissette strolled down the street carrying a shopping bag. She did not notice James in his car. He followed her to the main door to the flats and held it open after she had gone in, forcing her to turn. All she could do was stare into his eyes. She trembled and her eyes began to fill with tears. Two other people were waiting to get into their own flat.

'Lissette, sweetheart, please let's go in. We are holding people up.' He ushered her through the door but had no idea which flat was hers. 'What number is it?'

'Number 18.'

He held his hand out and she obediently gave him her key, and after following her in he did what he had longed to do for months. Cupping her face in his hands he let his lips wander hungrily over her lips, murmuring, 'You do love me, Lissette. Do you know what agony it's been wanting to hold you again? Lissette, please don't send me away. I love you so much. In fact, I won't allow you to send me away. Please say you love me.'

He held her close and let her cry. He realised it was not just this last 12 months' problems that were upsetting her but that her distress went much further back. He guessed that she hadn't completely got over losing her parents. She needed to let the grief out, then she would feel better. Whispering words of love and encouragement he held her tight until her sobs became more controlled and she became quiet in his arms. She was exhausted and eventually drifted into a heavy sleep. Determined to let her rest he kept his arm around her, and laying his head on hers he sat contentedly. Sometime later his arm had gone dead. He needed to get her into bed but had no intention of leaving her side. Gently he shook her awake.

'Lissette, wake up, sweetheart. We need to get you into bed.'

Helping her to stand as she got her bearings, he said, 'Which way is the bedroom?' She did not respond, just held on to him, led him into the passageway and opened the first door. She looked as if her legs would not hold her.

'Sit down while I help you undress,' he said, gently stripping her to her underclothes. He helped her between the sheets then sat on the bed to take off his shoes. 'I'll only hold you, Lissette. I respect and love you and there will be plenty of time to get to know one another when we are married.' After turning the light off he slid out of his trousers, took off his shirt and tie and joined her. He put his arms around her and held her tight. Lying there in the darkness he didn't allow himself the luxury of sleeping himself until Lissette was breathing evenly. While she slept she turned and held onto him; he had to fight to keep himself in check. All he wanted to do was make love to her but he needed to prove he was not like Nathan. Difficult as it was, he was intent on doing this right, for her sake.

Eventually, they both slept heavily, not waking until quite late. Eventually the telephone woke James, who picked up the receiver and said, 'Hello, Lissette Darcy's flat.'

'Who are you?' said the male voice.

'James Garner,' he replied curtly, 'soon to be Lissette's husband.'

'So, you are the man who has broken my sister's heart,' Is Lissette there'. 'Yes but she is still sleeping I will get her to ring you back when we have sorted a few things out'.

'And you must be John Lissette's brother? It was a misunderstanding and I hope that now I have resolved it. I love Lissette and would never hurt her intentionally. I will be taking her back home with me as soon as we have sorted out the lease on this flat and told her employers she will not be returning to work.'

'But she sold the tea room.'

'Yes, I purchased it as a wedding present for her.'

At that moment Lissette's voice broke in.

'You did?'

'Lissette, sweetheart, you are awake.'

'John, as much as I would like to talk to you I need to sort out some misunderstandings with your sister. So I will ring you soon and tell you when the wedding is; we will be expecting you to give her away.'

James pulled Lissette to him.

'Sleep well, my love?'

'Yes,' she answered shyly, realising that they had spent the night in the same bed. He urged her to get out of bed and into the shower.

'After breakfast we will talk.'

Lissette returned from her shower wrapped in a towel.

'I'd better go and take a cold shower,' James said, eyeing her almost-naked body. 'Promise me you will stay put and won't do a runner.'

'Never again,' she answered.

James feigned disappointment at there being no bacon. 'Never mind. I'm only hungry for you. Lissette, I'm sorry about what happened at the function. I was stupid and pig-headed. I couldn't stand the thought that Nathan might have touched you. I was jealous.'

'James, I didn't love Nathan, I sort of drifted into it. I'm just glad I found out what he was like before it was too late.'

'Lissette, I don't need to know anything else. I trust and love you. Let's not dwell on our mistakes. The future is what matters.

'Now, if we've got no bacon, what have we got?'

'Toast and coffee,' she said, smiling.

'Okay, that will have to do. After breakfast we'll sort out paying off the lease on this place, ring your work or visit them, then pack and go home.' She busied herself with making his toast and coffee.

James rang Lissette's office – another solictor's – and arranged to go in with Lissette to collect her belongings. They had coffee with the senior partner, Craig, and Lissette listened to them talk shop. They had lots in common. Finally James stood up and they made their way out. Like James, Lissette would be glad to get home.

Two months later they stood at the altar taking their vows. Her dress was white lace with long sleeves, high at the front and slightly lower at the back. Standing beside her was John, who had given her away. James had asked Rob Peake to be his best man. Ron and David were ushers, and completing the picture was Gill, Lissette's bridesmaid. As the vicar pronounced them man and wife James pulled her into his arms, kissed her and looked as if he would never let her go.

'Come on James, let her come up for air!' joked Rob.

James and Lissette were to spend the night in their home at Goodrington Sands. They would then honeymoon in Majorca for a month. In their bedroom that night James inclined his head towards the bed.

'Shall we?'

Lissette turned around. 'Is this a payment?'

Smiling, he replied, 'If it is, you will be paying for the rest of your life,' and with that he picked her up and placed her on the bed.

'Tonight will be unforgettable,' he said.

They reached for each other and were both consumed by passion.

Restless Spirit
By Barbara Machin

CHAPTER 1

Megan was 27 and very attractive. She was 5ft 4in; her blonde short hair framed her face. Her features were small but she had large violet blue eyes in a heart-shaped face and a petite, boyish figure. Most of the time she appeared to be a very serious young lady. However, when she smiled her face changed from pretty to beautiful. Megan had lived in East Anglia all her life, in the village of Thetford. It boasted its own famous forest, which covered most of the surrounding area. It was a popular with tourists, who came from all over the country to the Forestry Commission's visitor lodge. Thetford was also home to the Centre Parcs holiday complex. In other words, it was a desirable place for land developers. Megan hated to see the modern homes that were being thrown up around the countryside, spoiling the natural beauty of the area.

She looked at her watch. She still had 30 minutes before she needed to be at the school to collect Ben, her small son. He was almost eight, and today her mother, who would normally pick him up, was not well. The owner of the surveyor's company she worked for always allowed her to make-up the time if she left early, as and when she could. Today was one of those days. Megan thought back to when she was at college at 17. She had had a childhood sweetheart and they had been joined at the hip. His name was also Ben and he had had dreams of leaving Thetford after he finished college. He had been certain that if he went to London he would flourish and become rich. Ben and Megan had had their favourite spot; they would walk through an underpass which led to the ruins of an ancient priory where they would lie on the grass and share their dreams. Because they were so much in love, nature took its course. Soon it became their place. Then Ben finished college. He was very ambitious. He had just turned 22 and was restless. He needed to follow his dream. As they lay in the grass holding each other Ben had told Megan that he'd decided it was time to follow his dream and had promised to send for her when he was settled with a job and flat. Holding her tight they had made love for the last time. Megan promised she would be at the station to see him off the next day.

He had held Megan tight in his arms, promising to write as soon as he arrived. Megan never heard from him again, and three months later realised the folly of giving in to the pressure and ardour of young love. She was pregnant. Her son, also Ben, was a joy but it was hard work being a single parent even though her mum and dad gave her as much support as they could.

Megan reached the school gate as a dark grey Mercedes slid to a halt. The occupant moved his glasses from his face and opened the door. Then young Ben ran through the school gate and Megan bent to hug him. The man watched her take the child's hand and walk down the street.

How long he sat in his car he didn't know. What did he expect? It had been eight and a half years. Did he expect her still to be single? It had been a coincidence that he had been driving on that road and he had recognised Megan's slight form, the way she held her head high and her hair shining like burnished gold as the sun glinted on it. He had been about to rush over to her when he saw the child run into her arms.

He realised that she must be married. All the feelings he had for her had rushed back as he brought his car to a standstill. When he had gone to London, full of plans and hopes, it had not been easy for him to find work or a home. H had had to use his money sparingly in what he could only call doss houses, and he knew he couldn't ask Megan to live as he was. Eventually he managed to secure a job in a construction company and even found a half-decent room. But by this time he was working a lot of overtime because he had met another construction worker, Daniel, who had hopes and dreams himself. They worked hard to save enough money to set up their own development company, and almost nine years later they had become very successful. On seeing some land for sale near the M11 close to Thetford he had immediately decided to buy it. Building permission had been granted and, as his partner Dan was overseeing another development, he had offered to cover the Thetford scheme, all the time thinking of Megan.

He had not married, but he had women who threw themselves at him. None measured up to Megan. His current secretary was becoming a slight problem because she had set her sights on him. In the beginning he had been flattered, but that had soon worn off. At the moment she was trying to manipulate him into her bed. She obviously had her sights set well and truly on marriage, so going to Thetford had been a good move, although he had not reckoned on the rush of memories.

His meeting with Edward Jackson was not until the following day and he had to be on time because Edward needed to be out of the office quite quickly. He had said he would leave him in the capable hands of his secretary, who would do all the costings for him. This was why Ben had travelled up a day early, in case there were traffic holdups.

He decided that he would take a quiet walk for an hour or two before going back to his hotel for dinner and, walking slowly, he made his way to an underpass and realised he was at their special place, the ruins of Cluniac Priory of Our Lady of Thetford. Memories came flooding back. Everyone has regrets but suddenly all of his paled into a mere shadow against what he had lost with Megan who, judging by her little boy, must be very happily married. He strode back, thinking the sooner the deal was agreed the sooner he could return to London.

Megan made her way to her small cottage. Her mum, dad and gran had scraped up the deposit for her to ensure that she and her son were secure. She was managing to hold things together. The cottage was comfortable and had a flagged floor covered in a large green Chinese rug she had picked up from the Salvation Army charity shop. There was a plain cream settee and chairs to match the green cushions, and green curtains. There was also an open fire with a log basket in the corner. The kitchen had cream cupboards and a Belfast sink, and a jute rug covered most of the tiles. There was a small table and chairs in the corner. Megan removed Ben's coat and shooed him into the kitchen.

'Sit at the table, Ben, and do your homework while I cook tea.'

'Can't I watch telly, Mummy, please?'

'You have to do your homework first, then you can watch Children's Hour before you have a bath.'

'Please, Mummy?'

'No, Ben, if you don't do your homework there won't be any television at all. So the sooner you do it the sooner you can watch your programmes.'

'All right, Mummy, sorry.' He gave her a beaming smile. Megan's heart lurched. He looked so much like his father when he smiled.

Once Megan was satisfied that Ben had completed his homework, she set the table for his tea, which was his favourite – fish fingers and beans, with a slice of bread to make sure he was full enough.

'Eat that up, Ben, and if you eat it all you can have some sugar-free jelly with ice cream for afters.'

Megan had beans on toast and a cup of tea. Once Ben had finished, the routine was one hour of TV and then a bath. Megan would wash his school clothes and put them to dry, then would put out her office clothes and Ben's clean school clothes in readiness, to save time the next morning. Her neighbour, Sue, who had children, would take Ben to school with her two. Megan didn't like to keep them waiting. Megan would then read with Ben and help him with the big words. Ben loved this the most. Once he was in bed she would complete the daily chores. Megan was trying to save a little money with which to take Ben on holiday the following summer. It was hard, because he quickly grew out of his clothes. It looked like he would become quite tall. Her mind kept going back to his dad. He had been tall with dark hair and blue eyes. The hurt never seemed to go away. She had not dated again, because the shame of not being married was constantly with her. She had had offers but her son Ben was her life, now. Megan would not risk losing someone she loved again.

After an hour spent reading *Gulliver's Travels* with Ben and completing the chores, all Megan wanted was a bath and her bed. It was 8 o'clock already. She had promised to take Ben to the Charles Burrell paint shop museum in the morning, to see the traction engines and the factory where Burrell had employed 350 people; that would be Saturday taken care of. On Sunday Ben and Megan would go to her mum and dad's for lunch. This was supposed to be her day of rest, but she still hadn't got to the gardening; the weeding needed to be done and she needed to plant some winter cabbages and other vegetables. If her dad was well enough he would come and help but at the moment he was suffering with the cold that had put her mum in bed.

CHAPTER 2

After waving Ben off in the morning Megan made her way in the opposite direction towards her office. On arriving, Edward Jackson, who owned the company, called her into his office. He had promoted Megan to office manager. He was older than Megan at 41, and on several occasions had asked Megan to attend business functions with him. When she had she agreed to go she had enjoyed being with people of her age. He had made it obvious that he would like more but she had said, 'Let's just be friends for now and see what happens in the future.'

'Okay,' he had replied, but said they would speak about it sooner rather than later.

They were to attend an important function the following Saturday and Megan's thoughts went to what she would wear. Most of her clothes were dated; it seemed ages since she had bought anything new. Megan arrived in work on time and began to sort the post and enter cheques in the ledger against the outstanding accounts.

'Megan, I'm just slipping out,' Edward called. 'I've seen something I want to buy; it's kind of an extra bonus for you so no arguments when I get back. Just accept it gracefully.'

'No, please, Edward, there's no need. I'm happy having the same as everyone else.'

'No buts, Megan, you work harder than everyone else so that's an end to the conversation.'

At 2 o'clock Edward had not returned and Sally, the receptionist, opened her door.

'It's Mr Jackson's 2 o'clock, Megan.'

'Show him in, Sally, and make a pot of coffee for three and bring some of Edward's favourite biscuits.'

'Will do, Megan.' Sally returned Megan's ready smile.

Megan stood as she heard Sally say, 'This way, Mr Lawrence,' and looking up at the opening door. She was suddenly rooted to the spot and gripped the desk with her outstretched hand.

'Take a seat please, Mr Lawrence,' Sally said. 'Edward won't be long.'

'Megan!' he breathed. 'You look even lovelier than I remember. I'm Ben, you know?'

'A lot of time has passed since then, Mr Lawrence, so I'd prefer to keep this meeting on a professional level.'

At that moment the door opened and Edward walked in.

'I'm sorry to be late. These ladies' shops are a nightmare.' Quickly taking in Megan's pink cheeks and the way Ben was looking at her, he said, 'This is for Saturday, Megan. It will match your eyes. Now let's get down to business.'

After an hour spent going over the plans Edward looked at his watch, and said, 'I'm afraid I'll have to go now. Megan, can you cost these plans and give Mr Lawrence the quote, and then we will take it from there. I'll be back about 4.30. I'm pleased to be doing business with you, Mr Lawrence, but this other meeting was already booked when you rang me. I'm sorry.'

'Don't worry about it. I will be more than satisfied to stay with Megan,' Ben said, not taking his eyes from her face.

Edward went out of the office looking at Megan and wishing he didn't have to leave her with this Ben Lawrence, who appeared to be watching her every move. Next time they had a meeting with him he would make sure it was he who dealt with him. He had cared about Megan for a long time and he hoped she would soon feel the same about him. He had been too busy to get involved with anyone else but was aware he was getting older.

'So, alone at last, Megan,' Ben said, scrutinising her pink cheeks. I saw you outside the infant's school yesterday. You have a lovely little boy. You're married now?'

'You are here on business, Mr Lawrence, so let's stick to that. My private life is nothing to do with you.'

'It did have eight years ago,' he said, gazing at her and making her blush.

'That was just a phase. It's over. Besides, you forfeited the right to talk about that.'

'But it was good, then, wasn't it,' he persisted.

Picking up the papers on her desk, Megan said, 'Let's get this done and then you will be free to leave.'

Ben noticed she didn't wear a wedding ring.

'The little boy was yours, wasn't he.'

'I thought I had made myself clear. It's none of your business. But as its happens, he is mine, and I'm proud of him. Now, let's stick to why you're here, shall we. The sooner we complete the costings the sooner you can go.'

'For now,' Ben replied, 'but we need to talk about it another time to clear the air.'

Once the costings were done Ben stood up and said, 'Please don't think too badly of me, Megan. At least not until you hear the full story.'

'I don't think anything of you, Mr Lawrence, one way or the other.'

Ben then held his hand out but Megan put her hands behind her back. 'Goodbye, Mr Lawrence.' She opened the door for him to leave.

Megan sat at her desk. She was shaking with anger. How dare he! It was as if he expected to walk straight back into her life as if nothing happened. The cheek of the man. She vowed there and then he would never get to know that Ben was his. It would be his loss.

At around 4.15 the door opened and Edward walked in.

'Sorry about leaving you with Ben Lawrence. He didn't give you any trouble, did he?'

'No, nothing I couldn't handle, Edward.'

'You do have a baby sitter for Saturday, don't you?'

'Yes. Ben is staying at Mum's for the night.'

'Good. I'm looking forward to the weekend.'

'Edward, you should not have bought that dress.'

'I wanted you to give me your time and I don't pay you overtime. It's a bonus, and besides, I want to spoil you. You just say that little word yes and I promise you, you will want for nothing.'

'Not now. I'm not ready to commit to any man. But if I change my mind you will be the first to know.'

'Right, come on, you will have your hands full with what I purchased so the least I can do is take you home.'

'Thanks, Edward, I'd appreciate a lift. I do feel a little tired.'

Edward gathered the shopping while Megan set the alarm and locked the door. He saw her into the car and placed the shopping in the boot. Neither of them saw Ben sitting in his car nearby. Edward drove the short distance to Megan's mothers, saying, 'I'm coming in to say hello to your mum then I'll see you home.'

Ben pulled up further down the road and watched as they went into the house. He couldn't get Megan out of his mind. How he wished he hadn't left her behind. He realised he'd never stopped loving her. It looked as if Edward and Megan were an item. Did they live together? Ben thumped his dashboard in anger.

He then watched Edward and Megan return to the car. This time he didn't follow them. As the small boy had come out holding Megan's hand he had been chatting away with Edward. Ben waited until they were out of sight then made his way back to his hotel. There was no way he would destroy that child's life or Megan's if she was happy, which he hoped she was. But he knew he would never want anyone else and he only had himself to blame.

CHAPTER 3

Edward helped Megan out of the car and removed the packages from the boot. He waited for Megan to open her front door. Ben ran inside. He'd had tea at his gran's so he went straight to the telly. He'd done his homework, as Grandad had sat with him until it was completed. So Ben knew he would be able to watch until it was time for a bath.

Edward looked at Megan, thinking she might invite him in. But it was as if she read his mind.

'Would you mind if I don't ask you in? I have to get Ben ready for school in the morning and I've got a vile headache.'

'No, of course not. You go and get sorted and I'll see you at work tomorrow.' Unusually, he felt the need to give her a quick kiss on the cheek. He meant to make sure she knew he was serious about her.

Megan closed the door. She really did have a headache now. Her mind was all mixed up, a jumble of what ifs. She had waited so long to hear from Ben but now she just felt bitter. And she could do without the added stress of Edward wanting them to be a closer. Even though she knew that circumstances had changed her over the years, her love for Ben had not. But she was determined to make sure he never found out.

After washing Ben's school clothes and setting out the next day's clothes she gave him a bath and helped him with his reading. As soon as he began to doze off, she tucked him in and ran a bath for herself. She didn't feel like anything to eat, and after her bath she checked that everywhere was secure and fell into bed hoping to sleep. But sleep eluded her and she tossed and turned all night. She really didn't feel well the next morning. Her stomach felt as if there were butterflies flitting about inside. And she still hadn't looked at what Edward had bought her; she would quickly look before she went to work.

Once Megan had her son ready for school, she popped him to Sue's and shot back to quickly look in the packages. They contained a sapphire blue cocktail dress and silver shoes, with a matching bag and stole. How was she going to pay him for these? Determined to pay him back she thought she would have to dig into the money she was saving to take Ben on a short holiday. She had been looking forward to taking him. He didn't have many treats.

She realised she needed to get her skates on or she would be late for work, and Edward had been so kind, she didn't like to take advantage. The day passed with no more stress and she thanked Edward for the dress and assured him she would pay him back.

'No, Megan, I won't hear of it,' he said.

It was Friday tomorrow, her half-day. Megan would be glad of the extra time at home and it allowed her to fetch Ben from school herself. The museum visit the following day would be a rare treat for him as she was always busy at the weekend, and he had been talking about nothing else. Standing at the school gate waiting for Ben she didn't realise that once more she was being watched by Ben Lawrence.

As the child came out, Ben looked at him; he reminded him of someone. It must be Megan. He had to stop doing this. Still, he would not have time soon. He needed distraction so he had rung and asked his secretary to join him. Now he wasn't sure he had done the right thing. He needed a partner for a function on Saturday night. Perhaps it would have been better for him not to attend. He didn't want to raise Marie's hopes. She meant nothing to him, but he had asked and had assured her that it was work related, and now he needed to pick her up from the station. He had booked a room for her, but knowing her she would try to wheedle her way into his bed. He was no monk, but with Megan being so near, his heart was not in it. Marie was tall and slim with dark hair that hung to her shoulders. Pleasant to look at but no real depth of character and definitely a no-holds-barred girl.

Ben picked Marie up, and managed to keep her out of his bedroom, and on the following day ran her to the site and discussed the plans. She asked him to show her around the town. They strolled down the street and who should be walking towards them but Megan, holding her little boy's hand. She slowed down as she neared them.

'Megan, how nice to see you.'

'Hello, Mr Lawrence.'

'Now, who have we here?' he said, looking at Ben.

'I'm sorry, we're in a hurry,' Megan said, not giving him time to ask her son his name. Panic was rising in her throat.

Marie's voice floated back to her. 'Well, she was rude,' she said, looking at Ben.

'Perhaps she has a reason or she was in a hurry,' he replied. He was deeply hurt, however, and for him, the day was ruined. He wasn't looking forward to the evening event and would have preferred to prop up a bar and drown his sorrows. 'Let's head back and you can have a rest until we go out.'

'I can think of what we can do and it doesn't involve resting!' Marie said suggestively.

Ben was tempted, but kept seeing Megan's eyes. They had a sadness that had not been there eight years ago.

Looking at the smart clothes Marie was wearing he realised that Megan's clothes were clean and tidy but out of fashion. Her wardrobe must be sparse. He began to wonder what the child's father was like. Did he live with her, and if not, did he help support the child?

'Mummy, who is that man? Is he not a nice man?' young Ben asked.

'Why yes, of course he's a nice man. I'm just in a hurry, Ben. Remember you'll be staying at Gran's tonight because I'm going out with Edward. I don't often manage to go out, do I, and I want to make sure we have enough time to enjoy the museum before I drop you off, and see all the engines that Charles Burrell made. His hard work created jobs for more than 350 people. That's a lot isn't it?'

When Ben had explored the museum and had seen enough, Megan took him to his gran's and made sure he knew she would be back in time for lunch the next day. After lunch they would go home. After extracting a promise from him to be a good boy for Gran, she got ready to leave.

'Megan, can I have a quick word in the kitchen before you go?'

'Of course, Mum. What's the matter?'

'Ben Lawrence is back here. His aunt told me.'

'I know, Mum. I've seen him.'

'Why didn't you tell me?'

'Because he means nothing to me. He will never find out from me that Ben is his child. We didn't involve his family then and we won't now. We have brought him up and will continue to do so. He never wanted me so he would never have wanted Ben. Ben deserves better than a part-time father. No father is better than a part-time one.'

'Are you sure, Megan? Hasn't the child a right to know his father?'

'No, Mum, please. And if you see him don't tell him. Neither I nor Ben need pity from him.' Megan gave her mother a kiss. 'Thanks, Mum.'

How long Megan's mother stood in the kitchen she didn't know. She worried about Megan, remembering the nights she had listened to her darling girl cry over Ben Lawrence. Yes, on the surface, it looked as if Megan had forgotten him and made some sort of a life with her young son. It would be lovely if there could have been a happy ending, though. Megan had become bitter and didn't seem to want to get involved with any other men. She still thought that Ben should know his father, thought, but she had promised Megan not to say anything and a promise was a promise. She walked into the lounge to find Ben, who seemed quite happy and, so far, had not asked why he didn't have a daddy. But at some stage she was sure he would. What then?

Megan took a quick bath and washed her hair, eying the blue and silver cocktail dress that Edward had bought her. It had three-quarter length sleeves and a round high neck at the front which was dipped at the back. It was a deep sapphire blue and the top layer of the chiffon had a figured pattern of silver adorning it. The waist was nipped in and fitted perfectly, and the hip was slightly dropped and swirled out in a cloud of chiffon, finishing just below the knee. After slipping her feet into her silver sling-back strappy shoes she studied her reflection. From the top of her blonde head to the tip of her toes she looked years younger. Her hair shone and her skin did not need any make-up, but she still rummaged out her eye shadow and found a pot of blue. She also added just a touch of her favourite lipstick – Roman pink. Megan had worn the same colour ever since she was old enough to use make-up.

Once she was ready she sat and waited for Edward. Her mind turned to Ben. He was more confident and sure of himself than he had been when they were young, and Megan began to wonder what it would be like to be held close to him now. She remembered the sweetness of their young love. Why hadn't he come back for her? Megan gave herself a mental shake. She needed to stop this. He obviously didn't want her. He was like lots of men: he must have thought her easy. He had certainly taken his time, she thought bitterly. They had been joined at the hip since she was 13, and at 17 they had become sweethearts. Megan was 19 when he walked away from her, promising the world.

Suddenly the doorbell rang. Megan stood up, determined to push Ben from her thoughts.

'Why, Megan, you look great. I knew that dress would suit you.'

'I will pay you back, Edward, it's far too much for a bonus.'

'No, Megan, I don't want paying back. I won't hear of it. I like spoiling you. You look beautiful.'

'You don't look too shabby yourself, Edward.'

'Why thank you, kind maiden,' he replied, flashing her a smile.

Megan wished with all her heart that she could love Edward. However, her heart would always belong to the Ben she had known all those years ago.

She forced herself to follow Edward to the door, and locked it behind her. Edward took her stole from her hand, placed it around her shoulders and opened the car door. He was the perfect gentleman, and made sure her dress didn't get trapped in the door. They made their way to the function venue and once inside Edward held her elbow and steered her between the tables. He had asked for a table for two, and, although he was there to do some networking, he wanted Megan all to himself.

'There's someone over there I would like to chat to, Megan. Could you make a mental note of anything he says of interest, please? I can trust you to remember anything that will be beneficial.'

It was the chairman of the council's planning application department. Edward wanted to find out about any building work being planned in the area and to send his brochure in advance. Megan listened to their conversation, picking up snippets. Then she heard Ben's voice.

'Edward, I didn't know you would be here, and Megan, you look stunning.'

'Thank you, Mr Lawrence,' she replied frostily.

Ben wanted to ask Megan to draw a line under the past.

Turning to Edward Megan said, 'Could we go back to our table, Edward, please? I'm getting a headache.'

Edward put his arm around her. 'Of course, Megan. Excuse us.'

Suddenly Marie butted in. 'Ben, aren't you going to introduce me to your friends?'

'I'm sorry, Marie. Edward, this is Marie, my secretary. Marie, this is Edward, and Marie, if you had bothered to look in my appointments' diary you would have seen that we are doing business with Edward at the moment. And this is Megan, a friend from many years ago.'

'Pleased to meet you, Marie.'

Ben's troubled eyes followed Megan as she returned to her table.

'You didn't tell me you knew Ben Lawrence,' Edward said.

'I didn't think it was relevant, Edward. I knew him in another time, another life, many years ago. I try my best to forget it. Now could we just forget him and enjoy tonight.'

'Of course. Would you like to dance?' Megan nodded, and, after taking his hand, they walked to the dancefloor. She felt not only Ben's eyes on her but his companion's as well.

Edward held her closer than before. It was as if he was saying, She's spoken for, but although Megan was dancing with Edward her mind was on Ben. Was there another reason Ben had brought his secretary with him? Were they partners? Megan wished she had said no to Edward when he had invited her to this function. Why did Ben have to come back into her life after she had managed to put him out of her mind? Yes, her life had been uneventful, but she had felt safe and settled. Now, she didn't know how she felt. Her past had come back to haunt her. And, come what may, she was determined that Ben would not find out how she felt about him; that part of her life was over. If it hadn't been for the support of her family, she would have considered moving. Megan was realistic, and knew she couldn't manage without the support her mum and dad gave her.

At the end of the evening Edward had fallen quiet, too, and, feeling guilty, Megan did her best to compensate for spoiling his night after he had been so good to her and bought her the new clothes. She would still see that she paid him back.

Edward stood up and said, 'Are you ready to go, Megan?'

'Yes, Edward, I'm ready.'

Edward suddenly took hold of her hands as if to say, Please tell me I have a chance. Looking into her eyes he said, 'Promise we can talk about it soon.' Megan knew she owed him at least that.

'Yes, Edward, I promise. '

'Soon,' he insisted. She agreed. Then he took her by surprise and kissed her quickly on the lips. She did not know that he had done that because he had seen Ben watching them. He draped her stole around her shoulders and led her out of the conference centre to his car.

For Ben it was like a knife being twisted in his gut. He promised himself he would make Megan understand why he didn't send for her or come back for her. He could not get her out of his mind. He had not stopped loving her. Now it looked as if Edward Jackson had won her heart. He liked Edward but that was no consolation. Was he sleeping with Megan? In fact, was Edward her son's father? Megan's young son didn't resemble Edward Jackson, but he did remind him of someone. Try as he might, Ben couldn't think who; he couldn't quite figure out.

Back at home, Megan lay in bed wondering what to do about Edward. She knew he wanted an answer as to why couldn't she love him, and had told her repeatedly that he would like a relationship. Why could she not accept him and say yes? She knew her life would become easy. But she also knew it wasn't fair on Edward to do that. Megan endured a restless night and sleep evaded her, and when she rose in the morning she was heavy-eyed and weary. However, she still needed to go to her mum's for lunch and to pick up her son. She would need to smile through dinner and act as if the bottom of her world was not falling out.

She would do that for her little boy, who she loved above anything or anyone. She would smile through the day even though her heart was breaking. Why, Ben, why? she thought. What had happened to make you stop loving me? She was certain that he had loved her. Her son had made her life worth living when Ben had left and was the only part of Ben she still had. It was if he had been Ben's parting gift.

CHAPTER 4

Megan was at work the next day when she saw Ben come in and be shown into Edward's office. She looked in the diary and noticed that his appointment was not there. Also, Edward had not asked her to take notes. He must have arranged it himself.

Megan's office was next to Edward's; there was half a glass panel between them. Megan could see when Ben got up to leave and she could feel his eyes on her, but she was determined that she wouldn't look.

Megan kept her head down for the rest of the day and made sure that she kept busy. Edward looked into her office at around 4 o'clock to say he was leaving. He had an appointment and would she lock up.

'And by the way, I can see you don't care for Ben Lawrence so I have given him my mobile number and will deal with him direct. You won't have to see him. I won't have him upsetting you. Goodnight Megan, I'll see you tomorrow.'

Megan smiled. Edward's heart was in the right place; he was trying to take care of her. Perhaps Edward was the answer, but deep down in her heart Megan didn't believe he was, and she dreaded hurting him. When Ben had gone away she had learnt to be strong and to block him out of her heart. Now he seemed to have come back with a vengeance. Checking the time on the office clock she realised it was time to lock up and go home. The evening stretched out in front of her and back at Sue's, Ben was chattering ten to the dozen. Smiling, Megan thanked Sue and said, 'I'll bring him around in the morning.'

Ben skipped up his path beside Megan, rushing through the door and into their kitchen. He put his school books on the table and got straight down to his homework. The TV programmes he wanted to watch were starting earlier and he didn't want to miss them.

It was a full two weeks before Megan saw Ben again. She was not aware that he had returned to London for some business meetings. She had to admit that she missed the odd sighting of him, but then thought that perhaps it was for the better. If he didn't come back Megan thought she might be able to stop thinking about him. Her mind had been on him more than she cared to admit. She needed to settle back into her uneventful life.

Today it was Megan's half-day and it was at least three hours before she needed to pick up Ben from school. It was only on her half-day that she was able to pick him up; how she wished she was like other mums with a husband to help support them. Then she could pick him up every night.

Megan wandered into town, deep in thought, and before she knew it she was at the priory. She still knew exactly where their special place was. She sat on the grass, her mind wandering back to the days all those years ago. She relived the moments spent in Ben's arms. Ben might have forgotten her but he could not take away her memories. Deep in thought she was shocked into awareness when she heard Ben's voice.

'Megan, you remember, too, don't you?'

Megan couldn't answer. He was the last person she expected to see here. Suddenly she came to life. She needed to get away from there. She couldn't cope with this.

'No, please,' Ben said, urging her to sit down again and sitting down beside her. His strong arm held her there. 'Megan, look at me, please. I need to explain why I didn't send for you. I'm sure you couldn't know how hard it was.' Suddenly tears appeared in Megan's eyes.

'Please don't,' Megan said.

Ben suddenly leant over and kissed her, parting her lips to explore her sweetness. He couldn't help himself. He was like a dying man craving for a drink of water. Suddenly Megan stopped fighting and responded to his passionate kisses. His hands began to roam and explore her body. Megan suddenly came to her senses, and, taking him by surprise, pushed him off and jumped up.

'Don't think I'm easy prey, Ben Lawrence. Those days are over. Stay away from me.'

'No, Megan,' he shouted as she started to run away. 'You do care for me, I can tell.'

Megan ran as fast as she could, not looking back. Tears were streaming down her face. Things couldn't get any worse. Ben coming back had turned her life upside down. He followed her at a distance, not wanting to upset her more than he had already. But he knew Megan still had feelings for him. He badly needed to make sure that she was doing the right thing. Edward Jackson had hinted that he was soon to be married. Was Megan destined to be his wife? If so, Ben was sure she didn't love him.

He followed her to the village and was surprised when she headed in the opposite direction to her mother's house. The least he could do was make sure she got home safely. He could tell she was shocked by the depth of her own feelings.

After turning up a narrow lane Megan let herself into the last of a row of cottages. It was small with a small front garden. At least he knew where to find her if she insisted on ignoring him. He would be able to write to her and then she might understand.

The next day Megan's father called on her at work to say he would go and get the seedlings for the winter vegetables and that he would try to start weeding at the weekend. Edward came out of the office to ask how he was, and when he said his chest was still bothering him but that he needed to get Megan's veg patch organised Edward said, 'I've some spare time at the weekend. You just fetch the seeds and I can sort it out. Then you can make sure you stay warm and get well.'

'Are you sure, Edward?' asked Megan's dad.

'I'm sure. I'd do anything for Megan.'

'I know you would, lad, and I hope things turn out right for both of you.'

Edward put his hand on Ted James's shoulder to show he understood what he meant.

When Ted left, Megan looked at Edward and said, 'You can't keep doing things for me.'

'Megan, come into the office.' She followed him slowly. 'Sit down. I think I need to lay my cards on the table. You know how I feel about you, and that I'd like you to become my wife. I'll take care of both you and Ben. I know you keep telling me we will talk about it but I need you to know I love you.'

'Edward, I'm so sorry. I wish with all my heart that I could love you. You're the most genuine, kind man I have ever met. But it would be wrong of me to marry you. I'll never get married. I'll only ever love Ben's dad and I know that will come to nothing. You deserve better than me, Edward. You should not be second best. Someday, someone will make you a wonderful wife and you, dear Edward, will make a fantastic husband. I only wish I could love you. Can we still be friends?

'We can if I can be your knight in shining armour until I meet that paragon of virtue. For like you, Megan, I don't think I'll ever love anyone other than you.'

Tears sprang into Megan's eyes. 'I'd like that, Edward.'

Edward walked around the desk and kissed her tenderly on lips. At that moment Ben Lawrence walked into the office. He had seen the tender scene between Edward and Megan. Frowning at Megan, Edward said, 'I wasn't aware that I had an appointment with Ben. Nip into your office and do me the costings for Jones & Brett please. I'll deal with Ben.'

Megan walked past Ben and into her office, where she rifled through her filing cabinet to find the relevant papers to cost the work for Edward.

Later, Ben left Edward's office thinking he was right: Megan was to marry Edward Jackson and he had lost her. Everything was in place for the development to go ahead. He needn't be here all the time now and could return to London. Perhaps when he was there he could forget Megan, as she obviously intended to forget him. He had written to her a couple of times and his letters had been sent back, Return to Sender. After that he had thrown himself into his work. It was his fault. He should have found the time to come back and see her, although he still wouldn't have been able to give her a good home as he had been living hand to mouth. Now he had everything except Megan. He could have provided her with a much better home than she had now, and he would even look after the child. He wondered again who the child's father was. To be able to hold her again in his arms as he had at the priory he would forgive her anything. After all, she was no different to him. He had consoled himself in quite a few women's arms, but none of them had meant anything and if he had still been sure of Megan's love there would have only been her. He wouldn't have looked at anyone else.

Before he returned to London he decided to take a last look around the village. He headed to the cottages where he now knew Megan lived and as he walked towards the lane, he saw Edward Jackson's car pass him and turn towards her house. Edward parked outside her cottage. So, it was Megan that Edward was to marry. Ben's stomach lurched. He would still write to her tonight and make sure she was aware he had never forgotten her. Ben remembered some of the doss houses he had lodged in while looking for a job. She might be marrying someone else but he needed her to know the truth – that he would always love her.

He returned to his hotel and sat down to write the letter. He spent most of the night writing then screwing up the paper. He persevered, and at 3 o'clock in the morning he had a letter of sorts. He decided he would take the letter himself and put it through the door of her cottage.

CHAPTER 5

The next day was Monday and wearily Ben showered and packed his belongings. He waited until he thought Megan would be at work then drove to her cottage and slipped the letter through her letter box. He noticed the newly mown lawn and neat borders. If he had not been so intent on making money he might have been living there happily with the woman he loved. Now it was too late. He climbed back into his car, brought the engine to life and headed away from Thetford.

Life for Megan began to return to normal. The only difference was that she had received the letter from Ben. Could she believe that he had written letters and she hadn't received them? Megan loved her mum and dad and could not and would not believe they had kept her letters from her. Why would they do that? No, Ben must be lying. Perhaps he had said that because he thought he could carry on as before. Well, not this time. She would never again have a man in her life. Ben would be her only child and she would concentrate on him. Perhaps she would not be able to give him a lot of material goods but he would have all the love and care in the world.

Autumn turned to winter and Megan had bought a small Christmas tree, and she and Ben had excitedly decorated it with tinsel and baubles. She couldn't afford many presents, but by the time her mum and dad had added their bits and pieces he would have enough. And Edward always got him something, as well.

Up until then Megan had not shown Ben's letter to her mum, but now something was niggling at the back of her mind. She would wait until after Christmas and approach her mum then. Ben had only been here for a short time but his visit had unsettled her, and every night in her quiet moments she allowed herself the luxury of reliving their love affair. The hurt in her heart was far greater than before and the love she had felt for him was no longer lying hidden in a corner of her heart; it had burst out, filling every inch of her being. Looking at herself in the mirror Megan realised she had lost weight. She could also see the violet shadows under her eyes. This won't do my girl, I need to stay strong and healthy for Ben, she thought. The one person to give her joy was her little boy. He was waiting patiently for it to snow and he did nothing but talk about making his snowman, as he had done the year before. That and Santa Clause coming. Megan had to admit that she was looking forward to Santa's visit, too.

Back in London Ben threw himself into his work, but working harder and staying longer made no difference at all. His routine had now become work, home and overindulging in drink. The one thing his trip to Thetford had done was to make him celibate; the only woman he wanted was Megan.

On arriving home that night he looked in the fridge to see what there was to eat, and once again just had a sandwich. Then, reaching for the whisky bottle, he poured a large glass and sat down to think. He went upstairs to his bedroom to get a box from the top of the wardrobe, and searched through the photographs inside until he pulled out a worn snap of Megan. He sat for a long time holding his head. But it was no use him crying over spilt milk. Moving unsteadily he knocked the box onto the floor then, groaning, stooped to retrieve it. Lying on the top of the pile was a picture of a small boy. His hand shook as he studied the features of the child, and, turning it over, he saw the words 'Ben, aged seven' written on the back. There was no mistaking the picture of himself as a child. He had been the age of Megan's boy.

How had he not seen it? He had thought Megan's child reminded him of someone and now he knew exactly who: he was the father of that small boy and she had kept him in the dark. Why? He was certain now that he, Ben Lawrence, had a son. Why had she not told him? Now Edward would effectively be his father. He would have to insist that he be part of his son's life. She had no right. Damn it, he loved her, and he would have been over the moon if he had known. Why? he kept asking himself. He sobered up quite quickly then rang Daniel, his business partner, to tell him he needed to go back to Thetford the next day.

'I have a personal problem to sort and it might take a couple of weeks. But I will keep in touch. You can have the pleasure of fending off Marie!'

Dan laughed, and then said, 'Be careful, though, Ben, they've forecast snow. Why don't you take the Land Rover?'

'That's a thought. I'll do that.'

'Is everything all right, Ben. You haven't been the same since you went there last time.'

'I know, Dan, trust me, I'll tell you all about it sometime but right this minute it hurts too much. I'll be back in the new year. Have a great Christmas.'

'You too, Ben, and I hope you sort out what's bothering you.'

After packing a bag Ben returned to the office to collect the Land Rover, leaving his car there. Driving back home he remembered that he had been drinking. He never drove after drinking but had forgotten because he had been in such a hurry to prepare himself for the morning. He needed to be careful of how much he drank in the future. Since returning from Thetford he had been indulging too much. He needed to put the brakes on that, and to keep a clear head. All that night he lay awake thinking about what he had missed. The child must be coming up to eight if his calculations were correct.

In the morning he quickly showered and put on warm clothes. Daniel had been right: thick snow lay on the ground. Still, the main roads would be clear. Ben couldn't define the feeling he had inside him. He needed to concentrate fully on getting to Thetford safely. He had an excited but sickly feeling in the pit of his stomach. If Megan's child was his he wanted to be part of the boy's life. He remembered meeting Megan and the boy in the village and how she had nervously brushed him off.

It was Christmas Eve. Before leaving London he called at a store and picked up a couple of books and a toy truck. He remembered what Megan's favourite chocolates were and on impulse purchased a large box.

On pulling up in front of Megan's cottage the first thing he saw was the child building his snowman and, leaning over the wall, Ben said hello.

'Hello,' the boy replied. 'You are that nice man so Mummy won't mind me talking to you.'

'How do you know I'm nice?'

'Because Mummy told me. She said you were a very nice man. Mummy's making me some hot chocolate with marsh mellows. Would you like some?'

'Yes I would but first, what's your name? Mine's Ben.'

Excitedly the boy put his hand over his mouth. 'Oh! You have the same name as me. My name's Ben as well!'

'How old are you, Ben?

'I'm a big boy. I'm eight.'

Ben went pale. This was his son. She could not deny it. Looking at the small child he just wanted to fold him in his arms and hug him. At that moment Megan appeared in the doorway.

'Ben, take this drink and go inside.'

'But, Mummy, it's the nice man and his name is the same as mine and he wants some hot chocolate.'

'And I want some explanations now and I'm not leaving until I get them, Megan,' interrupted Ben. 'So don't try the Mr Lawrence thing and try to fob me off, because I know who little Ben's father is.' Megan went pale and began to shake, and quickly Ben was at her side. He led her into the cottage, noticing the clean but plainly furnished interior.

'Ben, show me to the kitchen and I'll make your mother a drink.' Ben smiled up at him and taking his hand led him to the kitchen where Ben senior made a drink of hot sweet tea. Taking it into the lounge he bent down to the boy and said, 'Do you think you could drink your chocolate at the kitchen table while I have a little chat with your mummy?'

'Yes Mr Ben.'

'Let me help by carrying your drink.' Ben took the boy's hand and they walked into the kitchen. He placed the drink in front of him on the table and suddenly hugged him.

'We won't be long, little man.'

Returning to Megan he sat down. 'Feeling better?'

'Yes,' she whispered. All the fight had left her. Her heart was racing. 'How did you find out?' Ben took the picture out of his pocket and placed it on the table.

'I thought when I saw him that he resembled someone I knew, and this confirmed it.' Megan found herself staring at young Ben's double. 'Why did you not tell me?'

'How could I? I didn't know where you were. But you knew where I was and you didn't see fit to come back, so quite obviously you were having your fun and had dumped me.'

'No, Megan, I did write to you.' He took out of his pocket a small bundle of letters. 'Look, it says "Return to Sender" – they have been opened by the post office and returned to me. Haven't I got feelings? I'm that boy's father and I didn't even know he existed. I've missed out on so much – eight years of his life – and I won't miss out on any more. I have to live with the fact that Edward will be his step-father but I'm his biological father. Just seeing him makes me want to hold him close. We can do this the hard way or the easy way. What is it going to be? I'm going to book into the hotel and if it takes me the rest of my life I intend to be part of his life. And I'll get to see you now and then, too.

'I've brought him a couple of presents. I'll get them from the car and leave you to think about how we are going to sort this out. Then I'll be on my way. I'd like your phone number to contact you so perhaps you'll be good enough to write it down while I go to the car.' He stood up. 'If things had been different, we could have been so happy, but we've both lost our way. Sad isn't it, Megan, two people in love who've thrown it all away. What a waste.'

Quickly he went to the car and returned carrying the presents. He placed them on the table. He picked up the slip of paper on which Megan had written her number and put it in his jacket. As he walked back to the car he looked back. Their eyes locked and the sadness in Megan's eyes broke his heart. It was a little after 2 o'clock and it was Christmas Eve. He needed to speak to Edward Jackson; he wanted to make sure that Megan was going to be happy. If he couldn't have her he would at least make sure she would be looked after.

Entering the reception of Edward's offices, he asked to see Edward. Sally picked up the phone and rang Edward. Ben went in.

'Edward, I was just passing when I remembered that you said you were going to get married soon. Would it be to Megan, by any chance?'

'Why do you ask, Ben?'

'I just need to know.'

'Ben, do you have a personal interest?'

'You might say that.'

'Well, whatever it is, Ben, Megan has no plans to marry me or anyone else. She turned me down. She told me she would never love anyone but Ben's father. I would have looked after both of them, you know. I wish I knew who he was. She has struggled for years bringing him up on her own. What was that man thinking of? She is lovely, generous, kind and considerate. She works hard. What was he thinking of leaving her when she needed him more than ever.'

'I can only say I didn't know and that I have only just found out that Ben is mine.'

'Yours?'

'Yes mine.'

'That explains why she was upset every time you came to the office. You aren't here to upset Megan again, are you?'

'No, Edward, I'm glad that I came to see you. I would never have known how she felt. I was willing to stand aside, thinking she loved you. Now I won't leave Thetford until she's my wife, and of course got to the bottom of who kept my letters away from her.'

'Make her happy then, Ben, that's all I ask. Don't hurt her again or you'll have to answer to me.'

Smiling, Ben left Edward's office, bought a huge bunch of flowers and made his way back to Megan's cottage.

When he arrived he walked up the path and rapped loudly on the door. Megan answered it. Her eyes were red from crying. After Ben had left earlier that day, she had been unable to control her feelings, much to her son's distress. He had climbed up beside her on the settee and implored, 'Please don't cry, Mummy, please don't cry,' until he was crying himself. They had sat together, hugging each other. Megan had forced herself to stop crying for Ben's sake; she had to calm him down. He had never seen his mum distraught – she had always been calm and loving with him.

'What now?' She kept her visitor at the door.

'I'm coming in, Megan, and I'm not leaving until you give me some answers.'

After gently pushing her inside Ben put the flowers down, and before either of them could say anything else, young Ben threw himself at his father, shouting, 'You made my mummy cry. She said you were a nice man and you are not. Go away. Go away now!'

Reaching down and holding the boy's small fists, Ben said, 'I'm sorry, young man, I promise I won't make your mummy cry ever again.' Bending down until he was at eye level he pulled Ben to him and held him tight. 'I love you and your mummy, Ben. I promise I'll keep you both safe and happy for the rest of my life, if your mummy will let me.' Lifting Ben up he sat on the settee and gently pulled Megan down beside him.

'I know, Megan.'

'What do you know?'

'I know you'll only ever love Ben's father and that's me. I'm right aren't I? Ben is my son and you do love me, don't you? Please say you do.'

Megan buried her head in Ben's jacket and whispered, 'Yes.'

'Oh, my darling girl, how are we going to tell Ben he has a daddy? And I'll forever be in Edward Jackson's debt. If I hadn't called to see him, I wouldn't have known. He told me you had turned him down and said it was because you would only love me. I'm not moving from here until we are husband and wife. What shall we do for Christmas dinner tomorrow?'

Megan lifted her tear-stained face and said, 'We were to go to mum and dad's.'

'Well, dry your tears and wash your face. I'll make us a cup of tea and then we'll go over to tell your mum she has another guest for dinner – her future son in law.' He drew Megan to him and kissed her, searching for the answer he needed.

'Mummy, who is my daddy? I heard Mr Ben say I had a daddy.'

Ben kissed his small son. 'It's me, Ben. Is that all right? I've always been your daddy. I just haven't been here. But now you and Mummy will be living with me so I'll always be here with you. And we'll go shopping and buy us a new house. Would you like that?'

'Yes, Mr... Yes, Daddy! Now I can tell everyone I have a daddy too!'

Ben was very happy as they drove to Megan's parents' but still needed to know why his letters had been returned. He didn't intend to upset anyone but he had guessed that her parents had sent them back because they worried about Megan going to London. A plan had formed in his mind: he would ensure the house they were to live in as a family would have a granny flat to house Megan's mum, dad and gran. He realised they would need to be near Megan, as they loved her so much.

Megan explained to her parents what had happened.

'I'm glad if this will make you happy, girl,' her mother said.

Her father added, 'I'm sorry, lad, we thought it was for the best, but we were wrong to return the letters and we admit it.'

'Well let's say no more about it,' said Ben, holding out his free hand; young Ben was proudly hanging onto his other hand.

'Grandma, Grandad, this is my daddy,' the boy said proudly.

Looking at Megan's mum, Ben asked, 'Can you manage another one for dinner tomorrow?' Megan's mum smiled her yes.

'Well, young man,' he said, turning to his son, 'are you going to stay here while your mum and I do a little more shopping for Santa Claus?'

'Yes, because Grandad is teaching me to play chess.'

Two months later Megan and Ben were married at the registry office. He had made an offer for a property that would house all of them. They went on honeymoon and Ben insisted that their son go with them. He couldn't bear to leave him for a full month.

As they boy slept in his hotel bed, Megan and Ben lay locked in each other's arms after making love. Kissing her, he asked, 'Are you happy?'

Megan nodded. 'I'll always be happy with you by my side.'

He groaned and pulled her to him again, whispering, 'I'll never leave you. I'll always be there at your side. No more going anywhere without you. I'll no longer be restless, as long as I have you here with me. I love you, Megan, and I will spend the rest of my life taking care of both of you.'

Lightning Source UK Ltd.
Milton Keynes UK
UKHW041128291119
354414UK00003BA/41/P